I0699085

SEE JANE DIG!

A West River Mystery

Jolene Stratton Philo

Midwestern Books
MB

Copyright © 2024 Jolene Stratton Philo

All rights reserved
No part of this book may be reproduced, or stored in a retrieval system, or transmitted in any form or by any means, electronic, mechanical, photocopying, recording, or otherwise, without express written permission of the author.

ISBN– 979-8-9880628-9-9

Cover design by: eBook Cover Designs

Published by Midwestern Books
801 W Washington Ave, Polk City, IA 50226

Contact: info@midwesternbooks.com

Dedication:
In memory of Gene Odell, who
told my husband about exposed
dinosaur bones in Harding
County, and in memory
of Gene's wife Carol, who
befriended me when we moved
to Camp Crook.
You are both missed and loved.

Chapter 1

I raised my voice to be heard above the noisy mass of children. "Put your lunch bags in the cooler and line up beside your buddies."

Eleven children stampeded into the entryway and did as they'd been told.

"When we go outside," I raised my voice another notch to be heard above unrelenting din, "you are to quietly walk, *not run*, to the vehicle you'll be riding in. Is that clear?"

Eleven children replied in unison. "Yes, Miss Newell!"

I patted down my overall pockets to make sure the Band-Aids and snakebite antidote I'd put in them were still there. This was my first field trip as Little Missouri's lower room teacher, and if I had any say in the matter, it wouldn't be my last.

Whew! My first aid supplies were were they belong.

I eased the door open. "In that case, let's go."

The children galloped past me and screamed as they ran across the scruffy playground.

Sigh.

I locked the schoolroom door and snatched up my shovel. It had been a housewarming present from my uncle Tim when he and my mother moved me to South Dakota last August. I balanced the shovel on top of the cooler and picked it up.

Grace, Keeva, and Elva, the three girls riding with me, came back to help me lug the load to the car. Before long, my VW Beetle was leading a short line of vehicles along a gravel road. No eating someone else's dust for me on our drive through the short-grass countryside where sprouts of vegetation tinged the tawny prairie a pale, hopeful green.

Being tapped to lead the field trip parade was, I hoped, a sign of confidence from my students' parents. Most likely because I had survived the first eight months of my rookie year unscathed. Not that everyone in town felt the same. The fact that I had found two corpses over the course of those months still caused some of Little Missouri's ninety-two citizens to give me a wide berth. Not so the parents of my students. They had welcomed me into their lives and treated me like family.

That said, I wanted to make it through today's field trip unscathed and with my dignity intact. I hated physical exertion *and* digging in the dirt *and* spending six hours in sunny, windy conditions. Yet that was today's agenda. Clearly, I hadn't been thinking about myself when arranging a trip to the new dinosaur dig at the old Lindgren place east of town. I'd been thinking about how the excursion would make science come alive for my dinosaur-crazy students. About how they could partici-pate in uncovering world-class paleontological discover-ies only a few miles from the remote South Dakota town where we lived. And about having one less day of lesson plans to write. Okay, so the last thing was all about me, but the rest were about the kids.

Grace Berthold spoke up from the back seat. "Are we there yet?"

I glanced at her in the rearview mirror. She and Keeva McDonald, her best friend in the universe, were holding hands and giggling. They were, in my opinion, the cutest brown-haired kindergarteners in the universe, too. Grace had brown eyes and a sturdy build. Keeva's eyes were blue, and she was rail thin. Despite my many first-year teacher faux pas, they still believed I could do no wrong. I loved them for that and hoped they would be first graders, or maybe even second, before their bubble burst.

The pint-sized passenger riding shotgun answered Grace and Keeva on my behalf. Such behavior was completely in line for Elva Dorgeson, third grader. She had stepped into the role of my apprentice upon entering my classroom last August. Though she was only eight years old, this wunderkind, with her red hair, blue eyes, and the last remnants of baby fat clinging to her frame, was astoundingly competent. Give her a few more years, and she would become the youngest student teacher in the state.

"Look out the back window." Elva turned around and pointed at the rear of the car. "We're less than a mile out of town. Miss Newell said it's twelve miles to the dinosaur dig. Twelve miles minus one mile is eleven miles."

Keeva's eyes grew wide. "Eleven miles is far."

"It is," Elva agreed. "Let's sing songs until we get there." She launched into "Goodbye Old Paint."

I chose to teach the song in music class because it

was in the key of C, meaning I could plunk out the melody with one finger on the out-of-tune piano in my classroom. I hadn't expected it to become a runaway classroom hit, but it had. Its popularity may have sprung from the mention of Montana in the lyrics. That state's eastern border was a mere two miles west of our school. In reality though, I suspected the song was popular because it was a love ballad to a horse. My students were nothing if not crazy in love with horses. This condition ran rampant among children raised in Tipperary County where the high school rodeo team was not only larger than the football team, but also made up of cowboys *and* cowgirls.

Elva and the kindergarteners launched into "Oh My Darling, Clementine" as I turned onto the lane to what was commonly referred to as the old Lindgren place. The gravel was in good shape until our caravan passed a prefab ranch-style house, its bright and shiny facade at odds with the "old" in old Lindgren. From then on, the lane to the dig site deteriorated rapidly. I drove the final half mile at a snail's pace, swerving to avoid deep ruts and sharp rocks. I was sweating when I reached the pasture where a dusty Volkswagen van and a mud-splashed pickup truck were parked.

I cut the engine and spoke to the girls. "Wait here a minute." I hopped out of the Beetle as Cookie Sternquist and Mary Borgeson, the moms who'd come in one vehicle, and Pam Barkley, who'd driven separately in case of an emergency, joined me in the parking area. We huddled together, trying to ignore the chill of the morning.

"Are we in the right place?" I asked.

A deep voice boomed from behind the van. "You are!"

A hefty man came into sight. His getup—a flannel shirt layered over a Fleetwood Mac T-shirt, beat-up work boots under baggy blue jeans, and a floppy-brimmed, battered brown hat—screamed, "I'm not from around here!" He doffed his hat, bowed low, and further cemented his outsider status by declaiming, "Professor Victor Vanderwinkle at your service." Then he stood erect and asked, "Which one of you lovely ladies is Jane Newell?"

With eyebrows raised, Cookie, Pam, and Mary looked at me. I raised mine in reply. The nutty professor examined each of them in turn and finally fixed his gaze on me. A blinding glare bounced off his bald head right into my eyes.

I slipped on my sunglasses and stepped forward. "I am."

He took in my ball cap, the camera hanging from its strap around my neck, my hooded sweatshirt under denim overalls, and my hiking boots. He sucked in his belly and straightened his shoulders. "Oh my." He rubbed his hands together and licked his lips. "You're younger than I expected."

He gave me the willies. Cookie, Mary, and Pam closed ranks around me. I guess he gave them the willies, too.

I motioned for the children waiting in the cars to get out. They burst out of their respective vehicles like zoo animals released into their natural environment. They surrounded the professor, sniffing and circling him like the interloper he was.

Second grader Tiege Sternquist bounded up to him with the spring and enthusiasm of Tigger. "What's your name?"

"Professor Victor Vanderwinkle."

Five-year-old Winter Skye Swensen, never at a loss for words but often less than tactful, put her hands on her hips. "That is a weird name. Where did it come from?"

"My parents." He winked at her and the other children. "It's quite a mouthful, isn't it? How about you all call me Vic?"

Renny Berthold crossed his arms and spoke next. "So Vic, where do you come from?"

At age nine and in the third grade, Renny was our classroom's senior spokesman. He was also the least motivated and least confident of my students, so his take-no-prisoners tone caught me off guard.

"I'm a science professor at Morningside College in Sioux City, Iowa." Vic gestured at my cap and hoodie, both of which bore that college's insignia. "Unless I miss my guess, it's where your teacher went to college, too."

The children whipped their heads in my direction.

"He's right," I confirmed. "I graduated from Morningside almost a year ago."

Renny uncrossed his arms and stood down. The other children stared at me as if I might be another here-to-day-gone-tomorrow interloper in their ranch community, like the professor. I'd been their teacher for eight months, but there were still times when these tough, country kids doubted that I was here to stay.

The professor pointed to the gap between the dirty pickup truck and the dusty van. "Now, come around this way, and I'll tell you about what brought me and my crew out here."

We fell into line behind him like cattle heading to a stock tank. Small fingers slipped into my free hand, the one not clutching my rattlesnake shovel. I glanced down, assuming it was my kindred spirit, second grader Cora Barkley. We both preferred sparkly shoes and fairy dust over dusty fields and dinosaur bones. But it was Renny who offered me a shy, wry smile. I smiled back. When he squeezed my fingers and held on tight, I didn't let go.

Victor—I'd never been in one of his classes but referring to a professor by his nickname was a bridge too far—threaded the needle between the vehicles, past a windmill and stock tank, and through a gate. It was held open by a slightly built young man. He waved at the children as they walked by. They were too busy staring at the do-rag partially covering his reddish-blond ponytail to wave back.

"Look, Miss Newell!" Stig Borgeson shouted in his piercing first-grade soprano. "It's a hippie, just like on TV. I never saw one of them before!"

There wasn't time for me to rush over to the young man and apologize on Stig's behalf. Victor hurried us alongside a large tent, its sides rolled up and held in place with Velcro ties. Rubber tubs filled metal shelves. A refrigerator and stove were plugged into outlets at the base of a yard-light pole. Pots and pans were stacked on makeshift counters, and two utility sinks stood near a hydrant. Garden hoses ran from the hydrant to the sinks. Five-gallon buckets sat beneath the sinks to catch gray water. The kitchen of my apartment had never looked so good.

Victor motioned for the children to sit at the picnic tables in an open area beyond the kitchen. Then he gestured toward a handful of hippies, the sort Stig had never seen before. They were working in a cordoned-off area about twenty yards east of us, chipping away at dirt with small chisels and whisk brooms. One by one, they looked up and waved or smiled.

The female hippie closest to the picnic tables jumped up and shrieked. "Jane Newell?" She picked her way to the edge of the cordoned area, ran toward me at top speed, and engulfed me in a hug. "Is it really you, Jane?"

"It is." I extricated myself from her smothering embrace and placed my hands on her shoulders. Anything to keep this young woman at arm's length. Then I examined her face, hidden as it was behind sunglasses and a bandana worn low over her forehead and tied behind her head. I searched for a shred of familiarity. Nothing.

I stepped back to put distance between us. "I'm sorry," I said, though I wasn't at all sorry. "Who are you?"

She whipped off her sunglasses and bandana and giggled as she undid her ponytail so her dark, wavy hair tumbled onto her shoulders. "Now do you know who I am?"

I stared at her, dumbstruck. My mouth gaped open. Finally, I spoke. "Beanie Lavender?"

*   *   *

"In the flesh!" Beanie squealed and danced around me like we were rocking out to "Crocodile Rock" at a high school sock hop again. She was taller and curvier than the pip-squeak sophomore I'd befriended during my senior year, but her exuberance remained infectious. I grabbed her hands and we partied and shouted the lyrics like it was 1973.

We didn't stop until Bennan Barkley, who, like his fellow first grader Stig Borgeson, was all cowboy all the time, yelled, "Miss Newell, you shouldn't dance with hippies. They hook people on drugs."

Doing my best Elton John imitation, I "Laa-la-la-la-la-la'ed" over to Bennan and said, "She's no hippie. She's Colleen Lavender. We went to high school together."

Beau Kelly, the third and shyest of my three first graders, whispered, "How come you called her Beanie?" He clutched Bennan and Stig's hands as if channeling their courage.

Beanie pranced over and squatted in front of him. "That's what all my friends call me. You can too." She put her right hand over her heart. "And I solemnly swear that I'm not a hippie."

Winter Skye narrowed her eyes and rocked back on her heels. "Then how come you all are dressed so weird?"

"Because we're paleontologists," Victor declared with gravitas that captured the children's attention again. "Serious scientists are too smart to wear their good clothes while they dig in the dirt all day. Do you know what we're hoping to find?"

"Dinosaurs!" the children screamed in unison.

Victor's eyes brightened. "That's right. Do you know what kind of dinosaur?"

Silence.

"We have reason to believe that during the late Cretaceous period, this area was a playground for Tyrannosaurus rex."

"Wow! The fence around it musta been higher than this." Tiege launched into the air with his arms raised.

When he came down, he conferred with the other children. "How deep do you think the post holes went?"

His classmates added their two-cents' worth simultaneously at top volume. Victor had taken less than five minutes to lose control of his audience. I decided to wait and see if he had what it took to recapture their attention.

He put two fingers to his lips. His high, piercing whistle shut my students down. An unseen dog howled in the distance.

I hadn't thought he had it in him. There was more to the professor than met the eye.

Victor stroked his chin dramatically. "I don't suppose you know any kids who would like to learn how to hunt for fossils, do you?"

His question unleashed a second round of pandemonium. Eleven children leapt to their feet and began yelling at the top of their lungs.

"I would!"

"Yes!"

"Can I be first?"

"Hang on!" Victor raised his arms like Moses in the wilderness. He held the pose until the children sat down and quiet reigned once more. "You must complete your paleontology training first."

He called the rest of his team over and introduced two more young women and two young men. Then he assigned the kids to groups headed by the college students. Elva and Cora went with Beanie. Tiege and Renny were assigned to Sheila, a tall woman with red, curly hair peeking out from under her bandana. Teresa, a solidly built brunette, high-fived her two charges, Winter Skye and Jeremy. Donald, the young man who had opened the gate when we arrived, rounded up Keeva and Grace.

Frank, a hefty guy with shaggy black hair and a two-day beard was assigned to Stig, Bennan, and Beau. He walked over to them and asked, "Where'd you get those cool boots, cowboys?" Just like that, he owned their little first-grade hearts. They looked at him like he'd just won the National Rodeo Finals.

For the rest of the morning, the college students led their charges on a tour of the dig camp. They took them to the lab tent and demonstrated how to use chisels, mallets, and paintbrushes. They even gave the kids time to practice. Then they took them to the camp kitchen for a snack of sliced apples and all the water they could drink. After that, they led the kids to the dig site and explained how they used the twine and tent peg grid system to document the location and position of fossils as they were unearthed. While all the college students were competent, Beanie stood out among them. Her ability to explain concepts in kid language and engage the children was exceptional.

The moms and I hovered in the background feeling superfluous. Other than the heft of the rattlesnake shovel I was toting, this was the easiest morning of my teaching career. I was getting ready to crow about it when Victor rang the dinner bell. He pointed toward a tiny, weathered shack beyond the far side of the lab tent.

"Line up in front of the outhouse so you can take care of business."

Though the day had grown warmer in the past few hours, I froze. The only thing I feared as much as meeting a rattlesnake was using an outhouse. The only thing

I feared more than either of those was meeting a rattle-snake while using an outhouse.

My students seemed to have no such compunctions. They lined up cheerfully, so I sucked up my courage, tightened my grip on my shovel, and swung into place as the caboose. When we were done lightening our loads, we washed our hands in a basin of cold, soapy water that sat on a rickety stand beside the outhouse.

I sent Renny and Elva to get the cooler from my car. Soon we were all sitting at the picnic tables cramming food into our mouths until our lunch sacks were empty and our stomachs were full. Once we'd eaten, the children became restless. The college students brought out Frisbees and invited the kids to play catch with them. After about fifteen minutes, the kids were sweaty and breathing hard. Victor clapped his hands and called for everyone to return to the picnic tables. My students trotted over, shedding jackets and sweatshirts and laying them on the picnic table.

Stig plopped down beside me. "Miss Newell," he shouted in my ear, "my hippie teached me how to throw a Frisbee!"

Victor clapped again and shouted above the din of the jostling, giggling kids. "How many of you are ready to dig in the dirt for fossils?"

The children raised their hands and screamed.

"I am!"

"Me too!"

"Can my leader come with me?"

Victor waited for the clamor to die down. It was a long wait. Finally he spoke again. "In a minute, your leader will take you to the kids' dig camp. They'll distribute your equipment and show you where to work. Remember you are scientists, so move carefully. We don't want to damage fossils that have been waiting to be found for millions of years, right?"

The children nodded, rose solemnly, and crept along behind their leaders. I tucked the "you are scientists" line into my mental classroom management file, picked up my shovel, and took my place at the end of the slow-moving line. When I reached the kid camp, the college students had arranged the children about two feet apart from one another and were supervising them. The kids were absorbed in their tasks, meticulously following their leaders' instructions to dig, brush away the dirt, and look for fossils. I got out my camera and tried to capture their junior-paleontologist vibes on film.

The afternoon was warm for late April, so we took a break after an hour. The children gulped down cans of cold pop and went back to work. At two forty-five, I announced it was time to stop. The children pleaded to stay longer.

"I wish we could," I tapped my watch, "but your parents are expecting us to return by dismissal time."

The air filled with groans and whines. Not from me. From the kids.

"Now, hand your tools to your leaders and thank them for a wonderful day."

The children thanked their leaders and then went a step further by hugging them. A few kids asked if they wanted to be pen pals—but forgot to collect addresses. I interrupted the warm fuzziness by insisting they end their goodbyes and by reminding them to pick up their jackets when we went past the picnic tables. The college students waved and scattered throughout the camp. Cookie, Mary, Pam, and I struggled to keep the children from doing the same.

Victor accompanied us to the parking lot and thanked the kids for their efforts. Then he presented each child with a junior paleontologist badge. I took a picture of him standing in the midst of them as they proudly held their badges. Victor thanked them once more and walked toward the camp.

I instructed the children to stand beside their buddy from the morning. Next I said, "Put your badges in your jacket pocket so yours doesn't get mixed up with somebody else's." All the children did as directed except for Renny, who panicked.

"Miss Newell," he said, wild-eyed and arms flapping. "I lost my jacket. My dad's gonna kill me. I gotta go look for it."

"No," I said. "You wait here with Mrs. Sternquist and the other moms. I'll go see if it was left behind."

For the sake of speed, I gave the rattlesnake shovel to Cookie and jogged down the path to the picnic tables. I did a quick scan of the area and spotted Renny's jacket under one of the tables. I fished it out and slung it over my arm. As I did so, something smacked against my hip. Hard. I groped for it to prevent it from smacking me again. My fingers closed around an object, its shape and heft similar to the mallets the children had used during the dig. Had Renny accidentally put one in his pocket? Or had he done it on purpose? With Renny, both were possibilities.

Leaving the mallet on the table was less complicated than returning it later, so I slipped my hand into the pocket and pulled it out. Only it wasn't a mallet. It was a fossilized bone similar to the specimens we'd seen in the lab tent. While I believed Renny capable of filching a mallet as a souvenir, I didn't think he would take a fossil. I'd watched him meticulously follow Sheila's instructions at the kid's dig camp and observed the joy on his small face when he received his junior paleontology badge. I could not believe he would knowingly steal a fossil. Perhaps Sheila had a better explanation. I ran to the lab tent hoping to find her there.

I yoo-hooed from outdoors before sticking my head in. "Anybody home?"

Silence.

Guess not. As I turned to leave, a pair of sunglasses poking out from under a table along one wall caught my eye. They looked like the ones Beanie had been wearing. I went inside and knelt to pick them up, and found Beanie lying face down on the dirt floor. She lay still. Too still. A rivulet of blood seeped from under her head and snaked toward me.

My body trembled as I reached forward, put a finger on her carotid artery, and waited. An eternity of ages passed until I felt a faint but steady pulse.

Beanie was alive! But just barely.

CHAPTER 2

I fashioned a pressure bandage out of the paper towels and burlap lying on the table and applied it to Beanie's wound. I reined in the emotions that threatened to turn me into a blithering fool and yelled for help. One of the women—Sheila I think—ran into the tent, saw us on the floor, and ran for reinforcements. I kept my emotions under wraps when Mary Borgeson came with her first aid bag and administered emergency care. I returned to the children, still blocking my emotions, and arranged for Cookie and Pam to drive the kids to town. I remained steady when Dick Phillips roared into camp with the ambulance, and when Victor and Donald carried Beanie on stretcher, with Mary trotting beside them holding up an IV drip bag. But after the ambulance took off for the hospital, and with my students on their way back to town with Cookie and Pam, my emotions took over.

"Don't let her die!" Huge sobs bent me double. "Please God, don't let my friend die."

A hand rubbed my shoulder. "Shhh," a woman's voice whispered in my ear. She guided me to a picnic table where she settled us both on its bench.

"She can't die," I sobbed.

"Sheila, would you get Jane something to drink?" Victor asked.

"And tissues, too," she said before she left.

Tears streamed down my face. A rope of snot inched toward my lips and threatened to slime my teeth. I clamped my lips shut and mumbled out the side of my mouth, "Call the sheriff."

"Already done," Victor reassured me. "He should be here any minute."

Sheila returned with a box of tissues. Teresa brought a can of Diet Coke. I mopped up rivers of tears and snot, then alternately sipped the pop and used the cold can to cool my eyelids, which felt hot and heavy. Sheila and Teresa kept up a steady stream of conversation until the county sheriff arrived.

The sight of him with his official uniform shirt tucked into blue jeans, his cowboy boots, and his regulation hat reassured me. Sheila and Teresa's faces said they were more impressed than reassured by his tanned face, neatly clipped dark blond hair, and blue eyes. An understandable reaction since Tipperary County Sheriff Rick Sternquist—brother to my student Tiege and son of Cookie—was a good-looking guy.

Half the town thought Rick and I would become an item after I moved to Little Missouri the previous August. But what with me poking my nose into a couple of his investigations over his strenuous objections, and then helping to crack the cases, the hoped-for flame between us had been snuffed out. Murder investigations tend to have that effect on people.

Nonetheless, he'd been clear-eyed enough to see the value of the forensic skills I developed while pursuing a criminal justice degree—a path shut down by my mother five minutes after she discovered what I was up to. He had appreciated how my abilities aided his investigations. Eventually, he allocated county funds to build a forensic lab and hired me to run it when I wasn't teaching.

These days, our relationship was purely professional, as was evident when he gave the dig crew a cursory nod and then spoke to me. "Good to see you brought your camera, Jane. Let's cordon off the area where you found the victim and get to work."

His objectivity shifted me into forensic investigation mode. I stepped forward and introduced Rick to Victor, who asked how he and his students could be of assistance.

Rick shook the professor's hand. "Once my deputy arrives, he'll take preliminary statements from all of you. Until then, stay clear of the crime scene and stay together where you can see each other."

"We'll stay right here and wait for the deputy." Victor's quick acquiescence to Rick's demands showed that the professor had caught the steely undertone beneath the sheriff's surface friendliness.

"Good." Rick went to the patrol car and pulled out his crime scene kit. He slung it over his shoulder and came to stand beside me. "Lead the way, Jane, and tell me what happened."

As we walked, I described stumbling upon Beanie in the lab tent. Every detail of finding her on the ground and keeping her alive was seared in my memory. The same was not true of what transpired after Mary arrived and took over. I blathered on about Beanie and Sioux City and Diet Coke and ropes of snot and how kind Sheila and Teresa had been.

Rick stopped me. "That's enough, Jane. People from the dig crew can tell me what happened after you left the tent. You say this woman's name is Beanie?"

"Her given name is Colleen Lavender. But in high school, we all called her Beanie."

He sucked in a sharp breath. "You knew her in high school?"

I gave him the Reader's Digest version of our friendship and reunion. "You should have seen how she related to the kids, Rick. She captivated them with her enthusiasm. What do I tell them if she doesn't make it?"

He held up an index finger. "Don't go there until we have reason to. For now, we are looking for the person who assaulted Colleen . . . er, Beanie." He made her nickname sound like a foreign language. "God willing, those will be the charges and nothing more serious."

The compassion in those words brought tears to my eyes.

"No, you don't." Rick held up his index finger again. "I already told you not to go there. Don't make me do it again. Now, get busy with that Tipperary County official camera around your neck."

That got my dander up. "I'm the one who paid for it!"

"True, but I requisitioned the film and built the darkroom."

I peered through the viewfinder and fiddled with the lens. "Is your deputy ever coming? I'd like to meet him."

"You mean to say you still haven't met Cardo?"

"I haven't, and what kind of name is Cardo?"

"He and his dad are both named Ricardo. He goes by Cardo to avoid confusion."

"Seriously?" I lowered the camera. "There are two more guys in this county with names that riff off 'Richard'?"

"What are you talking about?"

I ticked off names of the men I'd encountered in Tipperary County in the past eight months. "Richard Wentworth for starters, and his son Junior, also a Richard. Then there's you, Richard Sternquist. And did you know Rocko Vander Meer's given name was Richard? Not to mention Rikard DuPeuss. Now we've got Ricardo and Cardo." I paused. "There's someone else. Who am I forgetting?"

"How 'bout your boyfriend?" A smile tugged at the corners of Rick's mouth.

Oh yeah.

I ticked off another finger. "And Dick Phillips makes eight. What's the deal around here?"

"There's no deal Jane. You're just looking for something that's not there." He changed the subject. "Are you sure you haven't met Deputy Cardo before?"

"Positive. And not for lack of trying. Before he gets to where I am, I've been gone for five minutes."

"Speed is not his finest quality." Rick checked his watch, shook his head, and turned to leave. "I'm gonna start interviewing the dig crew without him."

"Go for it." I put the flash attachment on the camera and began taking photographs. First, close ups of the area where Beanie had lain. Then of footprints upon footprints surrounding the area where I'd found her. Finally, I stepped back and captured shots that encompassed the storage shelves and their contents, as well as the tables and the items lying on them. I began to sense that something in the lab was out of place. The feeling increased with every picture I took, and I took plenty—three rolls, if I counted the photos taken during our field trip when Beanie had still been a—

None of that Jane! Rick said not to go there.

I removed the camera from around my neck and set it on the table to wind the film into its bright yellow canister. When the tension released, I popped open the camera, removed the roll, and added it to its two predecessors in the bib pocket of my overalls. I felt positively kangaroo-ish.

That's when I realized that nothing in the lab was out of place. But something was missing. The fossilized bone from Kenny's pocket, the one I'd been holding when I saw Beanie lying on the ground, was gone. What had I done with it after I found her? I scanned the floor, the tabletops, and the shelves. I knelt down to shine a flashlight under the tables and into dark corners.

Once I was certain the bone was really and truly missing, I walked outside. With one hand I shaded my eyes against the sun to the west and searched for Rick.

"Sheriff?" I called in the most casual tone I could muster.

"What do you need, Jane?"

"Would you come here for minute? There's something you should see."

Or, I thought as Rick sauntered toward the tent, the wrinkle between his eyebrows saying he had noticed the concern in my voice, what was no longer here to see.

CHAPTER 3

Rick heard me out. Then he asked me to repeat what happened after I'd found Beanie. "What did you do?"

I closed my eyes, rewound my memory to before entering the lab tent, and narrated the events. "Renny's jacket was over my right forearm and the fossil was in my hand when I went inside the tent. I intended to set the fossil on the table closest to the entrance and take the jacket to Renny." With my eyes still closed, I saw myself catch a glimpse of Beanie's sunglasses, take a couple steps toward them, and bend down. I felt Renny's jacket slide down my arm when I saw Beanie and the blood soaking the dirt beneath her head.

My eyes flew open. "I dropped the bone and the jacket when I knelt to check Beanie's pulse. Sheila came running, saw me with Beanie, and went to fetch Mary. She brought her first-aid kit and began working on Beanie. She had me get her car keys so Cookie and Pam could drive the kids to town. She moved Renny's jacket out of the way—"

Rick interrupted. "What about the fossil?"

I closed my eyes once more. Renny's jacket lay crumpled under the long center table that ran the length of the tent. The jacket was next to Beanie's sunglasses, the lenses now cracked and dirty, one bow at an odd angle, the bridge snapped. Broken beyond repair, I thought, just like Beanie—

Uh-uh, Jane! Not while you're on duty. Not until you hear how she's doing.

I wrenched my attention back to the dirt floor under the table. Jacket. Broken sunglasses. And the fossil.

"I returned to the present and looked at Rick. "The bone was still on the floor when we all left." I pointed to a spot beyond the broken sunglasses. "Right there."

Rick turned on his flashlight and knelt to examine the dirt more closely. "I can't make out an impression of the bone."

"Because of the footprints?"

"No. Because the floor's been swept clean. With what, I wonder?" Rick stood and studied the cluttered tabletop. "You reckon it coulda been done with this, Jane?"

He picked up a paintbrush between his thumb and forefinger. It was the kind the kids had used that afternoon. He took an evidence bag from his pocket and dropped the brush inside.

I loaded a new roll of film and photographed the spot where the fossil had been when I'd last seen it. I took shots from several angles, always keeping Beanie's broken glasses in the frame as a point of reference.

Then I put the lens cap on the camera and rubbed the back of my neck. "I've got what we need from in here. What else can I do, Rick?"

He sized me up. "You look beat. How long's it been since you ate lunch?"

I shrugged. "Lunchtime, I guess."

"That was six hours ago. You need to go home. Me and Cardo can handle what's left once he gets here."

"See what I mean about me always leaving before your deputy arrives? I really want to meet him." I tried to suppress a stomach rumble and failed miserably.

"I heard that. Go home." He picked up the evidence bag with the paintbrush inside. "Take this with you and dust it for prints when you get the chance. By that, I mean tomorrow at the earliest. Not tonight. Do you understand?"

I reached for the bag.

He held it out of my grasp. "You promise to leave it for later?"

I let out an exasperated sigh. "Promise."

He handed over the bag. "I'll call tomorrow. Now go home and get some food in you. And then go to bed."

He's channeling your mother, Jane.

"Yes, boss," I scowled and trudged to my car.

A sweaty weariness engulfed me on the drive home. The two things on my mind when I parked the Beetle outside my apartment were a cold drink and a hot shower. Engrossed in an internal debate about which one to do first, I stuck the evidence bag with the paintbrush in an overall pocket and walked to the apartment landing. I climbed the steps and saw my rattlesnake shovel leaning against the railing. Pam or Cookie must have dropped it off. Next, I sniffed the air and caught a whiff of frying bacon. My stomach rumbled with joy.

I turned the knob. The door was unlocked. A few

months ago, such a discovery would have thrown me
into a panic. And for good reason. Early on, I'd had
a string of unwanted visitors sneak into my home—a
rich rancher named Junior Wentworth who thought
he owned the town in general and me in particular, a
Fly Ranch boy who was running for his life, and a state
trapper who wooed me with deworming remedies and
a Pepé Le Pew valentine card. However, not one of them
had commenced frying bacon upon arrival. Nor—I
sniffed the air again and caught a subtle blend of non-
skid pancakes and chicken manure mingling with the
bacon—had they brought enough fresh milk and eggs
for a week's worth of breakfasts.

Even so, past circumstances had instilled in me a
modicum of caution. I picked up the rattlesnake shovel,
pointed it like a spear, and eased through the door.
"Merle, is that you?"

The only answer was a wet, schleppy intake of breath
keeping time with the sizzle of frying bacon. My caution
was superfluous. I returned the shovel to its spot on the
landing. Before I could go inside, however, all five feet
four inches and one hundred fifteen pounds of Velma
Albright barreled down the sidewalk.

"Did that fool of an old man who insisted on taking
my keys to make you supper forget to tape the note I give
him to your door so you wouldn't bean him with that
shovel you been carrying around since winter let up?
How many times have I gotta tell you that snakes is more
afraid of you than you is of them?"

Her statement incorporated a gross overestimate of
my courage coupled with an even grosser underestimate
of the courage of snakes. Considering the head of steam

she had on her, I decided this was not the time to point out her error of judgment. She had long ago mastered the art of pointing out the errors of others without ever pointing out her own.

Velma was the school's official janitor, for which I was thankful, and my unofficial social secretary, for which I was not. I beamed at her. "Merle's inside. Want to join us?"

"Of course I do." She stomped onto the landing. Her black eyes glittered. A smear of black hair dye was visible along her part. She'd been touching up her roots again. "Soon as I heard what happened at that there dinosaur dig, I told the old buzzard to come over and make you supper. I don't know how you keep gettin' in these fixes. Ever since you moved here, you've been tripping over dead bodies wherever you go."

Not true. The body of Twila Kelly, mother of Beau, had been found before I moved to Little Missouri. I had found the body of Edgar Running Horse in the Long Pines last November when half the county had been up there looking for Christmas trees. Had I not found him, someone else would have. Rocko Vander Meer's pulse was faint when I tripped over him during the dead of winter. His injuries and the subzero temperatures soon did him in, but not until after I found him. Also, Beanie had been alive when I found her and when the ambulance took off.

A shiver ran down my spine. "Are you saying she's dead?"

A rare softness came into Velma's eyes. "You mean that girl with the vegetable name? Sweet Pea or something like that?"

"Beanie."

"That's it. I heard she was in bad shape when they got to Spearfish, so they sent her right on to Rapid City. Far as I know, she ain't dead . . . yet."

Velma meant well, I knew she did, but unless her lack of tact was soon diluted, my emotions would take over and I'd lose it again.

I took a deep breath. "Let's see how supper's coming along." I waved her ahead of me.

She went inside and yelled, "Jane is famished! How long till we eat?"

I followed her through the entryway and into the open L-shaped half of the apartment. She stopped beside the table located in the corner of the L. I went past her into the L's long wing and opened the living room windows. Then I walked over to the afghan lying on the couch and surreptitiously slid the evidence bag under the blanket. Putting it where it belonged in the locked forensic lab would have to wait until I could take the key from its hiding place after Merle and Velma cleared out.

Merle stood at the stove in the L's short wing. His sparse fringe of white hair needed a comb, the white stubble on his cheeks and jaw needed a shave, and his faded denim overalls and flannel shirt, buttoned tight at the neck and both wrists, needed a washing machine.

"I shoulda figured you two'd keep yappin' until I done all the work and got the food ready." He forked bacon from the frying pan into a cake pan lined with paper towels. "Teacher, you know I ain't one for rummaging through other folks' cupboards—"

Velma crossed her scrawny arms. "Are you saying Jane's frying pan and whatnot jumped into your hands by themselves?"

I went to the kitchen, took plates and glasses from the cupboard, and gave them to Velma. She arranged them on the table while I added napkins and silverware. Next, I got out butter, syrup, and a jar of Mom's homemade plum jam and carried them to the table. Merle opened the waffle iron and added the last batch of his non-skid pancakes to an already heaping platter. After he brought over the food, we sat down, and I said a quick grace. Velma and Merle ceased their sniping, and we all dug in. I ate quickly, knowing the ceasefire wouldn't last long. In fact my angels of supper mercies were revving up for a new round of hostilities when the phone rang.

The well-timed ring shored up my faith in the sovereignty of God. I ran for the phone on the kitchen counter, blocking Velma with my elbows before she beat me to it.

I snatched the receiver from its cradle and held it to my ear. "Jane Newell speaking."

"Hi."

My boyfriend, Dick Phillips, possessed a maddening ability to shrink a sentence into one word that contained the fewest syllables and letters possible. It was his trademark, one that had nearly ended our relationship before it began.

With two of the nosiest sets of ears in town listening in on conversation—make that three, as switchboard operator Betty Yarborough was likely on the line also—responding in kind seemed a wise course.

"Hi."

"She's in Rapid City. ICU. Serious but stable condition."

My bones turned to jelly. I leaned against the wall.

"Okay, thanks. Bye." I tried to return the receiver to the cradle, but the jelly in my bones refused to cooperate.

"Hey!" Dick said.

What a charmer.

"Yes?" I replied.

"Want to go to supper and a movie in Tipperary on Saturday?"

My bones recovered. I held out the receiver and stared at it. Had Dick taken leave of his senses? Was he unaware that asking me out over the phone when Betty was listening in was tantamount to broadcasting the question via a loudspeaker on Main Street?

"Yes," I mumbled.

"Want to leave at four so you can go to the grocery store first?"

"Fine." I hung up before he could whisper more sweet nothings in my ear and make Betty swoon.

Merle smiled. "Musta been Dick Phillips."

How could he know?

"What'd he want?" Velma asked.

They'd get word of our Saturday plans soon enough, so I stuck to matters of life and death. "He called about Beanie. She's alive."

Chapter 4

That night I dreamed of Velma wearing a Tyrannosaurus rex costume. She chased me around my classroom, gnashing needlelike teeth. A dustpan dangled from one ineffectual claw, a whisk broom from the other.

She advanced upon me, roaring, "No more glitter," with each earth-shaking footfall.

Merle appeared behind her. He lifted my rattlesnake shovel to his shoulder, sighted along the length of its handle, and pulled the trigger.

I stuck my fingers in my ears, anticipating the shot to come.

Brrring!

My ears rang, defying my efforts.

Brrring!

Velmasaurus rex and Merle the Mighty vanished, leaving a fog of confusion in their wake.

Brrring!

My phone was ringing, not my ears. I threw off the pillow and was headed for the kitchen when my alarm clock began to trill. I ran to my nightstand, depressed the alarm's plunger, and dashed to the kitchen again.

I snatched up the receiver and rubbed my eyes. "Jane Newell speaking."

"Sorry to call so early," the sheriff said.

"It's a welcome relief," I yawned. "I was having a bad dream."

"Ah."

The nightmare that was yesterday cut through my mental fog. "How is Beanie?"

"Still alive—"

Thank God.

"—and unconscious due to brain swelling. That's what they think it is, anyway."

"What's that mean for the investigation?"

"We keep doing what we're supposed to be doing."

Rick had been sheriff for a couple years and had several investigations under his belt. I, on the other hand, had served as director of the county forensic lab, previously known as my guest bedroom, for only one case. The main thing I'd learned while working that case was to assume nothing.

Which is why I stated the obvious. "So I'm supposed to develop the pictures from the lab tent and dust the paintbrush for fingerprints."

"Yes."

"I'll start after school today." *A ridiculous assumption.*

"Would you also write a full report of what you observed yesterday?"

"From when I found Beanie? Sure."

"No. From when you first arrived in the morning to when you went home."

Like I said before. Assume nothing.

"Sure. I'll make copies for both of us."

"Me and Deputy Columbo—"

"You said his name was Cardo."

"That's his first name. His last name is Columbo. Like the TV detective."

"You're kidding."

"Nope. Dead serious. As I was saying before you interrupted me, me and my deputy will write up our interviews with the dig team and get copies to you too."

"Anything else?"

"The hospital is supposed to provide our office with daily updates about Colleen. We'll pass them on to you when they come in."

"Thank you."

He hung up, and I was about to do the same when Betty's voice came down the line. "I'm gwad your friend is stiww awive, Miss Neweww."

My ability to translate the Little Missouri switch-board operator's words had improved exponentially since our first phone conversation last August. My admiration of her communication skills caused by her lip and cleft palate repair in the early 1900s had grown by the same measure.

Though I understood her perfectly my reply caught in my throat. Betty waited, but my words refused to come. She interrupted the silence. "My goodness, wook at the time! I better wet you go so you're ready when your students gawwop in wike a pack a frisky ponies. We'ww tawk again soon."

I rang the school bell an hour later. I don't know if it was the brisk, clear morning or yesterday's field trip

that rendered the children more wild than frisky as
they lined up. This being a Tuesday, the kindergarteners
weren't in attendance. Had they been present, the stam-
pede up the stairs and into the entryway might have laid
me flat. The children flung their lunch boxes into cubbies
and tossed jackets onto hooks. Then they ran into the
classroom and raced around their desks like they were
running barrels.

Cora and Elva pranced over. Cora spoke first. "You
know how I said I wanted to be a princess when I grow
up?"

Of the one hundred and sixty-five days of school thus
far, she'd reiterated her future career plans on at least
one hundred and sixty of them. "As a matter of fact, I
do."

She sighed a princess-worthy sigh of pleasure and
did a little twirl. "Mom says she can put sparkles on my
overalls, so now I want to be paleontologist."

Elva folded her arms. "I'm still going to be a rodeo
star. And a teacher. Who teaches rodeo and paleontology." She wrinkled her nose. "Can I do that?"

"Elva, you can do anything." Truer words had never
been spoken.

Tiege bounced over. "Miss Newell, look what I
brung!"

"Brought," I corrected.

His eyebrows furrowed as he thrust a book under my
nose. "That's what I said. I brung you this. It's all about
dinosaurs."

Beau, Stig, and Bennan galloped up next. Beau served
as spokesperson. "Us three played dino dig in Grandma
and Grandpa's backyard yesterday, and we found this."

He stuck under my nose what looked like a steak bone
gnawed clean.

Bennan traced the tooth marks with a grubby finger.
"We 'zamined it just like Frank taught us. I'm a hunnert
percent sure those are from a Tyrannosaurus rex."

"Wanna see?" Stig waved a magnifying glass.

I grabbed its handle before it went up my right
nostril. "Whoa there!" I hollered to the herd of wild
ponies who seemed determined to injure my schnoz.
"It's almost time for show-and-tell. We'll start as soon as
you're in your seats and quiet."

With that, they reined in their enthusiasm and trotted briskly to their desks—all but Renny, who had shown
none of his classmates' exuberance. He was slow and
subdued on his way to his seat. His behavior was quite
out of character for a kid who relished show-and-tell
more than a T-Rex with a stegosaurus bone.

The children took turns going to the front of the
room to repeat to their friends what they had already
told me. No one brought up Beanie Lavender, her
ambulance ride, or the fact that she was in ICU. I didn't
either. While Beau, Bennan, and Stig took the bone
and magnifying glass from desk to desk, I wrote a note
in my memo book. I wanted to call the principal, Mrs.
Dremstein, after school and get her advice about how to
handle the Beanie situation with the students and their
parents. When I finished, I watched Renny. Instead of
impatiently waving his arm until I called on him for
show-and-tell, he sat at his desk unmoving. His eyes
were downcast, his mouth frozen in a frown. I jotted a
second reminder to phone his parents after I'd talked
with Mrs. Dremstein.

After show-and-tell, I lassoed the children and led them through their lessons—reading, phonics, spelling, math, handwriting, and social studies. During science I mentioned the field trip. Renny's expression went blank and his body shrank two sizes. From then on, I steered clear of dinosaur talk. Once the children left at the end of the day, I called the principal. She said that for now, telling the students that an accident had put Beanie in the hospital was enough. I thanked her for her guidance and said goodbye. Then I asked Betty if Renny's mom was at home or at Round the Bend.

"I beweive she went home to fowd waundry. I'ww connect you, and I'ww hang up out of respect for teacher-parent confidentiawity."

This was new. Confidentiality had never concerned Betty before, but I wasn't about to object.

Trudy picked up right away. After a modicum of chit-chat, I got to the point. "Renny didn't seem like himself today. Is something bothering him?"

She sighed a worried-mom sigh. "Last night, he overheard a couple guys at the bar. They were talking about what happened at the dig. I could tell right away it got to him. He's had a big crush on Beanie ever since the first time the dig crew came here to eat. Maybe we shoulda talked to him about it last night, but we decided to wait until we heard how she was doing. You know anything?"

"This morning the sheriff said she was stable, but unconscious. I didn't say anything to the children today either. I wanted to ask the principal how to handle it first." I told Trudy how Mrs. Dremstein suggested framing it as an accident that had nothing to do with the field trip. "Does that sound okay to you? I wanted to ask you because Renny seemed so upset. I don't want to disturb him any more than he already is."

"He's got it in his head that he done something that got her hurt. If you tell him he didn't have anything to do with it, that'll make him feel some better."

"Good. And Trudy? I'll let you know right away if Beanie takes a turn for the worse. Renny needs to hear it from you instead of from kids on the playground or customers in the bar."

Trudy agreed, and we ended our call.

I set the receiver in the cradle. My hand stilled, and I stared at the phone without seeing it. As far as I knew, Renny was the only student in my class who had known anyone from the dig crew before our field trip. Plus he had a crush on the person who'd been hurt, and the dinosaur bone had been hidden in his jacket. Was that a coincidence?

Maybe so, but Rick had stressed the importance of following up on coincidences during an investigation instead of ignoring them. This coincidence involved one of my students. No way was I going to ignore it.

Chapter 5

Every cell in my body longed to go straight to the darkroom and start developing film. Instead, I stayed at my desk until every paper was corrected, every grade recorded, and the following week's lesson plans were done. By then it was evening and time for a long overdue supper. I ate and went to bed so I could get up and start my day job early. I ate breakfast at my desk. To free up my time after school for working in the dark-room, I prepared seatwork packets and center activities for the rest of the week. I flew around fast enough to break into a sweat before the children entered the class-room. Winter Skye, with her white-blond braids whip-ping every which way, climbed the stairs and marched to where I stood in the entryway.

"Miss Newell." She paused to put her hands on her skinny hips. "My mom said to tell you there's dinosaur bones sticking up in our pasture. I wanna dig 'em up for show-and-tell, but Mom says no. We oughta have another field trip so the whole class can see them. We can roast hot dogs!" She punctuated her speech with a sweeping gesture, nearly impaling Jeremy Gibson on her bony elbow.

"Kapow," he bellowed with his usual Batman enthusiasm. "Can we have s'mores too?"

The other children crowded around us and began talking.

"How come Jeremy gets s'mores and the rest of us don't?"

"That's not fair!"

"I don't like marshmallows. Can I make mine with just chocolate and graham crackers?"

"How come nobody told me about the picnic?"

The cramped entryway reverberated with indignation.

"Calm down!" I roared with the ferocity of Velmasaurus rex. To my amazement, the din faded. The children all looked at me.

Um, now what?

"There's no picnic and no s'mores—"

"No fair," they whined as one.

Oh, brother.

The day was more of the same with a pinch of dinosaur research thrown in to reduce the whine factor now and again. The high point of the day was dismissal time. Never had I been so relieved to watch my students race across the playground and toward their homes. I loved my scoundrels dearly, but at this moment my heart was with the three rolls of film that had been calling my name for hours.

Fifteen minutes later, the classroom was ready for the next day. I went to my apartment, changed clothes, and hit the darkroom. By the time the negatives were clipped to their clotheslines to dry, my stomach was growling. I made a fried egg sandwich for supper and ate it while typing the report Rick had requested. Every once in a while, I closed my eyes to replay how the field trip had gone down. The report took much longer to finish than the sandwich did, though the sandwich tasted better. Eventually I finished and removed the last page from the typewriter. I made two piles, one of the original pages and one of the carbon copies, which I took into the lab. Then I went into the darkroom again and began making prints. Darkness fell as I hung them on the clotheslines that were strung from wall to wall in the forensic lab. Satisfied with my efforts, I put on my pajamas. It was after ten, and I was about to crawl into bed when the phone rang. Who could be calling at this hour? I yawned on the way to the phone

"Jane Newell speaking."

"How are you coming with the report and the photographs?"

"I should have known it was you Rick. Don't you care about me getting eight hours of sleep at night?"

"I do. But I care more about the report and the photographs."

"Both are finished."

"Good. Do you have time to go over them right after school tomorrow?"

"Nope. I've got a haircut at Galva Swensen's. I should be back by five if you can come then."

"I'll be there by five fifteen. Want me to grab supper at The Bend on the way?"

Silly question. I said as much and asked about Beanie.

"The doctors say she's in a coma. No better and no worse."

"Does she have anyone with her?"

"Her parents got there last night."

"I know them. Beanie invited us to her house all the time. Mr. and Mrs. Lavender welcomed us even when they didn't know who was coming. Or when." I imagined them sitting on either side of her hospital bed, holding her hands and praying for her to wake up. "The waiting. The limbo. It must be hell for them." Anger kindled inside me and fueled my resolve. "We've got a mountain of evidence to sift through tomorrow. How late can you stay?"

"As long as it takes," Rick said with equal resolve before he hung up.

Images of Beanie's parents hovering over her hospital bed haunted my dreams. I was grateful when the ring of my alarm clock chased away their ghosts. I jumped out of bed and padded into the living room for a peek out the window. The sun was bright in a clear blue sky. The outdoor thermometer read fifty-five degrees.

Yes!

Never mind my lack of sleep. The weather convinced me that spring was here to stay. To celebrate, I put on a sleeveless dress with a matching jacket and my favorite sandals. Without warning, a voice interrupted the party in my head.

You told your dad you would be up front with them about new investigations. Call your parents right now, at the beginning of the case. They should hear about Beanie from you.

I glanced at the clock. If I called right now, Mom would still be home. I went to the phone and asked Betty to ring my parents' house. Mom picked up right away.

"Mom, it's Jane."

"What's wrong? Are you sick?"

"I'm fine."

"Then why are you calling? I need to get out the door soon."

"The new case Rick and I are working on has a Sioux City connection. I wanted you to hear about it from me first."

"Who died?"

"No one. At least not yet. But Colleen Lavender—do you remember Beanie?—was injured on Monday. She's in a coma at the hospital in Rapid City. It could have been an accident or she could have been the victim of an attack."

"How did she get to that godforsaken country of yours?"

It wasn't *my* godforsaken country, but in the interest of time I didn't quibble. I summarized the incident without divulging anything about the progress of the investigation. It was an easy needle to thread since progress had yet to be made.

"I need to get out the door, so I'm handing the phone to your father," Mom said when I was done. "Talk to you more on Saturday." And she was gone.

"Dad, are you there?"

"Affirmative, Janie-Jo."

"Did you hear my conversation with Mom?"

"Negative."

After I repeated the story, he said, "Thanks for telling the truth from the start. It feels good, doesn't it?"

I agreed, and we said our goodbyes. I glanced at the clock. Not leaving time to correct the papers I'd left on my desk wouldn't feel nearly as good. For the second day in a row, I ate breakfast at my desk and finished recording the last grade with time enough to get a fresh cup of coffee with five minutes to spare. I took a couple hearty slugs before I went outside with the school bell. Based on the children's startled looks and shrieks, it rang louder and longer than usual. The caffeine was kicking in. Considering the day ahead, I wanted it to keep kicking until long after dark.

Chapter 6

My students were as tame and serious this morning as they'd been wild and frisky yesterday. I assumed the change was due to Thursday being a non kindergarten day. Or maybe the kids hadn't imbibed coffee at breakfast. Due to the impossibility of proving a negative, I would never know.

What I did know was this—the absence of four very busy, very curious, and very time-consuming kindergarteners meant that today was my chance to have a heart-to-heart chat with Renny.

My opportunity arose while I was on recess duty after lunch. Most of Liv's students were playing kickball in the grassy area on the south end of the schoolyard. A few of her younger ones were playing pioneer days with the kids from my room. The exception was Renny, who was sitting on a swing and kicking at the gravel with the toes of his cowboy boots.

I went over to him and plopped into the swing beside him. "Why aren't you playing with the others?"

He shrugged and stared at the ground.

"Is something bothering you?"

A nod.

"Want to talk about it?"

A shrug.

My stellar interviewing skills were having little effect on this kid. I waited a beat and tried again. "I miss Beanie. Do you?"

This time he looked up before nodding. Progress at last!

"She was my friend in high school. In Sioux City."

He brightened. "Mine too. In Little Missouri. Not Sioux City."

"I'm glad you're her friend." I bumped the side of my swing into his.

He giggled. "Me too. 'Cause those other dig team people ain't her friends."

I stilled. "Did she say that?"

"No." He scrunched up his face. "But I could tell. They didn't treat her nice when they come into The Bend."

"Like how?"

"I dunno. Nobody ever saved her a seat. And they quit talkin' when she come in."

"Did everyone on the dig team act like that?"

He nibbled at a fingernail before taking it out of his mouth and saying, "Yup."

Before he could elaborate, Liv rang the bell. Renny jumped out of his swing, but he didn't run to get into line. Instead, he took my hands and pulled me up. Then he clung to one of my hands as we went to join his classmates. When we got to where they stood, he squeezed my fingers. I squeezed his in return before going to open the door. My gaze followed him as he and his classmates filed past. His lower lip quivered, and his eyes brimmed with tears.

There was something he wasn't telling me. I was sure of it, but it would have to wait until next recess. I gave him a tissue as he walked by. He dabbed at his eyes and blew his nose as he trudged to his desk. He sat down and buried his head in his arms.

Oh, Renny.

Following up with Renny during afternoon recess didn't happen because Tiege had a humdinger of a nosebleed that needed tending. And I couldn't talk to Renny after school because of my hair appointment with Winter Skye's mom, Galva Swensen.

Their ranch was about ten minutes west of town, and I parked next to a large, new pole building. Its northeast corner had been partitioned off to house Galva's hair salon. Garth's taxidermy business took up the remainder of the space. My life was complete without ever again setting foot into that part of the building. Winter Skye, on the other hand, was obsessed with taxidermy. I whispered a prayer of thanks when she didn't materialize and drag me into the little shop of horrors she loved so much.

I went straight to the shampoo station in Galva's shop. She made small talk as she washed and rinsed my hair. "I hear you got a big date with Dick Phillips Saturday night."

"Uh-huh," I said, not letting on that my concern for Renny had made me forget about our date.

She wiggled her eyebrows and combed out my tangles. "I can fix your hair real glamorous."

"Don't you dare. I already had to phone my parents about what happened at the dig site on Monday. The last thing I need is a call from them on Sunday asking if Dick and I are engaged."

"Are you?" More eyebrow wiggles as she picked up her scissors and began snipping.

I spoke through clenched teeth. "Don't go there, Galva."

"You are so much fun to tease." She laughed. "Winter Skye said she told you about our dinosaur bones. You want to see them?"

"I'm not dressed to go tromping through pastures."

"How about tomorrow around five? We can hike out there, and you can stay for supper afterwards." She began shaping my hair with brush and blow-dryer.

"Yes," I yelled above the noise and smiled at my reflection in the mirror. The next few days were shaping up nicely. Carry out with Rick tonight. Supper with the Swensens on Friday and with Dick on Saturday was fine by me. All in all, a nice break from cooking for one and eating alone.

"Can I bring anything tomorrow?" I asked while writing Galva a check.

"Just yourself," she said.

"See you then."

The sheriff was sitting in his vehicle when I parked in my spot beside the school. He hopped out when I did, and we entered my apartment together. I crossed the living room in a few swift strides and flung open the lab door. "Bring the food in here," I suggested. "We can eat while we work."

Rick set out the food while I unclipped the photographs and stacked them next to our meals. Then we sat down and ate while he read through my account of the field trip, asked questions, and scribbled notes in the margins. After an hour of that, he studied the photographs for another hour while I read through the statements he and his deputy had taken on the day of Beanie's accident.

When I finished, I asked, "When did Deputy Cardo make it to the scene?"

"About five minutes after you left."

"Is he intentionally trying to avoid meeting me?"

Rick snorted. "More like he's as lazy as they come. His top speeds are slow and slower."

"Why do you keep him on?"

"You'll see." He tapped a finger on a few photographs he'd set between us. "Does anything stand out to you in these?"

I studied the images one by one. They all pictured the circular area around where Beanie's body had been. Each shot focused on a different wedge of the circle. In every one, the dirt floor had been swept clean of shoe and boot prints. But in the far corner of one shot, a partial print remained. I pointed to it. "Do you mean this?"

"Yes." He picked up a second handful of photos. "Now look at these."

They showed the children wielding their tools at the kids' dig site. I was about to tell Rick that they had nothing to do with the previous ones when I noticed what he had. More boot prints.

I picked up those photographs and the one from the lab tent. "I'll enlarge these so we can compare the patterns to the partial boot print and the work boots at the dig site. I'll have them ready by tomorrow afternoon if I start now. While I do that, would you make a table of where the dig team members were—and when—based on their statements?"

"I can. But before I forget"—he took a sealed envelope from his jacket pocket—"I better give you this. Cardo handed them to me before I took off. He said you would want it."

I ripped open the envelope and took out the paper inside. It was a chart with the information I'd just requested from Rick. I showed it to him. "That's kinda weird."

"That's Cardo."

"Hmm. So what are you going to do while I'm in the darkroom?"

He thought for a moment. "Eavesdrop at The Bend and nurse a beer?"

"The Bend. Oh my gosh. I forgot to tell you about Renny." I filled him in. "Can it be a coincidence that the bone was in Renny's pocket?"

"There are no coincidences in an investigation."

Of course he said that.

"Do you want to talk to him?"

"I doubt he'll open up to me. We'll probably learn more if you keep at it."

"You're right." I glanced at my watch. Seven thirty. "You go eavesdrop at The Bend and give me a call in the morning for my report on the photographs."

He left. I locked the door behind him and shut myself in the darkroom. "God, thank you for Deputy Cardo," I whispered while pouring developing fluids into tubs. "At the risk of sounding greedy, would you light a fire under him so we end up in the same place at the same time? I'd sure like to meet the guy."

No answer. At least not an audible one. With an impatient sigh, I pulled out the negatives in question and began making enlargements. God might not have a tight deadline, but I sure did.

Chapter 7

My clothes and hair still smelled like the darkroom after I hung up the prints to dry and left the lab. I was beat after my long day, but the last of the caffeine I'd swilled refused to leave the building and let me go sleep. To rid myself of both Eau de Darkroom and caffeine brain, I stood in a hot shower for longer than would have been possible were I, rather than the school, footing my water and sewer bills. Then I curled up in bed with the new Stephen B. Oates biography of Abraham Lincoln I'd checked out from the bookmobile. Exactly when I fell asleep will remain a mystery, but the circle of dried drool on page fifty-two will bear constant, silent testimony of my ignominy.

My disgrace made itself known when the phone began ringing and my eyes flew open. I threw the offending tome under the bed and went to the kitchen. I rubbed my eyes and checked the time before I answered. Six thirty. Only a few minutes before my alarm clock was set to ring. No need to chide the caller for waking me too soon.

"Hi, this is Jane."

"And this is Rick. Are you done with the photos?"

"Uh-huh." I rubbed my eyes.

"Can I stop by after school to pick up them up?"

"That'll be fine. I have to be at the Swensens' at five o'clock, so don't be late."

"Maybe we oughta start scheduling our meetings in advance. Your social life is picking up."

"Don't I know it! See you later."

I hung up and went to the window. The day was dawning clear and bright. The temperature was already in the forties. Once again, I marveled at how spring had arrived in a rush and sent winter packing. My spirits rose at the thought of pleasant weather stretching out for months to come. A couple hours later, the children trooped in smelling of fresh air, sunshine, and joy.

This was a kindergarten Friday, so our classroom was a busy place. It was also more orderly than had been the case when they'd been here on Wednesday. The promise of creating May baskets for their parents during the final hour of the school day if they were good listeners may have been the reason for that. My skill at dangling carrots rather than sticks had grown exponentially since August. I complimented myself as the May basket hour drew near. Then I heard Mom's voice.

Don't break your arm patting yourself on the back, Jane.

I directed a metaphorical eye roll at the voice in my head, announced that art time had arrived, and laid paper cups and supplies for making May baskets on the front table. The treats intended to fill the baskets would come out shortly before dismissal time. As a child, I had loved making little paper baskets and filling them with popcorn and candy. Even better was leaving the baskets on my friends' doorsteps on May first, ringing their doorbells, and running away before they appeared. I wanted my students to have as much fun on May Day as I had.

Our classroom buzzed with coloring, cutting, gluing, and stapling as the kids crafted their masterpieces. The dinosaur coloring pictures and stickers proved to be popular, as was glitter. One by one, the children brought their creations for me to see.

Cora, Grace, Keeva, and Winter Skye twirled over in a shower of sparkles. Embracing her status as the kindergarteners' role model, Cora spoke for them all. "Do you think our mommies and daddies will like these?"

I eyed their glitter-encrusted baskets. "Of course they will."

Next came Jeremy, Bennan, and Renny with brightly colored dinosaurs complete with bat wings stapled to their paper cups.

"Kapow!" I said.

"Kapow!" they replied in unison as they giggled and flew to their desks.

Elva and Stig showed off their creations, which featured paint horses with dinosaur stickers as brands.

"Because we're gettin' ready to brand the new calves," Stig explained.

To which his big sister added, "But horses are prettier than calves. And this is art class."

Tiege bounced over with his basket. He demonstrated

how to depress the pipe cleaner he'd coiled into a spring. One end of the spring was glued to the bottom of the cup and a paper tyrannosaurus rex to the other. When he let go of the dinosaur, it sprang up like a prehistoric version of Tigger. I would call his parents this weekend and advise them to find their safety goggles before May Day.

Beau made his way to me last. He had drawn, colored, and cut out the figure of a woman. She had long, dark hair and a butterfly perched on her shoulder. His artistic skill was undeniable. The picture of his mother was a remarkable likeness.

He leaned close and whispered, "It's my Mommasaurus."

"She's beautiful, Beau. And so is this." I touched the butterfly gently.

"Grampa and Gramma say whenever one flies close, it's Momma coming to see me."

I fought against the wave of anger that rose within me whenever the injustice of Twila's death came front and center. Beau would live without his mother for the rest of his life. Junior Wentworth, whose actions had caused her death, would never pay for what he'd done to her. True, he was in prison for other crimes, but one day he would be free to resume his life. Later rather than sooner, I hoped, as I hugged Beau close.

"Miss Newell." Elva pointed to the clock. "It's past dismissal time."

I gave Beau a final squeeze and let go. Soon I was barking orders like a drill sergeant with a weekend pass. "Put your baskets in the box on the table at the back of the room. We'll fill them at the end of the day on Monday."

A few minutes and uncounted protests later, the kids were gone. Art supplies cluttered the table. Bits of paper littered the carpet, and glitter covered every surface. When Velma saw this, she would explode. Although her anti-glitter campaign was on hold until next fall due to a ceasefire I'd negotiated a few months ago, the sight of the glitter winking brightly could foment an anti-glue, anti-paper-cutting, and anti-anything-kids-enjoy campaign with me as its target.

I dashed around, gathering up paper scraps and hurling them into the wastebasket. The floor was paper free and I was scraping globs of glue from desktops with a putty knife when she arrived.

The smell of cigarette smoke and a low, guttural growl announced her presence. "You been givin' them kids free range with art supplies again, ain't you? Why you gotta use glitter—"

"—Ah, ah, ah!" I straightened and wagged my index finger back and forth. "That's out of bounds and you know it."

She scowled. "How was I to know you'd be spreading glitter around this room like fish food in an aquarium every chance you got way back when I agreed to it? That's extortion is what it is!"

"That may be your definition of extortion. Mine is being signed up for square dance lessons without my permission and discovering that every single young man in the county is on my dance card."

The mention of her high-handed tactics last January shut her mouth. With a huff, she yanked the vacuum out of the closet, and attacked the carpet with a ferocity that set the glitter trembling. I went back to scraping glue. The tension was thick enough to cut with my putty knife.

"You in there, Jane?" Rick yelled above the roar of the vacuum cleaner and Velma's mumbling.

"Coming." I abandoned my task and met him in the classroom entryway.

Velma switched off the vacuum, followed me, and crossed her arms when she saw the sheriff. "Rick Sternquist, I got a complaint to register with you."

"You and half the county," he replied with a smile.

"But mine's important. Your la-de-da part-time employee"—she cocked her head in my direction—"don't see fit to give me a key so I can clean that forensic lab you built on school property. What you got to say about that?"

He considered her request and said, "You make a fair point."

Velma beamed in triumph. I stared at him in disbelief.

"Soon as you add cleaning the rest of school property, like Jane's apartment and the playground after the Wentworth's bulls get loose, to your janitorial duties, I'll get you a key. Whaddya say?"

"Never mind." Her tone was so venomous I took hold of the rattlesnake shovel as she grabbed her feather duster and stomped into the classroom.

I gestured for him to follow me into my apartment and shut the door between it and the classroom entryway. "Stand guard for a second," I whispered. After I retrieved the key from its hiding place under the ice cube trays in the freezer, I motioned him into the kitchen. He waited there while I retrieved a large manila envelope from the lab and returned the key to the freezer. Then I handed him the envelope. "I haven't had time to examine them closely. It'll be Sunday before I—"

"Social life getting in the way again?"

"None of your business."

"Want me to pick up food at The Bend after church? We could meet here and review the case over lunch."

"Perfect."

"Thanks for working me in, Jane." He snickered on the way out. I considered hurling the rattlesnake shovel at him, but then thought better of it. Being teased for having a busy social life was a good thing. I leaned the shovel against the wall, squared my shoulders, and, armed only with kindness, entered my classroom to face the wrath of Velma. She was cleaning the blackboards, so I vacuumed the floor until the glitter gave up its winking. When I was done, I put the vacuum cleaner away and told Velma to have a nice weekend. She replied with an almost imperceptible wink. I acknowledged our ceasefire with a wink of my own and escaped to my apartment before she got her underwear in a bunch again. Being Velma's enemy was easy. Being her friend required going while the going was good.

CHAPTER 8

A half hour later, I hopped into the Beetle, drove south on Main Street, and turned west onto Highway 20. The glare of the sun made my eyes water. I pulled over and took out my sunglasses. The image of Beanie's broken pair lying next to her still body on the dirt floor flashed into my consciousness. My stomach twisted when I realized I hadn't asked Rick how she was doing when he stopped by. I stewed about how quickly I'd relegated her condition to the back burner.

See what happens when you put your social life first, Jane?

I was still stewing when I reached the Swensens' and parked beside their mobile home. Winter Skye was waiting on the landing. She ran down the steps and toward my car. I opened the door. She took my hand, pulled me to my feet, and danced around me with gleeful abandon.

"You're wearing your prayleontology overalls, Miss Newell."

Her pronunciation beat the dictionary's, hands down.
I didn't bother correcting it.

"Is it time for the hike?"

Her gleeful expression vanished. Her eyes grew steely.
"Everybody has to go potty first, even teachers. Bathroom's in there." Her unyielding body language brooked
no argument as she jerked a thumb toward the house.

On the way to the house, I passed a Weber kettle with
a mound of charcoal briquettes heating on its bottom
tray. My mouth watered in anticipation of a meal that
featured grilled anything for supper. I climbed the steps
to the front door and knocked. Autumn Breeze, the
second-to-youngest Swensen sister, opened the door
and invited me in. Spring Day, the second oldest, stood
beside her, with the oldest, Summer Rose, next in line.
Looking at the sisters was a preview of what Winter
Skye would look like four, six, and eight years into her
future. Their daddy Garth better start collecting sturdy
branches now, I reflected. He would need a steady supply
to beat off the boys once Summer Rose started high
school next fall and for years to come as his younger
daughters made their high school debuts.

"The bathroom's that way," the girls said in unison.

I made short work of my business. When I reap-
peared, Garth was handing walking sticks to his daughters. Galva distributed their canteens.

When she reached me, she said, "Let me loop this
around your neck so it doesn't get tangled with your
camera strap."

I bent my head. "Thanks."

"We're off!" Garth held the door open and handed
me a walking stick when I walked by.

The girls trooped out first, then me, then Galva. The girls raced to a barbed wire fence west of the driveway. Garth and Galva fell into step on either side of me.

"What's it like to be outnumbered by so many females?" I asked Garth.

"It come on so slow, one kid at a time, I guess I got used to it." He trotted over to the girls, stepped on the bottom strand of wire, and raised the middle one to create a gap for everyone to crawl through.

Galva put a hand on my back and gently pushed me forward. "You're next, Miss Newell."

My stomach fluttered. A memory floated to the surface . . .

Uncle Tim stood next to a barbed wire fence. Aunt Wanda was next to me. She gave me a little push. "Go on, Janie-Jo. Crawl on through."

"It'll scratch me."

"I won't let that happen," Uncle Tim said, using his foot to hold the bottom strand to the ground as he raised the middle strand high. "See?"

"It happened last time."

"Oh for heaven's sake, Jane," said Mom, who stood behind Dad holding onto the handles of his wheelchair. "You're ten years old! Everyone else went through. Do you want to miss all the fun?"

As a matter of fact, I did. Because, contrary to what my sister, brother, cousins, and Uncle Tim believed, traipsing through a pasture filled with hidden divots and rocks, cow pies and horse apples, and worst of all, the rattlesnakes Dad said lived in northwest Iowa, was not fun. Sitting at home reading Laura Ingalls Wilder's

*description of walking through the prairie barefoot?
Now that was fun.*

"Please don't make me," I begged.

"Just try," Dad said.

*I did my clumsy best to wiggle through the gap that
had been child's play for everyone else. My reward was
a scratched arm and a rip in my pants. Mom and Aunt
Wanda safety pinned it shut, but to my everlasting mor-
tification, my cousins said my underwear still peeked
through . . .*

Here I was again, still mortified and anticipating the
disaster about to happen. I pushed away my fear and
walked to the fence, determined to show the Swensens I
was a fearless country schoolteacher.

Galva crawled through after me and surveyed the
damage I'd sustained. "The rip in the seat of your overalls is too small to see the color of your undies," she said
before examining the scratch on my cheek and asking,
"How long since you had a tetanus shot?"

"Last fall." I said nothing about the leg injury I'd sustained the previous October while diving through a gap
in another barbed wire fence. Saying that would demand
an explanation about why I was in a pasture in the first
place. With a bull. On a moonlit night. Galva picked up
her walking stick and motioned for Garth and me to do
the same. "No need to change our plans then. You can
clean up the scratch after the hike."

I watched the girls speeding ahead of us and breathed
in the scents of alfalfa and wet earth. "What a beautiful
afternoon. I'm so glad winter's over."

Garth barked a short laugh. "We're not out of the woods yet."

"What do you mean?"

"Spring snowstorms come pretty regular. They can dump a lot of snow clear into May."

My jaw dropped. I looked from Garth to Galva. "You're kidding, right?"

Their expressions said they weren't.

Winter Skye turned and cupped her hands around her mouth. "Hurry up, you guys! We got a ways to go yet!"

We guys quickened our pace. I concentrated on avoiding cow pies as we hiked across the grassy pasture that rose gently at first and then more steeply. After about fifteen minutes, we reached the top of a rise. Below lay a series of bald hillocks, a blackish-gray moonscape, wild and desolate.

"Over here!" shouted Winter Skye who stood atop a hillock and gestured at what looked like a dead tree stump beside her.

Garth and Galva helped me skitter down the steep incline and over to her. "That's not a tree stump!" I exclaimed as we drew closer. "It's a dinosaur bone!"

I lifted my camera and peered through the viewfinder. I snapped pictures of Winter Skye and her sisters posing beside the exposed dinosaur bone and then close-ups of the bone itself. I imagined how Uncle Tim and the rest of the Moy family would react when they saw the pictures when I went to Sioux City this summer. The girls scrambled down the hillock and ran to another and another and another, all decorated with dinosaur bones.

I followed after them, taking shot after shot until I ran out of film.

"Does the dig team at the old Lindgren place know about this site?" I asked while snapping the camera back into its case.

Galva nodded. "They came out and looked at it when they were scouting the area."

"I don't get why they didn't set up camp here instead of where they are now."

Garth put his hands in his pockets. "Scuttlebutt is that the rancher who bought the land made the college an offer they couldn't pass up. We don't have that kind of money."

"Who bought it?"

Instead of answering, Garth squinted into the sun, put two fingers in his mouth, and whistled. "Time to head home, girls! Chores are waiting!"

They circled around like a herd of young ponies and galloped toward the rise at the edge of the grassy pasture. Once they were out of sight, he said, "Well, after Pete Lindgren fell and moved to town, Richard Wentworth bought it. He's got deep enough pockets to pay a fair price for the ranch and persuade the college to dig there."

What Garth said fit my impression of Richard Wentworth Sr. His disdain for the common people of Tipperary County had prompted me to christen him with a nickname—Richard the First. His wife Corinne was his complete opposite. She was my sewing buddy, and I was certain he'd kept her in the dark about the transaction, as was typical for him. I knew through painful experience that their son, Junior Wentworth, had inherited his father's underhanded way of doing business. But he was out of the picture, sitting in a prison cell. If God was the God of justice he proclaimed himself to be, Junior would be behind bars for a good, long time.

Garth broke into a trot. "If you don't mind, I'll go on ahead and put the steaks on the grill."

Steak?

My mouth filled with saliva and drowned out all thoughts of Richard the First and his son. I picked up my pace.

"What's your hurry?" Galva asked.

"Oh, I want to clean up the scratch on my cheek. It's stinging again." This was true, though it wasn't honest. The real reason for my haste was greed. And gluttony. I hadn't tasted a grilled steak since I'd moved to Little Missouri. Tonight, I planned on claiming the biggest piece.

CHAPTER 9

Dad fired off a series of questions during our phone call on Saturday morning. "What kind of steak?"

"T-bone."

"Rare or medium rare?"

"Not rare at all. Just medium."

"Grass or grain fed?"

"I have no idea."

"How can you call yourself the daughter of a cattleman?"

"Because you raised cattle instead of sheep?"

He chortled and snorted.

"Give me the phone, Harold." Mom's voice sounded closer with every word. "What did you say to him, Jane? He's laughing so hard he can't talk."

"It was a joke about sheep."

"Sheep are no laughing matter to him. You know how he hates them." She lowered her voice. "Have you gotten anywhere on the—you know . . ."

I didn't know what she was getting at. "On the what, Mom?"

"Oh for heaven's sake, Jane," she hissed. "Have you and that sheriff gotten anywhere on your new case?"

"I'm not allowed to discuss ongoing investigations."

"Not even with your mother?"

Especially not with my mother! Without a second thought she would leak anything I said to the Little Missouri spy ring she'd formed with Velma and Betty.

"Not if I want to keep my side gig."

"That hardly seems fair."

"To quote the wise woman who raised me, life isn't fair," I said with maximum sass.

"Can we talk about school, or is it off limits too?" she sassed in return.

We dropped the sass and swapped stories about field trips, spring fever in students and teachers alike, and what flowers and vegetables she had planted in her garden's rich, black soil. Then I described the dinosaur May baskets my students had made for their parents.

"After May baskets come Mother's Day cards."

The hint she dropped would have broken my toe had we been standing next to each other. I picked up a pen and scribbled "Mother's Day card" on my shopping list.

"I don't want to run up your phone bill, Jane. Besides, Tim will be here any minute to play cards with Harold while Wanda and I go grocery shopping. I'll talk to you next week."

"Tell Dad goodbye. I love you both."

"We know that, Jane. Bye now."

After Mom hung up, Betty said, "Your mom and I are going to chat this afternoon when she's done shopping.

Wouwd you wike me to remind her to say 'I wove you' to you?"

"If you want." Unless the senior member of Mom's spy circle had more influence than her children did, I doubted that my mother would change her ways. But it was worth a try. "Thanks."

Betty ended the call. I went into my classroom to grade yesterday's papers, write lesson plans, and organize seatwork and centers for the upcoming week. I wanted to have everything ready before Dick picked me up, so I could fully enjoy our date. I finished around noon, ate lunch, and turned my attention to my apartment. I spent the afternoon doing laundry, cleaning, and laying out church clothes for tomorrow, as well as a week's worth of school clothes. Choosing what to wear on our date took much longer. After much debate, I settled on my favorite pink blouse and my nicest blue jeans. Then I showered, spent an inordinate amount of time on my hair, and did my makeup not once but twice, because I wasn't satisfied with my first attempt. Just before four o'clock, I put on my espadrille flats. They could be counted on to communicate the right amount of special occasion without giving the impression of trying too hard. Which was exactly what I was doing.

Dick arrived right on time. I opened the door and took in his new jeans and a blue checked button-down shirt that accentuated his tan. He looked as uncomfortable as I'd ever seen him, and that's saying something. After I invited him inside, he managed to croak out, "You look really nice," before he blushed as red as I'd ever seen him. That's saying something too.

He swallowed a couple times and cleared his throat. "You ready to go?"

"Just a sec." I collected my purse and shopping list from the kitchen table before saying, "Now I'm ready."

He pointed to the cooler beside the door. "I can carry that."

"Thanks." His burgeoning conversational skills impressed me. So did the fact that I'd remembered the cooler for storing the frozen foods on my list.

Dick's conversational skills ceased their burgeoning on the drive to Tipperary. Perhaps the demand I'd made a month ago—that he speak in complete sentences during our dates—had already run down his battery. To give him time to recharge, I provided a steady stream of talk, more or less a rerun of my earlier conversation with my parents. He listened attentively, laughed at the funny bits, but otherwise remained silent until he parked in front of the grocery store.

"Are you okay with this as our first stop?" he asked.

"Sure am," I replied. He came around to open my door, but I beat him to the punch. We raced the few steps to the grocery store. He got there first and held the door, gesturing for me to enter ahead of him. I conceded defeat and went inside.

"Oh look! It's Jane!"

I recognized Teresa's voice before I located her in the checkout lane. She and the rest of the dig team waited as the clerk rang up the contents of their shopping carts.

"Hello there!" I took Dick's arm, and we walked over to them. "Do you have any news about Beanie?"

Sheila nodded. "We visited her this morning."

"How is she?"

Victor grimaced. "Still in a coma, but out of ICU. She's been moved to a semi-private room. Number 305 if you want to send a card. Her parents are able to be with her all the time now."

Sheila looked at Dick. "Aren't you one of the EMTs who took her to the hospital?"

"Yeah."

"Beanie's primary physician told her parents that she's still alive because of the attention the EMTs provided."

Dick shrugged away the compliment. "All I did was drive the ambulance, but I'll let Mary Borgeson know. She's the one who took care of Beanie. The doctor was right. Mary's very good at what she does."

Sheila took his hand in both of hers. "I saw how gentle you both were when you settled her into the ambulance. Thank you." She put her arms around his neck and hugged him long and hard.

To describe the pause that followed as awkward is an understatement. Dick blushed. The dig team members and the checkout clerk stared. No one spoke.

Finally, I broke the silence. "So," I said a tad too brightly, "you came here after visiting Beanie to get groceries?"

Victor recovered first. "We usually come about nine on Saturdays. We take showers at the high school locker room, then go the laundromat. We eat lunch here in town, get groceries, and drive back to the dig site. We're running late today since we went to Rapid."

"That's a long day," I said. "Dick and I will leave you be so you can finish up and get on your way."

After saying goodbye, I took out my list, found a cart, and steered it to the first aisle. Dick took a cart for himself, and we shopped in companionable silence. Once our purchases were bagged and paid for, we took them to his truck and put the cold stuff into our coolers. He shoved them and the rest of our bags in the front of truck bed and covered everything with a tarp.

We stopped at the hardware store, the drug store, and the gas station before Dick drove to the #3. He ordered a T-bone and was surprised when I ordered the chicken instead. I told him about supper at the Swensens' and our hike to see the dinosaur bones in their pasture. He asked question after question, displaying a curiosity he'd kept hidden until now. We talked so long we almost missed the movie. *Smokey and the Bandit* was well underway when Dick purchased our tickets, and we took our seats in the American Legion Hall. I waited for him to take my hand. When he didn't, I took his. He didn't protest. In the light that came through the translucent windows on either side of the hall, I saw him blush.

After the movie, we got in his truck. I slid to the middle seat, fastened the lap belt, and snuggled into him. Once he stopped blushing, he said, "I don't know about you, but the way the sound bounced off the walls, I couldn't make heads or tails of what the actors were saying. Were you able to follow the plot of the movie?"

"No," I confessed. "The acoustics were so bad I couldn't hear a word."

He started the truck and backed onto the street. "Next time we want to watch a movie, we'll go to the theater in Bowman or Belle Fourche."

Next time.

I sighed and put my head on his shoulder. I liked the sound of that.

Chapter 10

I stood outside the church on Sunday morning, steeling myself to be interrogated about my date with Dick the minute I set foot in the foyer.

Be brave, Jane. Be very brave.

I inhaled and went inside.

Pam Barkley rushed toward me. "How's that college student doing? Have you heard anything?"

I exhaled relief and inhaled guilt upon realizing that my reprieve came at the cost of Beanie's misfortune. I repeated what Victor had said the night before.

"At least her parents are with her," Pam said. "That counts for something."

Mary Borgeson and Cookie Sternquist, along with a few others, drifted over and caught the tail end of our conversation. I repeated Victor's update for their benefit and said to Mary, "Beanie's doctor was impressed with the EMTs who brought her in. They said she's still alive because of you."

With everyone's attention on Mary, at least for the

moment, I kept my eyes on the door. When Dick walked in, I intercepted him and asked, "Want to find a pew now to avoid small talk?"

He nodded with a grin and we made a break for it.

Was I proud of using him to avoid an inquisition? *No.*

Would I do it again to achieve the same ends? *In a heartbeat.*

He chose at a pew halfway down the sanctuary and motioned for me to enter first. Once we were settled, he whispered in my ear. "Do you like Monty Python-type humor?"

"Uh-huh."

"*The Last Remake of Beau Geste* is at the Belle Fourche theater this weekend."

My eyes widened. I'd been bummed about missing the *Beau Geste* spoof when it made the rounds in Sioux City. It wasn't the kind of movie that would find a home on prime-time television anytime soon.

"Want to go Saturday night?"

"Yes!"

Pastor Petersen hurried down the aisle. Cookie went to the piano and played the introduction to the first hymn. We stood, and Dick pulled out a hymnal. His strong, clear baritone was at odds with his soft, halting speaking voice. We stood and sang and sat and prayed along with everyone else, but I found following the sermon to be impossible—for good reason. When we sat down, my full skirt poofed over the space between Dick and me and floated onto his pant leg. When I went to move it away, he grasped my fingers and hid our intertwined hands under the fabric. I spent the remainder of the service wondering who had seen what Dick had done, what the fallout would be, and bracing for the interrogation we'd escaped earlier.

After the benediction, Dick exited our pew and waited for me. We walked into the foyer together. Several of my students' moms—Pam Barkley, Mary Borgeson, Cookie Sternquist, Galva Swensen, Trudy Berthold, and Linda Gibson—flanked together and advanced on us.

Here it comes.

Rick Sternquist cut in front of them. They halted. I stood still. Dick bolted for the door.

I resisted the impulse to sink to my knees and thank God for his miraculous intervention. Instead, I adopted my role of serious forensic investigator and asked, "Are you ready to work on the case, Sheriff?"

"Are you?" Rick headed for the exit.

I swung into place beside him. "You have no idea."

Once outside, we decided he would pick up lunch, and I would go to my apartment to lay out the evidence and look over the case file. When he arrived, I was still adding to a list of items to discuss with him. I went through the list while we ate, beginning with a second look at the conversation I'd had with Renny.

"He misses Beanie. Says they're friends. She would talk to him when the team came to The Bend."

Rick set down his burger. "Why wasn't she hanging around with the people she came with?"

"According to Renny, they gave her the cold shoulder."

"Hmm. The other two college girls on the team—I forget their names—"

"Sheila Hundley and Teresa Kroll."

"Thanks. I ran into them at Burt and Iva's store Friday, right after I broke up the glitter fight between you and Velma. They were going on about how close they'd gotten to Beanie during the dig and how bad they felt about her accident. That doesn't square with what Renny saw. Do you think he was telling the truth?"

"I do. Mainly because I can't think of a reason for him to lie. Whereas Sheila and Teresa . . ." I trailed off.

"I see what you mean. Maybe it's time for Deputy Cardo to go to the dig site to ask a few more questions." Rick took out his notepad and pencil and began to write. "What else you got?"

I told him about my conversation with the dig crew at the grocery store in Tipperary. "You know, we could go to the dig site next Saturday when they're gone and compare their boots to the prints in the photographs."

"That'll only work if they don't wear their boots to town. I've mailed the photographs you enlarged to a hiking outfitter in Rapid. He should be able to identify the brand and maybe even provide a foot size."

"Can Cardo find out who wears which boots without making them suspicious?"

"That's his specialty." Rick wrote another note and asked, "You have anything else?"

"Yes." I related how Garth thought the dig team had been persuaded to set up camp at the old Lindgren place. "Did you know Richard the First owns it now?"

"Yep. I thought you did too."

"I wouldn't have planned a field trip on Wentworth property if I had."

"I wondered about that when I heard where you were going. I figured it meant you were gaining maturity."

I threw my napkin at him.

"Shoulda known better." He threw it back. "How'd you learn about the dig in the first place?"

"There was an article about it in the college alumni newsletter. Let me get it." I went to my classroom and pulled the field trip folder from my file cabinet. I returned to the kitchen, took out the newsletter, and handed it to him. "Here you go."

He skimmed it. "Mind if I make a copy at my office? I'll return the original."

"Sure." I ate a french fry and asked, "What do we do next?"

"I'll look into the Wentworths' connection to the college. It seems like a far stretch, but who knows? Once I hear from the outfitter, Deputy Cardo can start the new round of interviews." He tapped his notebook with his pen. "Could you talk to Glen and Trudy? See if they noticed any tension or factions among the members of the dig team? That sort of thing."

"Sure. Anything else?"

"Oh yeah." He put his pen in his pocket and stood. "The doctor called Friday and said that Colleen Lavender's holding her own. She's in stable condition and her vitals are good. He thinks her brain swelling is going down."

"Isn't there a test he can do to be sure?"

"He said there's this new thing called a PET scan take pictures of the brain, but they're too new and expensive for regional hospitals. At least for now."

I accompanied Rick to the door. "So we wait."

"And ask questions and poke around. And pray that Beanie wakes up so this remains an investigation of attempted murder."

"That's a good prayer." My hands clenched as I remembered how I'd begged God to heal my dad over and over. "But God doesn't always answer good prayers."

"It may feel like he isn't listening, Jane, but he does answer. Not the way we always want, but in the way that always proves best." He smiled sadly, gave my shoulder a gentle squeeze, and left.

I thought about what he'd said. Slowly, I unclenched my fists and stared at my palms and wondered what I'd been holding onto. My heart whispered a single word in reply.

Hope, it said. *Hope.*

Chapter 11

For the rest of the afternoon and evening, I put the case out of my mind by spreading craft supplies on my kitchen table and making dinosaur-themed May baskets. Once they were finished, I put them in a cardboard box and stored them in the lab—I like to shake things up like that now and then—until morning.

Bennan was the one who shook things up when he arrived the next morning. "It's May Day!" he yelled as he ran through the door. "Can we put candy and stuff in our May baskets now?"

I ruffled his hair. "What did I say on Friday?"

"That we'd do it right before school got out." He pouted and his eyes grew watery. "But I can't wait 'til then."

Tiege bounded over. He sank to his knees in front of me, clasped his hands, and begged. "Have pity on us, Miss Newell. Please?" He scrambled to his feet, knocking over Keeva and Winter Skye in the process.

"Hey," they squealed in unison. "Watch what you're doing!"

Tiege apologized with a maximum of dramatic, dangerous gesticulation. At this rate, his remaining classmates were going to go down like pins in a bowling alley.

I took his hands and lifted them high. "Kids, the only way to reach your desks is through London Bridge." I began singing and so did they, ducking under the bridge and giggling as they trotted to their seats.

Calm reigned during the Pledge of Allegiance, then abdicated its throne when I asked if anyone had something for show-and-tell.

Stig waved his hand, all excitement and eagerness. "Me, me!"

His sister Elva's hand shot up. "Me, too. Both of us. Please, Miss Newell."

Stig's behavior was typical, but Elva's caught me off guard. I was curious about her reasons for throwing caution to the wind and granted them joint permission. Stig galloped to the front of the room. Elva followed at a more dignified canter.

Stig hopped from foot to foot as he spoke. "We're branding tomorrow and—"

Elva broke in. "And we get to miss school to help."

What?

I'd never heard of such a thing. From the ensuing cacophony, I gathered that this practice was a Tipperary County staple. The other ranch kids reported on their upcoming absences—Tiege on Thursday and Winter Skye next Monday.

I looked at Keeva McDonald. "What about you?"

"Saturday," she said.

At least her parents had their priorities straight. Probably because, being a teacher herself, Keeva's mom believed education should be their top priority.

Keeva continued. "Dad wanted Friday, but Mommy said we can't afford her losing a day's pay."

Well, hmph.

The town kids piped up next, reporting on whose parents were picking them up after school on what days to take them to which brandings. That turned out to be every town kid attending every branding.

But not you, Jane.

I stood. "It's time to start reading lessons. "Kindergarteners, bring your workbooks to the front table. The rest of you can begin your seatwork."

The morning and early afternoon hummed along. During the last recess, I passed out the May baskets I'd made for my students. They were surprised when they came inside and saw them on their desks. Doubly so when I allowed them to nibble their goodies—popcorn, peanuts, and M&M's—while they worked on dinosaur reports during science class. When the moment came to fill their parents' May baskets, the kids were too full to pilfer any of the treats in them. The children didn't suspect the method behind my madness. They left school, holding the baskets they'd made high as they ran across the playground.

I took a handful of leftover goodies to my desk to snack on while correcting papers. No sooner had I picked up my red pen than a knock sounded at the door. I shoved a handful of popcorn in my mouth, went into the entryway, and looked out the window. No one was there. Weird. I returned to correcting and was gaining steam when there was another knock. Again, I went to the entryway, peered out the window, and saw no one. Weird and getting weirder. After the third knock, I opened the door and discovered three May baskets on the top step of the landing. A blur of motion caught my eye. A child ducked around the corner of the building and burst into a fit of laughter.

This scenario repeated itself until twilight. I netted more May baskets than children in my classroom. Some of the upper-grade students must have gotten into the spirit of the day too. I carried the baskets inside and sorted through their contents. The popcorn would go stale before I could eat it all, so it went into the trash. I filled a plastic container full of peanuts and put it with my baking supplies. The candy went into a plastic zipper bag.

In one basket, I found a note from Mary Borgeson.

Miss Newell,

You want to come to the ranch tomorrow after school and see what goes on during branding? You can catch the tail end of working the calves and stay for supper with the crew. We have plenty of food, so don't bring anything and don't bother to call. Just show up.

Mary

I grinned like a big dope, whether because of Mary's thoughtfulness or because of the horseshoe-shaped basket she had fashioned out of a paper plate and pipe cleaners, I couldn't say. The grin remained as I put the bag of candy in the freezer and arranged the brightly colored baskets on my kitchen counter.

I was admiring them when the phone rang. "Jane Newell here."

"Good. You're home."

"Is that you, Dick?"

"Uh-huh."

Where had his complete sentences gone? I waited for him to manufacture a few. He didn't.

"Do you want something?"

"What? No."

I felt my grin fade. "Then why did you call?"

"Oh." Pause. "Yeah." He coughed. "To cancel our date. I have to work at Fly Ranch this weekend."

The complete sentences were back. That was good. The content of those sentences? Not so good.

"Do you really mean cancel?" I asked, hoping I'd misunderstood. "Or do you want to postpone until the weekend after next?"

"Cancel."

"As in that one date or us dating altogether?"

"One date. I have to work the next three weekends. *Beau Geste* will be gone by then."

Much as I hated Dick's one-word answers, his sentences were almost worse. Still, I pressed on. "Why are you working three weekends in a row?"

"It's a long story."

"I've got time."

"I don't." He paused. "Did you get my May basket?"

"I got fifteen of them. Did you sign yours?"

"Um, no." Dead air. "My break's over. Happy May Day, Jane!"

"Happy May Day to you too, Dick Phillips!" The sarcasm dripping from my reply may have had something to do with him hanging up before I finished talking.

"You were a wittwe hard on him, Miss Neweww," Betty said.

"Do you know why he canceled?"

"Not yet."

"Will you tell me when you find out?"

"Do you promise not to bite my head off?"

"Yes."

"Then it's a deaw. Bye, Miss Neweww."

"Bye, Betty."

I fought tears as I hung up. Then I marched to the freezer and took out my candy stash. I fished out the chocolate Easter bunny that had been in one of the baskets. I wiped at my tears and bit off a rabbit ear.

Though the bunny was a little stale, eating my feelings had never tasted so good.

Chapter 12

After devouring the last of the chocolate bunny, I thumbed through my recipe box for Mom's Early Bird Coffee Cake. Mary said not to bring anything tomorrow, but I wasn't about to show up for supper empty handed. I found the card, laid it on the counter, and decided to get up early to throw it together in the morning. It would be fresher that way. After a light supper, I flipped on the television and spent the evening with three of my favorite guys—Hawkeye Pierce, Johnny Fever, and Lou Grant.

Merle's scrawny rooster and the dawn roused me in plenty of time to make coffee cake. It was out of the oven and cooling on the counter when Beau Kelly led his classmates into the entryway. He inhaled the homey scents of nutmeg and cinnamon drifting in from my kitchen and licked his lips.

"Yum!" he said. "Did you make us cookies?"

Here was a disadvantage of living in an apartment next to my classroom that I hadn't foreseen when

I'd accepted my job. Even my baking life faced public scrutiny. "It's coffee cake," I said, "to take to the Borgesons' this afternoon."

The handful of children present—which in the absence of the kindergarteners and the Borgeson kids consisted of Beau, Bennan, Cora, Tiege, and Renny—volunteered to see if the cake was any good.

"Nice try," I said. "Now get to work."

We rattled around the half-empty classroom, eyeing the clock between lessons. Eva, Stig, and the kindergarteners—traitors every one—were having fun at the branding as we toiled at our desks. When the hands on the clock reached dismissal time, Tiege shot up faster than a pterodactyl. The other children followed suit. I raced to open the door and set them free. Within a half hour, my classroom was ready for the next day. I changed into old blue jeans and a sweatshirt. With the coffee cake in hand, I hopped in the Beetle and traveled twenty bumpy miles to my first branding. When I nosed my car between two of the beater pickup trucks parked helter-skelter along the Borgeson's lane, the air was thick with dust. On the short walk to their doublewide mobile home, I regretted my decision to leave the cake pan uncovered. Maybe the crumb topping would hide the grit settling on it.

Mary came outside and swatted my leg with the dish towel she held. "You weren't supposed to bring anything." She bent closer and inhaled. "It smells delicious."

"Where should I put it?"

"On the screened-in porch with the other desserts. But let's go to the kitchen so I can tell you the latest about Beanie."

My heart skipped a beat. "She woke up?"

She walked me to the kitchen, which was empty. "Not even close. But her pupils are becoming more reactive to light, and that's a good sign. No guarantee, but in this situation, a little hope is better than none at all."

She hesitated. "Also, you oughta know I invited the dig crew to the branding. Mainly 'cause I don't think they eat real good at their camp. And a little bit because I thought you'd like another look at them. I mean, one of them has to be Beanie's attack—"

"Mom!" Elva shouted as she burst into the kitchen. "Miss Newell's car is here. Have you seen her?"

"She's right here, Sweetie."

Elva flew at me and wrapped her arms around my waist, nearly knocking the pan out of my hands. "I was afraid you didn't get the note in our May basket and weren't coming."

I handed the cake to Mary and lifted Elva's chin until her eyes met mine. "How could I miss a note in a horseshoe basket? Of course I came. Now"—I pointed to the pan Mary held—"can you show me where to put this?"

Elva led the way to the screened-in porch. She grabbed my hand once the cake was delivered and pulled me outside. "Come see what my brother found." She dragged me across the yard and into the pasture behind the machine shed. Renny, Stig, Beau, and Bennan were on their hands and knees around a hole in the ground. From the shovels lying every which way and the dust that coated every inch of them, I guessed the hole was their doing.

Stig jumped up. "Miss Newell!" he yelled. "We dug up a dinosaur."

Before he could elaborate, Tiege rounded the side of the machine shed and declared with a grand, sweeping gesture as Sheila Hundley and Donald Gaddy came into view, "I brung the fossil experts. Stand back, everybody, so they can examine our dig."

Sheila and Donald knelt beside the hole and peered inside. Then Sheila cleared her throat and said, "It's my scientific opinion that you have discovered the bones of a bovinasaurus. Do you agree, Donald?"

He nodded. "Most definitely."

They didn't crack a smile until after all the kids except Elva ran off at breakneck speed shouting, "Mom! Dad! We dug up dinosaur bones."

Then Sheila and Donald began to laugh.

"Those are cow bones, right?" Elva asked.

"Right," the fossil experts gasped.

Elva looked ready to give them a piece of her mind when the dinner bell rang. "I gotta go help my mom," she said and ran off.

Sheila, Donald, and I followed at a slower pace.

"How's the dig going?" I asked.

Sheila shrugged.

Donald waited a moment and said, "Not good. Beanie's accident is bumming us out. It kinda feels like we're holding our breath, waiting for her to wake up. It's like a bad dream. You know what I mean?"

I wanted to ask why he believed Beanie's attack was an accident, but we reached the food line before I could. Sheila and Donald drifted over to where the rest of the dig crew was clustered in the yard. Victor gave me a half-hearted salute. I countered with a half-hearted smile, then got into line behind Glen and Trudy Berthold.

"Who's minding the café?" I asked as we filled our plates with barbecued beef, baked beans, and potato salad.

"Fannie McDonald," Trudy said. "She does a real good job."

"And who's in the bar?"

Glen fished a Diet Coke from the drinks cooler for me and beers for him and Trudy. "Velma Albright. We'll see how many customers she costs us." He pointed to an empty picnic table. "Wanna sit with us?"

"Sure." Once we were settled at the table and had taken the edge off our hunger, I relayed what Renny had said about how the other people on the dig team treated Beanie. "I wanted to tell you because he considers Beanie to be his friend. He's really worried about her."

They thanked me, and the conversation dried up. I had the distinct impression that, like Renny, they knew more than they were willing to say. When Pam Barkley and Galva Swensen plunked down beside us, I was grateful.

"Do you know who brought this?" Pam pointed at her half-eaten slice of my coffee cake. "I want to get the recipe."

I raised my hand. "It was my doing. I'll send the recipe home with Cora and Bennan tomorrow."

"I want it too," Galva said before leaning in confidentially. "Betty said you weren't very happy when Dick had to cancel your date for this weekend. Have you forgiven him yet?"

Trudy jabbed her fork into thin air. "After the cockamamie stunt he pulled, he doesn't deserve forgiveness."

"What cockamamie stunt would that be?" I asked. "What are you talking about?"

Galva shook her head and held up her palms. "I thought you already knew, or I wouldn't have mentioned it."

"It's not our place to tell you," Trudy agreed. "But I seen Dick around here somewhere."

"He was down by the cattle chute in the corral last time I saw him," Pam said. "You can go ask him."

I drained my can of pop and banged it on the table. "If you'll excuse me, ladies, I think I will."

CHAPTER 13

I crossed the lawn in a snit and was weaving my way through the vehicles along the lane when I realized I didn't know how to get to the corral. In my way of thinking, I had two options. One was to spoil my emotionally satisfying dramatic exit by going back and asking for directions. The other was to follow my ears toward the sound of calves bleating and heifers bawling, and let my nose guide me to the mingled odors of manure and burnt flesh wafting on the breeze. It was a no brainer.

I veered left into the pasture and up a steep hill. The noise and aroma intensified as I climbed. The view at the top of the rise stretched for miles in every direction. The vast landscape evoked in me the sense of awe and fear it always did. My attention shifted to the riotous clamor below me. A couple teenagers were waving their hats and chasing a frightened calf toward a chute that connected the corral to a fenced pasture. The chute had gates at both ends, and a lone heifer stood bawling near the gate on the pasture side. The calf ran toward her. And who was waving the calf toward corral-side chute but Dick Phillips. The calf galloped into the gate, and he clanged it shut.

I zigzagged down the hill to avoid cow pies and horse apples partially hidden by shoots of greening grass. I imagined small rattlers coiling in wait underneath the clumps of manure and gave them a wide berth. The indirect path slowed my descent and provided ample time for fueling my snit. Why hadn't Dick told me what he'd done? I could be eating dessert with friends instead of dodging poop and snakes and who knew what else.

Dick was latching the gate when I walked up behind him. "I think we're done," he told the teens standing on either side of the corral fence. "Go on up to the house and see if there's any food left."

I tamped down my snit and smiled at the kids. "Don't worry. Mary won't let anyone go hungry."

They tore up the hill as Dick whirled around to face me. "I'm afraid you missed all the action."

"I didn't come down here to see the branding." I pointed to the half-dozen boys who were jostling and chasing each other up the hill. "Are they from Fly Ranch? Do you need to keep an eye on them?"

"Nah. They're all ranch kids from around here."

I slowed my pace to put more distance between them and us. The fire behind my words was obvious when I spoke. "I came here to ask you a question."

"Okay."

"Why do you have to work for the next three weekends? Everyone knows except me, and no one will tell me."

"Oh. Well. You aren't going to like it."

"I already don't like being the only person in the county who's out of the loop."

He rubbed the back of his neck and veered away from me. "Sorry about that."

I stopped climbing and put my hands on my hips. "I want an explanation, not an apology." Then I realized my stance was a fair imitation of Velma at her most belligerent and dropped my arms to my side. "How bad can it be?"

"What's your definition of bad?"

"Tell me."

He rubbed his neck again. After a long pause, he stared over my shoulder and began to talk. "Well, the northern lights were real bright the other night. Me and Joe, the other counselor on duty, brought the boys up on the flat roof to watch until curfew. Once our shift ended, me and Joe went on the roof again."

When he paused, I asked, "What's so bad about that?"

"Just wait." He inhaled and then blew out a deep breath. "When the lights died down, I decided to jump off the roof."

"What? That's crazy."

"Not really. My brother and I used to jump off the roof of our barn and never got hurt. It was higher than the dorm roof, and I knew how to aim for the grass, crouch, and bend my knees to cushion my landing. No problem."

"But?"

He grimaced. "Joe decided to try it. He jumped before I could tell him how to do it."

"And?"

"He landed on the cement sidewalk and broke his

foot. He's out of commission for at least three weeks. I'm covering his weekend shifts."

"What on earth possessed you to do something that stupid?"

"I don't know how to explain. But I am sorry, and I'll make it up to you. I promise." He moved closer to me looking as hang dogged as a human could.

I refused to let go of my snit. "I'm going to need time to think this over. I'll call you when I'm ready to discuss it without clubbing you on the head." I lit out, oblivious to cow pies and any rattlesnakes dumb enough to lurk beneath them. All I wanted was to be far away from Dick until I could cool off and think straight again. I was still fuming when I went to the dessert table to collect my cake pan. It was empty. Good. My early exit wasn't going to deprive anyone of dessert. I grabbed the pan and whirled around, almost bumping into Pam Barkley. Our eyes met.

"Oh," she said. "You heard."

"The man's a jerk."

"No. Junior's a jerk. Dick's just—"

"Stupid?"

"Sure. But aren't we all stupid now and then?"

"You can defend him all you want. But just like I told Dick, I need to think about this for a while. I want to go home."

"Can I walk you to your car?"

Her kindness made my eyes well up "Thanks, but no."

I walked away, ducking my head to hide my tears. After I got into my car, I set the pan onto the passenger seat beside me and peeled out. The pan slid onto the floor when I rounded a curve in the road too fast. That made me slow down, and I arrived home still in one piece. Dusk was falling when I parked. I felt around for the cake pan and came up empty.

I got out, went around to the other side, and opened the door. No sign of the pan. I slanted the seat forward and felt around. There it was under the front seat. As I retrieved it, paper crackled. My fingers searched and found it. I pulled out a paper sack and set it in the pan. Once inside the apartment, I left everything on the kitchen counter. It could wait until morning. I was tired and in need of a shower to wash away the ranch dust coating my clothes and skin.

Unless the water could wash away the disappointment and anger deep inside me, along with the dirt, I wouldn't get much sleep tonight.

Chapter 14

Midnight came and went before I drifted off. Merle's rooster, heartless creature that he was, cut me no slack, and I rose with the chickens. I plodded to the bathroom replaying my conversation with Dick. I still wasn't happy about what he'd done, but I wasn't mad at him anymore. That emotion had been replaced with the conviction that I'd responded badly. Not just to him. To Pam also.

I started yawning. It took two cups of strong coffee and a bowl of oatmeal to make it stop. The yawns started up again during show-and-tell, despite the excitement generated by Tiege's announcement about the bones he and his friends had dug up next to the Borgeson's pole building. He asked if he could borrow my rattlesnake shovel so he could re-enact the discovery on the playground. When I said no, he hid his disappointment with a dramatic announcement: "The fossil experts said we dug up a bovinasaurus."

Elva was waving her hand before the words left Tiege's mouth. After being called on, she pursed her lips and said, "Bovine is a fancy word for cow. They were saying you dug up cow bones."

Tiege's fellow paleontologists howled in protest. I was mid-yawn and unable to silence their hisses and boos. Elva stood her ground until her cool stare quieted the children. At eight years old, she knew a thing or two about how to react when the going got bad. The thought sobered me. I swallowed my yawns, sent Tiege to his seat, and delivered an impromptu speech about how to politely disagree with someone. The children might not have gained much from the lecture, but I sure did.

I fought the yawns until lunchtime. Because I rarely grew drowsy while using my camera, I loaded it with a fresh roll of film. I told the children I would take pictures of them to use in the Mother's Day cards they would make during our next art class.

The children mugged for the camera every chance they had. They didn't learn much during science and social studies. Then again, I stayed awake. Plus, I snapped some pictures guaranteed to melt their mothers' hearts. Even so, I wasn't sad when dismissal time rolled around and I bid them a weary farewell. Tiege and Elva began arguing about dinosaur fossils and cow bones as they crossed the playground. I listened attentively until they were halfway to their parents. At that point, they were under their parents' jurisdiction. Then I retreated to my quiet classroom, laid my head on my desk, and fell asleep.

A snore woke me, and my head jerked up. I'd slept for over an hour, but the nap had done me no favors. I had a crick in my neck. My eyes were bleary. I stood and rubbed at the sore spot. Then I went to the kitchen to get an apple and make an egg sandwich. I took the food to my desk and ate while I worked. When I was done, I carried my empty plate to the kitchen and set it beside the sink. That's when I saw the dirty cake pan and a tattered bag on the counter.

I filled the pan with water and left it to soak. I tossed the greasy, torn bag toward the wastebasket and missed. The bag flipped and landed on the floor, revealing Renny's name written with Magic Marker. How had his lunch bag from the field trip ended up in my car? More importantly, what had been growing inside it since then?

I spread a newspaper on my kitchen table, went into the lab for a pair of latex gloves, and pulled them on. I held my nose as I picked up the bag and shook its contents onto the newspaper. A shriveled apple core tumbled out first. Not too disgusting. Next came a napkin wrapped around bread crusts covered with fuzzy, green mold. Totally disgusting. The mold and the napkin were fused together in places. In other spots, I could see writing on the inside of the napkin. Weirdly interesting.

I got tweezers from the lab and carefully eased the bread and the napkin apart. Then I scraped away as much of the mold as I could without destroying the napkin. I unfolded it and tried to decipher what was written on it. Between the mold, grease stains, and tears in the napkin, what I could make out—*n ou k p th at T Send dy?*—was precious little to go on. Still, it was more than I had five minutes ago.

My weariness sluiced away, and I was fully awake. Rather than plugging random letters into the blank spots, I asked myself a series of questions.

Who had the bag belonged to? *Renny.*

Could anyone else have known it was his bag? *Definitely.*

In that case, had someone put the note into the bag for Renny to find? *Perhaps.*

If not for him to find, then who? *Most likely Trudy.*

I ran into the lab, returned with my yellow legal pad and a pencil, and copied the letters onto the legal pad.

n ou k p th at T Send dy?

Operating from the fact that Trudy worked at The Bend, I filled in what made sense.

T Send was "The Bend." I was sure of that.

dy were the last two letters of Trudy's name. I rewrote the note with the gaps filled in thus far.

n ou k p th at The Bend Trudy?

Now to puzzle out the rest of the question. Odds were in favor of *ou* being the last two letters in "you" and that *th* was followed by an *e.* Now the sentence said, "____n you k____ p the _____ at The Bend Trudy?

The only common word that ended in *n* to start a question was "can." I tried it and studied the result.

Can you k___p the ______ at The Bend Trudy?

I read it out loud, saying the letter sounds for *k* and *p* with no sound in between them.

"Can you 'k' 'p' the at The Bend Trudy?"

I was close, but "the" didn't make sense. I replaced "the" with "this" and read the sentence out loud again. "Can you 'k' 'p' this at The Bend Trudy?"

I read it again, only faster. "Can you kp this at The Bend Trudy?"

Light dawned. I yelled the sentence at the top of my lungs. "Can you keep this at The Bend, Trudy?"

I dropped my pencil, carried the legal pad to the phone, and rang Betty. When she picked up, I yelled, also at the top of my lungs, "I need to track down the sheriff. Immediately!"

Chapter 15

"Miss Neweww," Betty trilled, "This is your wucky day! Cookie cawwed Mary Borgeson not two minutes ago about the pie pwate she forgot to bring home. She needs it to make pies for the Sternquist branding tomorrow. Mary said she'ww give it to Cookie in the morning when they drop off their kids."

"And how, exactly, does that make this my lucky day?"

"Weww, Cookie said Rick's on the way from their ranch to Wittwe Missouri right now, and before he weft he said he'd stop by the Borgesons' and pick it up, even though it's out of his way, and give it to Cookie when he goes to hewp them brand tomorrow."

"So you're saying Rick may drive by the school at any minute?"

"Exactwy."

I hung up, snatched my jacket, then ran outside. I didn't stop running until I was standing in the middle of Main Street facing north. I put on the jacket, though the weather was pleasant enough to go without, and waved my arms to avoid becoming roadkill. It worked. The drivers who passed by eyed me quizzically and steered wide. I wiggled my fingers as though impersonating a windmill in the middle of Little Missouri's busiest street was completely normal. When the sheriff's vehicle came into view, I added jumping up and down like a crazy person to my windmill impression. The speed with which Rick braked and rolled down his window said my efforts were highly effective.

"Why are you standing in the middle of Main Street and waving like a crazy person?" he asked.

"To flag you down. Park and come inside. I have something to show you."

When he came into my kitchen, I stuck my legal pad under his nose. "Get a load of this!"

He pushed my arm away, squinted, and read, "n ou k p th at T Send dy." His forehead wrinkled. "Is it in code?"

"I didn't mean the top line." I pointed to the final line of writing. "I meant this."

"Can you keep this at The Bend, Trudy?" He shrugged. "Jane, you're going to have to help me out. I still don't get it."

I motioned for him to sit at the table and told him about finding the paper bag and the note. Then I filled him in on my conversations with the Bertholds at the Borgesons' branding. "I had the distinct impression they were holding something back. This note proves it. But as Renny's teacher, I'm not in in a position to press him or his parents."

"You're not, but I am." Rick stood. "Mind if I use your phone to call Trudy and see about stopping by for a chat in a couple minutes?"

"Be my guest." While he made the call, the exhaustion that had disappeared in the excitement of finding the note slammed into me again.

"See you in a minute," he said, before hanging up and turning to me. "She's not real excited about talking to me. It'll be tomorrow evening before I can fill you in on what she says. Sorry about that."

He was gone before I could swallow my yawn and say his apology was unnecessary. I was too tired to care about anything but sleep. I fell into bed fully clothed and slept through the night and the neighborhood rooster's cheery morning greeting. When my alarm clock rang, I wondered where my pajamas had gone. I rolled onto my back and stared at the ceiling until memory returned.

The note!

A surge of adrenaline made me spring out of bed, my mind racing with tasks to attend to before school. Seal the note and paper sack in an evidence bag. Write up reports about finding them and my conversations with Renny and his parents. Prepare the fingerprint kit and my camera for dusting and photographing the note and sack after school. Eat breakfast, take a shower, and change my clothes. I sniffed an armpit and decided that no matter how much I wanted to work on the case, a shower was my first priority.

When I opened the door and welcomed my students, I looked and smelled presentable. I'd ticked every item off my to-do list. Even better, the day turned out to be an easy one. Tiege was at his family's branding and Thursday meant no kindergarteners. The six students in attendance had been at the Borgeson branding on Tuesday, so much of the novelty had worn off. The children concentrated on lessons at the table and seatwork at their desks, so I was able to grade most of their papers during the school day. Finishing the remainder of my tasks once the kids were gone didn't take much time. I was in the lab and dusting the bag and napkin for fingerprints by four o'clock, photographing them by four fifteen, and developing negatives in the darkroom by four thirty. At that point, I lost track of time. I was hanging up the last of the negatives to dry when a faint knock sounded.

"Just a minute!" I hollered before opening the darkroom door just enough to squeeze through. "On my way!" I hollered again, hoping my visitor wasn't Dick. He hadn't crossed my mind since I'd found Renny's lunch bag, and I wasn't ready to talk to him yet. I hurried to the entryway and was relieved to see Rick standing on the landing. I opened the door and invited him in.

"I figured you were in the darkroom and would forget to eat. I brought you supper." He held a Round the Bend white paper bag in one hand and a diet Coke in another. He took the bag to the kitchen table and took out a cheeseburger, side salad, and fries.

"Nothing for you?" I asked.

"This was branding day at our ranch, remember? I ate there."

While I ate, he filled me in on what Trudy had said. "Once I let her know about the note, she told me about a conversation she'd had with Beanie before the field trip."

"How long before?"

"She wasn't sure. Maybe a week. Two at most." Rick took out his notebook, flipped a few pages, and read what he'd written. "Beanie came to the bar and asked about dropping off a few items at The Bend. She said there wasn't much privacy at the dig site, and she wondered if Trudy would hold onto them for a few days. Trudy said she'd do it, but Beanie never came by again."

I stopped eating and thought for a minute. "My guess is that she wasn't able to stop by on her own. When she saw Renny at the field trip, she decided to slip the note and the fossil in Renny's jacket pocket after he left it at his picnic table."

"You're probably right. I'll set up a meeting with Renny and his parents for this weekend and see if he confirms it." He scribbled in his notebook and snapped it shut.

"I'll take his fingerprints tomorrow so I can eliminate them. They've got to be all over his lunch sack." I tapped my chin. "Then again. I could take all the kids' fingerprints and make them part of their Mother's Day cards so Renny doesn't get suspicious."

"You are a wily one, Miss Newell. Remind me not to get on your bad side." He stood, took an envelope from his back pocket, and set it on the table. "Cardo wrote up the interviews he's conducted so far. See what you think of them. I better get back to the office and see what happened while I was at the ranch."

"Hang on a second." I went to the lab and returned with a manila envelope. "Here are copies of my reports. Everything's there except the fingerprint analysis. I'll finish it up on Saturday and bring it to church."

"That depends on whether or not there's church on Sunday."

"What are you talking about?"

"There's a blizzard coming."

"You might as well quit making outlandish statements just to get a rise out of me. I'm not the greenhorn I was last August."

"It's not an outlandish claim. There's a blizzard coming."

"There is not," I said. "It's spring. My students are making Mother's Day gifts in art class tomorrow. It doesn't blizzard in May."

"Maybe not in Iowa, but you live in South Dakota now. If you don't believe me, watch the weather report on television and then find your snow shovel. You're gonna need it." And with that, he put on his hat and left.

CHAPTER 16

The way Rick sauntered down the sidewalk looking like he didn't have a care in the world convinced me that the blizzard business was a prank. "Not funny, Buster," I muttered and checked the outdoor thermometer. Fifty degrees. "Not funny at all."

I turned on the television. Not to watch the weather, but to catch *Barney Miller* and *Soap*, my favorite Thursday night shows. When they were done, I turned off the TV and pulled out my flowered cotton jumper and white blouse. The blouse had collected a few wrinkles since I'd ironed it over the weekend, but the jumper would cover them. I was debating whether to wear my white, stack-heeled sandals or my espadrilles—the former matched the outfit better, but the latter were more comfortable—when the phone rang.

"Hello, this is Jane."

"Have you heard about the big bwizzard coming in tonight?"

"Did the sheriff put you up to this, Betty?"

"What are you tawking about? Didn't you watch the six o'cwock news?"

"I was busy."

"You better watch it at ten if you know what's good for you."

"I will."

Silence.

"Is there something else, Betty?"

"Weww, since you asked, as a matter of fact there is. Me and Vewma—"

Uh-oh. What had they cooked up now?

"—heard about the argument you and Dick had at the Borgeson's the other day. Earwier this evening, we cawwed your mother and broke the news to her."

I bit my lip, inhaled deeply, blew out a long breath, and responded with a cool "What exactly did you say?"

"That you and Dick are no wonger dating."

"WHAT?" So much for staying cool. "Where did you get that idea?"

"Me and Vewma heard you was upset and wit outta there driving way too fast. Your mom had her hopes up about you and Dick, so we was trying to wet her down sorta gentwe."

From past experience, I knew Betty's gentleness resembled that of the stubborn, old mule in their front yard. Velma's was of the riled-up rattlesnake variety. I pinched the bridge of my nose and counted to ten and then twenty before answering, hoping my gentleness would surpass the sum of theirs combined.

"Betty, Dick and I haven't decided whether we're still dating or not. Also, you and Velma had no business calling my mother. This is between Dick and me and nobody else."

"That's what I towd Vewma, but she said if I was chicken, she would caww Doris hersewf. That wouwda been reaw bad."

She had a point.

"Shouwd I caww your mother and straighten things out?"

"Thanks for the offer, but no. I will take care of it. Goodbye, Betty."

"I'm reawwy sorry, Miss Neweww. I know you're gonna be mad at me for a good, wong whiwe, but would you do me a favor anyway?"

"What is it Betty?"

"Watch the weather at ten."

I slammed the phone receiver into its cradle with the gentleness of a rattlesnake riding a mule and got ready for bed. When I left the bathroom after brushing my teeth and washing my face, the kitchen and living room felt cold. Wind whistled through the cracks between the windowpanes. I checked the outdoor thermometer again. It had dropped fifteen degrees since Rick left. I turned on the television, sat on the couch, and snuggled under an afghan.

Rick had been telling the truth. The blizzard was already raging east and south of Tipperary County. Sheridan, Wyoming had six inches of snow. Billings, Montana had four. Winds were rising, and the blizzard was moving in our direction. The snow was predicted to hit Little Missouri around midnight. The highest predicted totals were for northwestern South Dakota. The weatherman looked directly into the camera. "Ranchers, this storm could devastate livestock. Tonight is your last chance to move your animals to sheltered locations. By morning, it will be too late."

I imagined ranchers bundling into their winter clothes and saddling their horses. I pictured men and women riding to the pastures where heifers and ewes grazed and nursed their young offspring. I saw ranch kids opening gates as their parents and their herding dogs coaxed the animals into more sheltered areas where stock tanks and hay bales waited on the leeward side of windbreaks. I asked God to protect the animals and begged him to keep my friends safe.

"Amen," I whispered. Then I hunted for my snow shovel and found it in the supply closet hiding behind a pile of red playground balls. After turning up the furnace thermostat, I went to bed wondering what the outside world would look like in the morning.

The answer was white. White on the playground. White on Main Street. White blowing on the wind. I was about to check the rooftops when the phone rang.

It was Mrs. Dremstein. "School's cancelled. Will you let Liv know?"

I was about to do so when Betty rang me. "Sheriff's on the wine."

"Can it wait until Liv and the other parents know that school's been cancelled?"

"I'ww take care of them. The sheriff's deawing with an emergency. I'm connecting you now." And she was gone.

"Jane?"

"Rick? What's up?"

"The dig crew could be in trouble. There's a convoy of

snowmobiles leaving Little Missouri real soon to check on them. The plan is to bring the crew to the school and house them there if they need to be relocated. It's the only place in town big enough."

"How long will they be here?"

"Until the storm passes through and their camp dries out."

"I don't have enough beds. They'll have to sleep on the floor. What will I feed them?"

"Don't get ahead of yourself. They may be tucked in all warm and cozy at the ranch house near their camp. We're heading out now. I'll send word if I can. Gotta go."

I hung up and wandered around the apartment trying to decide what to do first. A shower and laundry made the most sense. After that, I would rewrite my lesson plans, rendered obsolete by the snow day, because twiddling my thumbs until I heard from Rick would drive me nuts. I finished everything and was about to start twiddling when the phone rang. I picked up immediately.

"Jane, Dan Barkley here. Rick radioed the Forest Service and said the power lines are down out by the dig site. Their crew stayed in the ranch house last night, but it doesn't have power either. The rescue party is loading everyone onto snowmobiles now."

"Are they all okay?"

"Cold and hungry from what I gathered, but they'll be fine once they get hot food in their bellies and a good night's sleep."

I repeated what I'd told Rick earlier. "They'll have to sleep on the floor. I don't have enough food for them, either."

"Me and Scott Gibson are bringing Forest Service cots, blankets, and pillows in a couple minutes."

Betty broke in. "The Kewwys wiww dewiver sandwich fixings from the store for wunch, and the Berthowds are sending supper from The Bend."

"What, no breakfast?" I quipped.

Betty assured me it would arrive soon. "Oh, another caww is coming in. Bye."

"I'll sign off, too," Dan said. The line went dead.

I replaced the receiver and wandered around the apartment as visions of how breakfast might arrive danced in my head. Cereal boxes skiing over the snow drifts. Pop Tarts blowing in on the wind and into the toaster. Milk cartons sprouting wings and—

A knock sounded, and I went to let in Dan and Scott. But it wasn't them. It was Merle. He was covered in snow from the top of his Elmer Fudd hat to the tips of his overshoes. The large cardboard carton he carried was frosted with snow as well. Merle limped inside and set his load on the kitchen counter. He pulled out the contents of the box one by one. A gallon of milk from his prized cow, Snippy. A quart jar of watery buttermilk. An enormous ball of butter. Two dozen eggs. A jug of syrup. A huge slab of bacon. Sacks of flour and sugar. Boxes of baking powder and salt. And a waffle iron.

Breakfast had arrived.

Chapter 17

"You gonna help make non-skid pancakes for these pal-ee-intol-ee-gers who ain't got enough sense to dodge a blizzard or what, Teacher?" Merle rubbed his hands together and blew wet, schleppy breaths to warm them. The snow on his eyelids and brows melted and ran down his wrinkled cheeks like tears. "You got measuring spoons and cups and bowls and pans in this kitchen, or do I got to go home and git my own?"

He'd already tracked snow from the entryway to the sink. A patch of wet carpet was growing under his galoshes. "I'll lay out what you need while you're in the entryway taking off your wet things."

He gimped away. I started a pot of coffee before gathering the bowls and utensils he needed to mix waffle batter. I was rummaging through a drawer for measuring spoons when a knock sounded at the door.

I shouted at Merle. "Would you see who it is?"

"You think I don't got it in me to bring folks in from a storm without you bossing me around?" he groused.

Cold air rushed in when Merle let in the visitors. Shivering, I went to see who they were. Two men came in, their faces hidden under ski masks. The Forest Service insignias on their parkas made me suspect Dan Barkley and Scott Gibson had come to call. They entered the kitchen, their arms straining around stacks of blankets as their boots deposited tiny mounds of packed snow with every step.

"How much more do you have to bring in?"

Dan reeled off a list. "Pillows and cots. Folding chairs and card tables our wives insisted we bring. They didn't think those college students would fit in your students' desks."

Bless Pam Barkley and Linda Gibson. Their solution was considerably better than my plan to have them picnic on the floor. "So a couple more loads?"

"At least," said Scott.

"In that case, let's put everything in my classroom for now." I squeezed past them, shuddering as my socks hit wet patches of carpet, and gestured for them to follow me into the school half of the building. They piled the blankets on the counter near the sink. I gave them my key so they could unlock the classroom door and bring the rest of the stuff in without going through my apartment.

I went to the kitchen again. Merle had found the frying pan and was setting it on the stove. "Did you know you can cook bacon in the oven?" I asked him.

"Nope."

I exchanged the frying pan for cookie sheets and turned the oven to four hundred twenty-five degrees. "I'll show you how. Just arrange the bacon strips on cookie sheets like this, put them in the oven for ten or fifteen minutes, and take them out."

"That's it?"

"Uh-huh."

"We-ull, you learn something new every day."

As I slid the pans in the oven, the roar of engines came from the schoolyard. I wiped my greasy fingers on a rag and went to the window to see what the commotion was. A line of snowmobiles drove onto the playground. Drivers dismounted and then assisted their blanket-wrapped passengers through the snow toward the building.

I ran through to the classroom, thrust its door open, and shouted, "This way!"

The drivers coaxed their charges up the landing stairs with promises of hot coffee, dry clothes, and warm quarters. Dan and Scott met the dig crew in the entryway, peeled off their ice-encrusted blankets and wrapped them in dry ones before guiding them to folding chairs in the classroom. Victor and his team looked rough— blue-lipped, teeth chattering, their thin clothes no match for a blizzard.

I went straight to the phone and rang Betty. "The dig team's in bad shape. They need more hot coffee than my pot can handle. And I don't have enough mugs, silverware, dishes, towels, and washcloths. They could use undergarments, socks, warm clothes, hot water bottles, and heating pads too, if you can find them. And I need it all five minutes ago."

"No probwem, Miss Neweww."

After the call, I had Dan and Scott set up the card tables in my living room. While they did that, Merle began spooning batter into the waffle iron. I poured stingy rations of coffee into every glass and cup I owned and distributed them to the iced humans waiting in my classroom.

"Jane, can you spare a minute?"

I recognized the voice and hunted for its owner. He was in the entryway hiding in his snowmobile suit and ski mask.

Rick removed the mask. "Is there somewhere private we can talk?"

"You're kidding, right?" I stared at him in disbelief.

He stared back, his expression grave and unflinching. The only unoccupied rooms were the lab and my bedroom. The former was locked, and I wasn't about to take the key from it's hiding place in front of my guests. Velma would wheedle its whereabouts in no time. That left the latter.

I glared at him. "Leave your boots on the entryway rug and follow me."

Once we were in the bedroom I shut the door. "What is it?" I snapped.

He shifted from one leg to the other. "We both know there's a ninety-nine point nine percent chance that Beanie's attacker is on the dig crew. We also know that person is aware that you are part of the official team investigating the incident, so I'm putting safety measures into place."

I hadn't had a spare minute to think about the matter. Suddenly, I was grateful Rick had insisted on having this discussion in private.

"Deputy Columbo will be here any minute."

"I've heard that before."

"He heard Merle is making non-skid pancakes. He'll

be here. After we eat, we'll move the dig team guys to the empty classroom in the trailer to the north of the school yard. Cardo will bunk with them for the duration and Velma—"

Velma?

"—has volunteered to bunk with you in here while the women sleep in your classroom."

"Not Velma."

"She's the greatest deterrent to crime in the county. And she said she'll cook and clean, too."

There was that. "Okay, she can stay. But make it clear that even with a blizzard raging, she has to go outside to smoke."

"Already did."

"So you are staying for breakfast?" I asked as we went into the living room.

He nodded. "But not to help with dishes."

Velma shot out of the kitchen—

When had she arrived?

—and nearly barreled into Rick. "Gonna eat and run, are you Sheriff?"

"More like drive my snowmobile to Highway 20 and check for stranded motorists."

She poked a finger at his nose. "Until then, you are in charge of setting tables. And you"—she poked the same finger at my nose—"are in charge of telling the jokers who are hauling the coffee pots and whatever else you told Betty to round up, to take off their boots and leave them on the newspapers I spread in the entryway of your classroom. I don't care how bad this blizzard is and how cold them dig team fools got. There is no excuse for the kind of mess being made. No excuse—"

"Stop your bellyachin' and do something useful, Velma," Merle bellowed. "Go tell the lumps of ice in the other room that there's enough non-skid pancakes and bacon ready to satisfy a dinosaur."

I looked from Rick, who was setting out plates and silverware at Mach speed, to Merle whose eyes were shooting daggers at Velma, to Velma who was shooting them right back, to Scott and Dan who were escorting the dig team into the apartment, and finally to a short, dark-haired man bringing up the rear. His substantial midsection made his shirt buttons strain. Of more interest to me than the buttons was the sheriff's deputy insignia on the sleeve of his buff-colored shirt.

I inched my way through the breakfast crowd until I stood before him. He held out his hand, and I gave it a hearty shake.

"Deputy Columbo, I presume?"

Chapter 18

The deputy tipped his head ever so slightly to one side. "Call me Cardo." He clicked the heels of his cowboy boots with a dash of European flair that seemed incongruous in a county populated by cowhands and ranch families. "Now, if you'll excuse me, I must see to our guests. After what they've been through, their appetites must be enormous."

"Guests" was a generous description of the five people who straggled into the living room. "Drowned rats" would have been more accurate. Cardo escorted them to the card tables, and they sank into the chairs clustered around them.

A large urn labeled "Property of the US Forest Service" was filled with fresh coffee. I began filling thick white cups, the kind Trudy and Glen used at Round the Bend, and set them at each table. Sheila and Teresa thanked me as they wrapped their hands around their cups. They appeared more interested in warming their fingers than in wetting their whistles. Sheila's blanket slipped off her shoulders, revealing her damp T-shirt. Soggy socks peeked out from beneath the part of the blanket that didn't quite reach the floor.

My eyes searched for Velma and located her near the window staring at the storm, her expression as hospitable as the blizzard raging outside.

"Velma, would you take Sheila and Teresa into my bedroom and find them some dry clothes?"

"I can do better than that," she growled before stomping into the other half of the building. She returned with a pile of clothes under each arm. She thrust them at the two women and barked, "Put these on."

Even half-frozen people listened when Velma barked. Sheila and Teresa took the clothes and fled into the bedroom.

Velma leveled her gaze on Rick. "How come you're just standing there, Sheriff? Go into Jane's classroom and get some of the men's clothes the Bertholds sent over." She flicked a hand at Frank, Donald, and Victor. "Take these three yahoos with you. They can change in the boys' bathroom."

The students and Victor's response was more boo-hoo than yahoo. Rick didn't point out their ungrateful reaction to the generosity they were about to enjoy. Instead, he obeyed Velma, and the three men trailed behind him like sheep.

I collected their damp blankets as they walked by and threw them in the dryer. When our guests returned in their new clothes, I handed them the afghans from my couch as well as the blankets and quilt from my bed.

They draped them around their shoulders and dug into bacon, scrambled eggs, and non-skid pancakes

as fast as Merle put the food on the tables. The only
sounds to be heard were the clink of silverware on
plates, coffee being slurped, and repeated requests for
more food. Merle happily complied and regaled them
with the origin stories of the butter, buttermilk, and
eggs.

"Where'd the bacon come from?" Victor asked, his
patronizing tone impossible to miss.

"The grocery store down the road. Where'd ya
think?" Merle glowered and snatched away the bacon
platter before Victor could take a third helping.

The students smirked as their professor busied himself buttering a waffle and pouring syrup. When had
they lost respect for him?

I stood. "I bet you could all use hot showers."

They straightened.

"The good news is that there's a shower in my apartment. The bad news is that it's the only shower in either
building."

They drooped.

"And you'll have to keep them very short, or we'll run
out of hot water."

Groans all around.

Deputy Cardo rose to save the day. He suggested that
once the men had eaten their fill, they retire to the other
building to set up their cots. They could use the bathroom sinks and all the hot water they wanted to clean up
and then get some sleep. He droned on, elaborating one
stultifying detail after another.

I was seized by a desire to escape the logistics
involved in providing hospitality for unexpected houseg-
uests and their keepers. But I couldn't. Until the blizzard

blew itself out and the dig site became habitable, my life would be composed of such details.

The more I thought about the next few days, the more hemmed in I felt. The weather prevented so much as a momentary escape outside. My guests' neediness prevented an escape into my bedroom with a book. Worst of all, Velma's watchfulness prevented an escape into the forensic lab. She would seize the opportunity and snoop to her heart's content. So here I sat, not ten feet from my darkroom where photographs of fingerprints waited to be analyzed, Cardo's reports waited to be read, and my yellow legal pad and a sharpened number two pencil waited to record clues and possible suspects. I closed my eyes and begged God for a double dose of patience. "I won't endure the next few days without it," I pleaded silently, "so send the patience immediately. If not sooner."

The scraping of chairs pushing away from the tables and the chatter of voices put a quick end to my begging. Merle launched into a little speech as the breakfast crowd carried their dishes into the kitchen.

"You may be thinkin' there can't be nothin' better than my non-skid pancakes and bacon"—he narrowed his eyes and aimed his next words at Victor—"from the grocery store. But you just wait till I serve up the soup that's simmerin' in my kitchen."

I leaped up. The legs of my chair tangled around my feet. I wrestled with the chair until it collapsed and fell on the floor. The expressions of my guests telegraphed a growing fear of being trapped in this apartment with a crazy woman. Pretty rich, I thought, when one of them was Beanie's attacker. But even that lowlife did not deserve to come down with salmonella or botulism after eating Merle's soup. He kept a pot of the vile stuff simmering on the back burner of his stove for nine months of the year. And I certainly didn't want to nurse Merle's victims back to health or clean up after them.

"Merle," I said and then took a moment to collect myself and sound alarmed, "you were a lifesaver this morning. Let's all give him a hand."

Everyone applauded enthusiastically, grateful for hot food and full stomachs. The dig crew applauded the longest, perhaps to warm their fingers, which still retained a bluish tint.

I went on. "Your offer is much appreciated. However, the Bertholds volunteered to bring supper from The Bend tonight."

Unfazed, Merle said, "I'll bring it at noon then."

"I believe the Kellys are sending lunch."

"They already brung sandwich fixings," Velma said. Joy at popping Merle's bubble was written all over her face.

Merle couldn't hide his disappointment. "We-ull, I best git on my way then." He limped toward the entryway.

"Can you bring more eggs, buttermilk, and butter tomorrow morning?" I asked. "I could use a hand making enough coffee cake to feed this crowd."

His limp diminished as he raised his index finger in the air as if testing the direction of the wind. "You can count on ol' Snip and me to do whatever we can, Teacher. What time should I git here?"

"Six thirty."

"I'll be here at six."

Rick left. After he and his snowmobile headed for Highway 20, the rest of us got busy. Deputy Cardo enlisted Dan and Scott's assistance in moving Victor, Frank, and Donald to the other building. Teresa and Sheila flipped a coin to decide who would use the shower first. Sheila won.

As she hurried off, I said, "Towels and washcloths are in the vanity cabinet."

Velma put on her best imitation of a smile and turned to Teresa. "Honey," she said.

Honey?

"Honey," she repeated, "you go to Miss Newell's classroom and help yourself to one of them pairs of pajamas. They're on the front table right next to the blackboard. I'll join you real quick, and we'll git your cot set up. I bet you could use a nap."

Teresa nodded and shuffled off. Velma waited until she was gone to speak. Really it was more of a hiss. And she didn't call me honey.

"You and me know that one of these so-called guests attacked that friend of yours with the vegetable name. What is it again?"

"Beanie."

"That's it. Well, I ain't gonna let that happen to you. I'm gonna bed down in that forensic lab right next to your bedroom." She held out her hand, palm up. "Give me the key."

"Velma, I'd rather have you sleep in front of my bedroom door. That would make me feel much safer." I enclosed her hand in both of mine. "Don't you agree, honey?"

Her lips tightened. Her eyes blazed. The floor shook

beneath her feet as she stormed out of my apartment and into the classroom. She slammed the door, and the sound reverberated throughout the building. I asked God to forgive me for unleashing Velma's anger on Teresa. Unless she was Beanie's attacker, I amended. In that case, Teresa deserved the wrath of Velma. And much, much more.

Chapter 19

After they showered, Sheila and Teresa took to their cots, each woman cuddled up to a heating pad and covered with blankets. Velma bent her anger and energy toward the entryways of the apartment and the classroom. Both areas looked like they'd been hit by a tornado followed by a blizzard. Deputy Cardo brought over a big armload of sodden clothes and put them in the washing machine. I tossed in Sheila and Teresa's damp clothes, added detergent, and started the load. The deputy ran the sink full of hot, soapy water and began washing breakfast dishes. I picked up a dish towel and joined him.

He turned off the faucet and pitched his voice low. "Is it wise for us to discuss the case with Velma around?"

I held a finger to my lips, tiptoed to the entryway, and tiptoed back. "She's not on the apartment side of the building, and door between us and the classroom is closed. She's not very good at sneaking up on people, so as long as we speak softly, we should be okay."

"Have you read through the interviews I conducted at the dig site?" he whispered.

"No. Rick delivered them"--I checked my watch--"about fifteen hours ago, but there hasn't been time."

"It feels more like fifteen years, doesn't it?"

"Does it ever. The reports are locked in the forensic lab. Since the day the bolt lock was installed, Velma's been on a mission to get inside. The reports will have to wait until she leaves."

His eyes darkened. "Some of your other guests may be itching to get into the lab too. When I showed up at their camp to take their fingerprints, they all tried to slink away. In my book, every one of them is more of a suspect than they were at the start of the investigation."

I opened the silverware drawer and began putting knives, spoons, and forks into their compartments. "Maybe they don't want you to know about something they've done that's unrelated to what happened to Beanie. College kids are famous for making dumb decisions. It could be they've been picked up for possession of marijuana and don't want Victor to know."

"True, but why didn't their professor serve as an example by being first in line instead of trying to disappear right along with them?"

"Maybe he's got a criminal past, too." I put a finger to my lips again and listened for any sign of Velma lurking nearby. The faint squeak of her wheeled mop bucket was all I heard. "Okay, go on."

"I believe that may be the case. Though his proclivities may run along the lines of bedding young coeds rather than imbibing illegal substances."

"What?" The silverware drawer slammed shut on my thumb. "Ouch!"

We froze and waited for Velma to tromp into the kitchen to check on the commotion. She didn't. Cardo turned on the faucet until the water ran cold and motioned for me to put my hand under it. When the throbbing died down, I turned off the faucet and sucked on my thumb. Still no sign of Velma.

"Do you think Victor's got something going on with one of the women at the camp?"

"I picked up some vibes between him and his research assistant that indicate more than a working relationship."

"You mean Sheila? The one with red hair?"

"That's the one." He set a clean plate in the dish rack.

My internal bell jangled, but I couldn't tell why. "Did you sense any other strange vibes?"

"Such as?"

"Who gets along with whom among the crew and who doesn't. Cliques among the students. That sort of thing."

While he thought the question over, I listened for Velma. Nothing.

"Are you asking whether or not they liked Beanie? Whether or not she'd been accepted into the group?"

"Yes."

"No one mentioned anything like that. Even college students aren't dumb enough to admit that kind of thing about a victim who's fighting for her life. But I did get the impression that they feel guilty about how they, or some of members of the team, treated her."

I told him about what Renny had observed and the

note in his lunch bag. Cardo let out a low whistle. He suggested we capitalize on our forced togetherness over the next few days. We would treat them like friends rather than suspects. Get to know them while we played board games and cards. Find out about their families and their hopes for the future while we all cooked, did chores, and watched television. Get them to let down their guard and disclose secrets about the person who'd put Beanie in the hospital.

Cardo set the last mug in the drainer. "That's a good job done."

"It is."

He unstopped the sink and watched the water whirl down the drain with a sucking sound.

"All you done was a few dishes." Velma's growl made us both jump. "That don't come close to what I been doing in those entryways. And I suppose you was so busy chitter-chattering that you ain't noticed what time it is."

I consulted my watch again. "It's eleven thirty."

"And?"

"And what?"

"Do I gotta spell it out for you?" Her eyes bugged out. "It's almost time for L-U-N-C-H!"

"With breakfast ending so late, I thought we would push lunch back until one."

She shook her head vehemently. "We gotta work backwards from supper. Glen Berthold is bringing hot meals at six o'clock. He wants to be safe in his house by dusk, and it'll come early with clouds as thick as what we got today. It's real easy to git lost in a blizzard after dark."

She was right about that. A few months ago, I'd

nearly lost my way playing cat and mouse with a killer at night during a snowstorm. I shuddered, recalling how close I'd come to ending my life as a human popsicle. I didn't like giving in to Velma's bullying, but if serving lunch at noon meant Glen would be home safe and sound before night, I could ignore her method in favor of his welfare.

"Then we better git a move on." She took Cardo by the elbow. "You come with me." She directed her next words to me. "And you move the laundry along."

I did as instructed and started making hot chocolate. I was pouring Snippy milk into a large pot when Velma and Cardo returned. She carried a paper grocery sack in each arm.

He set a cooler on the floor and straightened. Velma set the sacks on the counter and unloaded bags of potato chips, two packages of Hydrox cookies, Styrofoam cups, plastic silverware, paper plates, and napkins. Cardo piled the contents of the cooler—lunch meat, cheese, bread, condiments, a green salad, and three kinds of salad dressing—beside everything else.

I stirred the milk so it wouldn't scorch, while they arranged the food and tableware on the counter, buffet-style. While I whisked cocoa and sugar into the milk, Cardo bundled up and went to wake the men. I asked Velma to stir the hot chocolate so I could get a few things from my classroom before the crowd arrived.

She plucked the whisk out of my hand. "You could wake up them girls while you're over there, if it ain't too much trouble for you."

Manipulating her was far too easy, I thought, as I

went over to rouse Teresa and Sheila, which had been my real reason for leaving the kitchen. They were fast asleep.

"Time to wake up," I whispered. They didn't budge. I repeated the message three times, increasing my volume with each repetition. In the end, I had to shake their shoulders gently to get them to wake up. No doubt Velma had methods that would have been faster, but mine were kinder.

Sheila and Teresa made a pit stop in the bathroom. I returned to the kitchen to relieve Velma of hot chocolate duty. She declined my offer, demanding instead that I fill a pitcher with water in case anyone wanted that. Which is why, when everyone filed into the kitchen, she was presiding over the pot of hot chocolate when she announced, "I figured you all could use a treat and made up this batch of cocoa."

I was placing the water pitcher next to the Styrofoam cups when I caught sight of the smug expression she wore.

"Just who manipulated whom?" it seemed to say.

Chapter 20

A few hours of rest, warmth, and dry clothes had worked wonders for the members of the dig team. Lunch proved to be a lively affair as they tore through it with astonishing speed. When the meal was over, all the food was gone. The hot chocolate pot and the coffee urn were empty. The only snacks in the apartment were the May basket candies hidden in my freezer. I wasn't going to share it with this horde of locusts when the mid-afternoon munchies hit. I took the plate with two pounds of Snippy butter from the refrigerator and set it on the warm patch of stovetop right above the pilot light. As soon as the butter softened a little, we would make cookies.

One of the men whooped, and I turned to see what the commotion was. Frank was prancing around Donald and Victor, waving a long straw at them. "Are you jealous, suckers? I drew the first shower!" He ran for the bathroom.

"Towels are in the vanity," I said as he went by.

"You take longer than five minutes, and I'll turn off the water," Victor shouted.

Donald cleared away the paper plates and other trash from lunch and threw everything in the garbage. Teresa scrubbed out the hot chocolate pot. Sheila moved the clothes in the dryer into a laundry basket and lugged the basket over to the couch. She sat down and started folding.

While his students pitched in, Victor sat and stared at his watch. Five minutes later he stood, stalked to the bathroom door, and pounded on it. "Get a move on, Frank. Your time's up." Then he rounded on Donald, who was wiping down the card tables. "There better be hot water left for me when you're done. You shouldn't have let me draw the short straw."

Donald took the professor's appalling rudeness in stride. The two women exchanged furtive glances. Cardo also caught their guarded looks. We raised our eyebrows in concert. Velma missed the drama. She stood at the living room window watching the storm. Snow fell to the ground, only to be snatched by the wind and hurled into drifts.

"There's a foot at least, and it ain't letting up one bit," she fretted. "This could be real bad for the ranchers."

"How come?" Sheila took a T-shirt from the laundry basket.

Velma went to sit beside her and absently pulled a pair of men's boxer shorts out of the basket. She folded and unfolded the undergarment as she spoke. "Spring storms are the worst there is. Calves and lambs can wander away from their mamas, lie down, and die in this weather. Heifers'll pack together tight for warmth and suffocate. And the sheep have been sheared and don't have no way to hold in their body heat. I've seen ranchers lose half their herds come April and May." She balled up the boxers in her fists. "Some of 'their operations won't come back from that."

A single tear rolled down her cheek, and I remembered why I put up with her grumpiness—why I counted her as my friend. It was because she loved the people in this county and their way of life. She knew more about the obstacles they faced and their perseverance than I ever would. She cared more too.

She swiped at the tear with the underwear and then stared at her makeshift hankie. Comprehension dawned. She squawked, threw it in the laundry basket, and advanced on me with fire in her eyes. "How come you didn't say nothing?"

I hustled over to the stove and lifted the butter dish. "Who wants to make cookies?"

Everyone but Victor, who was again staring at his watch, converged in the kitchen before Velma could reach me. Within the hour, the aroma of fresh chocolate-chip oatmeal cookies baking in the oven was making our stomachs growl. Snow pounded on the windows, demanding to be let in to try the cookies too. I turned a deaf ear to the storm. Cardo and I piled decks of cards and board games onto the tables in the living room. Teresa, Frank, and Sheila tended the cookies. Victor kicked Donald out of the bathroom. Donald filled the urn with water, measured coffee into its basket, and plugged it in. Before long, Cardo, Donald, Sheila, and Velma were playing Sorry! at one table. I set up the cribbage board at another. Frank, Teresa, and I sat down and waited for Victor to finish his shower and join us. He emerged all clean and shiny ten minutes later.

The deputy and I exchanged glances while Frank shuffled and dealt cards. Our clandestine game of table talk was about to begin.

After counting my hand and pegging, I asked Frank, "Who taught you to play cribbage?"

"I grew up in a no-cards-allowed home," he said while the others played their hands. "So not my parents. Luckily my first roommate's family plays cribbage, hearts, spades, poker. You name it, he can play it. He devoted his freshman year to bringing everyone on our dorm floor up to speed. He was a good teacher, but a terrible student and flunked out after one semester. I almost did too." He grimaced and then counted his crib.

"How about you?" I asked Teresa when Victor picked up the deck and shuffled.

She giggled and tucked a strand of hair behind one ear. "I grew up on a ranch in Nebraska. We weren't allowed to play poker, but cribbage and other card games kept us entertained in the winter. There wasn't much else to do in weather like this."

While I organized my hand and decided what to throw in the crib, I overheard Donald at the other table explaining the "seven" card's usefulness. "Is this the first time you've played Sorry!?" he asked.

"My parents worked all the time. They didn't have time for me," Sheila retorted.

I thought of my dad, who wheeled up to the kitchen table as soon as I got home from junior high . . .

"Grab a snack and get over here, Janie-Jo! There's no

*time like the present for a round of cribbage." He took
the board and deck of cards from his lap and set them
on the table.*

*I laid a couple cookies on a napkin and sat next to
him so I could shuffle and deal every hand, then pick
up his cards, fan them out, and put them in his hand. I
munched a cookie while we played. I pegged points for
both of us, waiting for the request he was sure to make.*

*"Say," he pointed to my napkin, "how about you get
me a few of those too. For quality control purposes." . . .*

The memory warmed me but didn't reach to the next
table. Sheila's frostiness rendered Donald immobile until
Cardo reminded him to take his turn.

"When did you learn cribbage, Prof?" Frank asked
Victor.

My attention shifted to our quartet again.

"I grew up on a farm in Kansas." He tipped his chair
onto its back legs and gestured toward Teresa. "The win-
ters there aren't as bad as Nebraska's, but they're equally
boring. My family worked its way through a beat-up
copy of Hoyle's card games. When I got to college, I was
able to concentrate on my studies in college instead of
falling into the hole Frank's trying to claw his way out
of."

Frank was either impervious to his professor's barbs,
or he'd mastered his poker face when he learned to play
cribbage. I looked at each of Victor's students in turn.
Their faces were as impassive as Frank's, but the easy
camaraderie of a few moments ago had evaporated.
From what I saw, the distrust and tension Victor had

cultivated among his team could have led to the attack upon Beanie.

In light of that observation, I was in favor of Velma's plan to camp in front of my bedroom door. Executing an army crawl beneath her cot in the dead of night to get to the bathroom sounded reasonable. Better an obstacle course in the dead of night than being dead in my bed come morning.

Chapter 21

To everyone's delight, Victor announced he was going to the other building for some peace and quiet. No one begged him to stay, though Deputy Cardo insisted on going with him, as it wasn't prudent for anyone to venture outside alone.

The deputy returned a quarter of an hour later covered in snow. "The drifting is spectacular," he said from the entryway as he took off his boots. "Snow is piled high on the landings for this building, but the wind has swept the ones at the other building clean. Victor and I cleared the landing in front of the apartment entryway, and we shoveled the sidewalk too. Our herculean efforts will be erased within the hour. Before I left Victor, I insisted we locate Liv's shovel so he can get back here for supper."

The atmosphere in the room relaxed in the professor's absence. We played games all afternoon. Glen Berthold's call to take supper orders was our only interruption. My losing streak in cribbage was legendary, as were the details I coaxed out of my competitors.

Frank liked to eat more than he liked to cook. And he hated college. "I signed up for the dig team," he confided, "to get away from Morningside for a month."

Teresa said she was the youngest person on the dig team. As she described her upbringing on a ranch, it was clear she had more practical skills than her cohorts. She didn't realize how much she contributed to the team, but Sheila's respect for the younger woman spoke volumes.

Sheila had plenty to say about Victor. He'd earned an undergrad degree in geology at the University of Kansas, his Masters and Doctorate in the same field from the University of Michigan in Ann Arbor. Though Sheila didn't outright say he knew what he was doing at the dig site, she did say his scientific rigor was unquestioned. His handling of artifacts went by the book. He kept meticulous records. Still, she didn't think he'd arranged the dig in order to contribute to his field. He'd done it to beef up his resume and land the job of his dreams at his undergrad alma mater.

Donald said little, perhaps because his mouth was usually full of cookies. Then he pushed his chair away from the table and swallowed. "Deal me out this hand. I gotta go to the bathroom and then get more cookies."

When he was out of earshot, Teresa threw her cards on the table. "How does he do it? It's like he eats whatever he wants, and I gain my freshman fifteen *and* his."

Frank's bangs fell over his eyes. He shook them away with a toss of his head. "You mean his junior fifteen."

"Wait," I kept my voice low, "Donald's a junior?"

"He looks about fifteen, doesn't he?" Frank gathered our cards and shuffled them. "He was sick a lot as a kid, and it stunted his growth. But not his sense of adventure. He'll try anything."

When we heard a snowmobile roar to a stop outside, we ran for the window. I flipped on the light above the landing and tried to open the door. It wouldn't budge.

Cardo pressed his forehead against the living room window and cupped his hands around his eyes. "It's drifted shut again." He cranked the window open and yelled through the screen. "The shovel is leaning against the north side of the landing."

The snowmobile driver dismounted. Soon we heard metal scraping against cement, then a short silence, then Glen Berthold's voice. "Open the door. My hands are full."

Cardo did Glen's bidding. He walked in and thrust a big box at the deputy. "Take this. There's another."

He returned with the second one and gave it to Velma. "It's gonna be a brutal night, but the forecast says the storm's gonna blow itself out by morning."

He left on a gust of wind and disappeared into a wall of falling snow. While he was invisible, his snowmobile was not silent. The sound of it persuaded Victor to leave his peaceful hideaway in favor of the burger, fries, and beer Sheila had said was his usual order at The Bend.

We claimed our meals quickly and ate in front of the television while we watched the weather. We had originally found what Glen said about tomorrow's forecast too fantastical to believe, but the weather reporter confirmed it. The snow and wind would end in the night. By morning, the temperature would start rising and top out into the fifties during the afternoon.

"Yes!" Frank raised his hands, one of them clutching

what remained of his double cheeseburger. "We'll be sleeping in our own tents tomorrow night."

Teresa giggled nervously. "Not a chance. Camp's going to turn into a muddy mess when the snow starts melting. We'll be lucky to make it back by Sunday evening. You all better pray for sunshine to dry up the mud."

I did so immediately.

After supper we watched *Wonder Woman.* Even Linda Carter in her skimpy little costume wasn't enough to keep the guys awake. Sleep deprivation caught up with the dig crew. They soon began nodding off right where they sat.

Velma switched off the television during a commercial and put her hands on her hips. "You all might as well start your beauty rest now so you're ready to shovel show before breakfast tomorrow morning."

They headed to their sleeping quarters without objecting. Before long, Velma and I were the sole occupants of my apartment. I called first dibs on the bathroom, where I brushed my teeth and did my business. She was setting up her cot when I came out of the bathroom. I fled into my bedroom, locked the door, and climbed into bed with a book.

She was asleep when I unlocked my door in the morning and peeked out at her. I got on my hands and knees, pushed my clothes ahead of me, and army crawled under her cot and out the other side. She was still sleeping after I showered and dressed. When Merle arrived at six on the dot, the scraping of the shovel on the landing finally woke her.

She shot out of bed, hoisted her overnight bag, and

ran for the bathroom. "How come you didn't wake me sooner? Do you want Merle to see me in my nighty?"

As a matter of fact, I did, though admitting it struck me as unwise. I was too young to die.

A fully clothed Velma burst out of the bathroom soon after and stomped into my classroom. Merle and I heard her rouse Teresa and Sheila with dire threats of no breakfast. Then she stomped to the entryway and yelled that she was putting on her parka and boots and going to wake the men in the other building. A half hour later, the dig crew had completed its digging and came inside. They were greeted by the aroma of Early Bird Coffee Cake and Merle's distinctive old-man scent. They shed the winter gear on loan from the Forest Service, filed into the kitchen, and loaded their plates with coffee cake, orange wedges, and scrambled eggs. If we kept eating like this, every one of us would pack on our freshman fifteen. Even Donald. Even Velma.

I tried to conjure a picture of her as a collegiate. Impossible.

Frank and I were doing dishes after breakfast when the phone rang. "Go answer it," he said. "Donald'll take your place. Right, Donny?"

I set my dish towel on the counter and picked up the receiver. "Hello, this is Jane."

"Jane, you aren't going to believe this!"

"What won't I believe, Mom?"

"Little Missouri was mentioned on Sioux City's six o'clock news last night. The weatherman said you had eighteen inches of snow on the ground by then. How much do you have now?"

"I'm not sure. The drifting makes it hard to tell. I'll ask Cardo."

"Around two feet," he replied. "But not for long. Your thermometer is already sitting at thirty-two degrees. The snow'll start melting soon."

Sheila jumped up. "Perfect weather for playing outside. Anybody want to go with me?"

The other students roared as they went to the entryway and began putting on their winter gear.

"Jane, who is this Cardo person? And who is making that commotion? Do you have guests?"

After I brought her up to date, she said, "So you're saying that everyone on the dig team is staying at the school? Even though they are all suspects in your current investigation?"

"Yes."

"I don't like the sound of this. Did you get any rest last night?"

I told her about Velma's sleeping arrangements.

"What if she's the next victim?"

"Mom, you've met Velma. Who would be dumb enough to attack her?"

She laughed. "Certainly not me."

Velma snatched the receiver from my hand. "Doris, you stop worrying about your daughter. My cot's got enough room for me and Jane's butcher knife."

My butcher knife?

"Now, Doris, all them college kids just run outside to play in the snow. Don't you think it would be nice for Jane to be with them instead of in here with old fogies like me and Merle?" She motioned for me to vamoose.

I wasn't going to argue with a woman who slept with

a butcher knife. I put on my winter clothes and trundled outside.

"Over here, Jane," Sheila hollered.

I waded through the snow. It was almost up to my waist in places. In front of a tall drift, the others were shaping a . . . I didn't have the foggiest idea of what they were sculpting. I took a page from my asking-kindergarteners-what-they-were-making book, I asked Sheila to tell me about it.

"It's a Snowosaurus rex."

Aha!

I scooped up a mittenful of snow and smoothed it onto what I hoped was the snowosaurus's neck. Then I took a page from the one-of-you-attacked-Beanie book and lied through my teeth. "Of course it is."

Chapter 22

We filled the playground with eerie, white terrible lizards. Then we divided into teams and commandeered the dinosaurs to serve as makeshift forts for a snowball fight. We stockpiled ammunition to our hearts' content before we began peeking above our dinocades and hurling snowballs at our enemies. We stayed outside, embodying the children we'd been a decade ago. When Burt Kelly arrived on his snowmobile with several sacks of groceries, we were famished but loath to abandon our fun and go inside.

I felt like we brought the best of our former selves into my apartment along with the food. Donald humored Velma by laying fresh newspapers in the entryway and lining up our boots according to her exacting standards. The rest of us pitched in and fixed a lunch familiar to the children we had once been. Cold air and exercise transformed Campbell's tomato soup and grilled cheese sandwiches made with Wonder Bread and Velveeta into a meal fit for royalty.

Teresa, Cardo, and I took our food into the living room and sat together at one of the card tables. She closed her eyes and bowed her head. I followed suit, embarrassed by how easily I had shed the practice saying grace when others were present.

She opened her eyes and picked up her sandwich. She dunked it in her soup, then used it to point to the lab door. "Why is that always locked?"

How many times have you tried to open it?

To keep from saying what I was thinking, I bit into my sandwich and chewed slowly. How much should I reveal to her? Cardo nodded encouragingly.

I decided to go for broke. "You know I work part time for the sheriff's department, right?"

Her face was blank at first. When comprehension dawned, she said "Oh! So that's why you took so many pictures after Beanie was—after her accident."

There it was again. The subtle shift from attack to accident.

"Right. And I developed the film in a darkroom behind that locked door."

Partway through our conversation, Frank took a seat next to us. He eyed the distance between the door and the south wall of the apartment. "That's a sizable darkroom."

"No. It's in a small corner of the big room."

"What else is in there?"

"The same stuff you'd find in any forensic lab. Latex gloves. Evidence bags. A microscope."

Victor was listening in from the other card table where he sat with Sheila and Donald. Velma began rattling pans in the kitchen, so Victor raised his voice to be heard above the din. "A fingerprint kit?"

I nodded.

"Lists of clues and suspects?" Donald added.

"Yes. Those are kept in a filing cabinet." I broke off a corner of my sandwich. "It's locked too."

Sheila laughed. "It sounds very Nancy Drewish."

"More like Miss Marple."

Everyone laughed.

"But enough about what I do. Tell me why you joined the dig team. And why is the dig site near Little Missouri? This is no St. Mary Mead."

"For paleontologists, Tipperary County is better than St. Mary Mead," Victor said. "Ranchers are constantly stumbling over fossils."

"How do paleontologists learn about their discoveries?" I asked.

"The ranchers know to call the geology department at the School of Mines in Rapid City. Word travels from there."

"Is that how you heard about this site?"

"Actually my research assistant heard about it and told me," Victor said.

"I didn't know you had a research assistant."

"She's right there." He pointed to Sheila.

I turned to her. "Where did you hear about it?"

"A School of Mines professor. He presented a paper about this area at a conference I attended last year. I talked to him afterwards, and he gave me names of several ranchers to contact. Some from Tipperary County and some across the border in Montana."

That fit with what Garth had said.

"I contacted them by phone and arranged to visit their ranches last summer. Sort of a fact-finding tour. I reported to Vic about what I'd seen, and we chose the old Lindgren place."

She isn't mentioning the Wentworths. That says something.

Sheila stared at Victor, her eyes challenging him to say more. He dropped his gaze before she did. Velma broke the tension between them when she came over and demanded our supper orders. When she was done, Victor and Sheila acted like they were on the same side again.

I turned to Sheila and asked, "What made you decide to become a research assistant?"

"I want to become a paleontologist. Being a research assistant is good for my resume and allows me to work a couple other jobs and save for grad school. I worked my way through my undergrad degree. I can do it again."

I returned to the conversation about the dig site and asked Victor, "Did you have to get permission from anyone other than the rancher who owns the place?" I intentionally omitted the name of the new owner.

"We got a permit from the county just to be on the up and up," Victor said. "We also signed an agreement with the owner that any fossils found on private land would be housed by the college but remain his property. The agreement also states that museums that acquire them will provide fair compensation to the landowner."

You didn't mention the Wentworths either.

"Is that customary?"

"It depends on the landowner. Some donate fossils to museums. Some don't."

I knew which camp Richard Wentworth would gravitate toward.

Victor went on. "It's also a means of discouraging people from smuggling fossils and selling them on the black market."

"Is that common?" I asked.

Victor shrugged. "Hard to know. The black market isn't known for its transparency. But there are plenty of rumors. More each year."

Cardo cleared his throat and winked. He wanted me to move on.

"Okay, so I've heard from your professor and from Sheila." I gazed at the other students. "What about the rest of you?"

Frank picked up his empty soup bowl and paused before going into the kitchen. "I'm here marking time until the end of the semester. Then I'm getting a job on a road crew and telling my parents I'm done with college."

Teresa said she was a science major. "I joined the dig team to decide whether my concentration should be geology or chemistry." Her habit of looking through her eyelashes at Donald as she spoke made me think she'd gone into science because it was a male-dominated field.

Donald planned to be a high school science teacher. "I hope working on the dig will give me ideas about how to run the summer camp. I want to get kids who learn best by doing interested in science."

"Do you know how to make plaster fossils?" He directed the question to me. "It would be a good activity to help your students connect better with what they learned during the field trip."

"Can you show me how?"

"Do you have any plaster of Paris?"

"There's gobs of it in the supply closet. I don't know where it came from."

Velma scowled. "The teacher before you ordered the filthy stuff. The glitter too. She made messes right and left until I laid down the law. It's hard to believe, but she was worse than you." Her glare ordered me to drop the matter.

I turned to Donald and linked arms with him. "I'm always game for a good art project." I grinned cheerily at Velma and then steered him toward the supply closet. "The messier the better."

Chapter 23

Donald and the rest of the dig crew made working with plaster of Paris look simple.

"How did you get so good at this?" I asked, after one after another of my plaster castings came out wonky.

"Loads of practice," Teresa said. "We use the stuff every day at the dig site."

I took her words to heart, rolled up my sleeves, and made casts of anything I could press into the wet plaster we poured into paper plates and bowls—pencils, scissors, a mascara tube, combs, buckles. You name it, I tried it. The cast of the meat fork I was working on when the phone rang was a true masterpiece.

Frank picked up the receiver and held it to my ear as I carefully removed the meat fork and swished it in a bucket of water to dissolve the crumbs of plaster clinging to it.

"This is Jane."

"And this is Trudy. Do you know if Velma has your supper order ready yet?"

"She does. Want me to get her?"

"In a sec. Glen said to tell you that he and the sheriff was at the dig site about an hour ago. He says the snow's melting already, and the electricity is on again. Rick asked Richard Wentworth if the dig team could sleep in the house out there tomorrow night. He said it was okay and that they could use the washer and dryer."

"The team will be glad to hear that."

"Can you get Velma now?"

I dried my hand, took the receiver from Frank, and covered the mouthpiece with my hand before shouting Velma's name.

She appeared from the hallway to the bathroom, feather duster in her hand. "What's so darned urgent you gotta interrupt my janitor duties?"

"Trudy wants the supper orders."

Velma drew a wrinkled paper from her pocket, took the phone receiver, and read them out. After she hung up, she surveyed the fine layer of plaster dust that coated the kitchen. With sinister calm, she announced she was going to the other building to clean Liv's room. "I'd rather go hungry than eat with folks who got no respect for school property or the people who is in charge of keeping it clean." All bristles and sharp edges, she pivoted on her heel and stomped off.

"She has a point," Donald said. "We ought to clean this up."

I got my own caddy of cleaning supplies, but waited until Velma slammed the door behind her to get a few more things from her janitor's closet. We divvied up the chores—even Victor agreed to run the vacuum—and got to it. When Glen brought the food an hour later, my apartment sparkled. I went to the phone and asked Betty to ring Liv's room and persuade Velma to join us.

"I'm no miracwe worker," Betty said.

"Tell her we cleaned up the plaster mess."

"Why didn't you say so? I'ww give it a try." She disconnected.

Velma arrived a little later and remained silent during the meal. I passed along the news from Glen and the sheriff. It caused a stir of excitement amongst the dig crew and put everyone, including Velma, in a celebratory mood.

"You got any toothpicks?" she asked me.

"I do." I went to the kitchen and got the giant box I'd purchased when Dick and I had gone grocery shopping. It seemed forever ago. I set the box in front of her. "Here you go."

Velma's expression morphed into something that almost passed as pleasant. "Anybody up for a game of poker? We can play for toothpicks."

Eager to humor her, we readily agreed. An hour later she rose and gathered her loot, enough toothpicks to keep her out of a dentist chair for a decade. She cracked a yawn that exposed an expanse of white teeth with nary a cavity, evidence that she had employed this little scam before.

"I think I'll set up my cot and go to bed right this minute. I'm tired enough to fall asleep no matter how loud you blast the television." When we didn't react, she tightened the thumb screws. "Tomorrow's gonna be a big day. I told Merle to be here at six o'clock—"

In other words, five thirty.

"—to make a big batch of his non-skid pancakes

again. You gotta be done eating and packed up by seven. That's when the Forest Service is sending trucks to take you back where you belong."

Frank wrinkled his forehead. "Why not the snowmobiles?"

"There won't be a lick a snow left by morning." She loosed another unconvincing yawn along with a dramatic stretching of her arms. "Now if you'll excuse me, I need to visit the ladies' room before I get my beauty rest."

"Men, I believe we have received our marching orders." Cardo stood and pocketed the deck of cards along with my half-empty box of toothpicks. "What do you say to another friendly card game sans Velma?"

He and his charges left without a backward glance. Teresa and Sheila went to their sleeping quarters. I used the bathroom after Velma, took an empty tin can from the garbage, and dashed into my bedroom before her cot blocked the door completely. If nature called tonight, I would use the can for a commode. Even if my aim was off, it was better than crawling under Velma and her butcher knife.

Kitchen noises and the sensation of a bladder about to burst woke me in the morning. I dressed quickly and eased the door open. Velma's cot was gone, so I ran through the kitchen at full speed, nearly knocking Merle down on the way, and made it to the bathroom just in time. A few minutes later, I returned to the kitchen where I served as Merle's assistant. The morning proceeded precisely as Velma had said it would. The dig team ate their fill—a massive amount of food—and Scott Gibson and Dan Barkley picked them up and delivered them to the old Lindgren place. Scott and Dan returned in their Forest Service trucks to pack up the cots, the blankets and pillows, the parkas and boots, the card tables and chairs. They offered to drop off Merle and his waffle iron at his house. He accepted.

Velma stood at the window. "Why didn't the old fool walk home? It'll take longer for them to drive him home."

"I think you know the answer better than most."

"He is a lonely old fool." Her gaze softened.

I went to the window and stood beside her. Scott helped Merle into the truck and then squelched through the mud to the driver's side.

After they drove off, Velma's shoulders slumped almost to her belly button. "I just don't have the energy to tackle the mud that got tracked into your classroom this morning. You mind if I let it dry and come back this afternoon?" She sounded worn out.

How well had she slept on the cot the past two nights cozied up to a butcher knife? "That'll be fine, Velma. Maybe you should take the day off. I can take care of it."

Her shoulders went as stiff as a starched cotton shirt. "Not up to my standards, you can't. Plus, I got to tidy up the room where the men bunked and give the bathrooms a lick and a promise. I'll be back in a few hours." She put on her coat and crossed the playground, her hood thrown back, her face upturned to catch the morning sun.

I went into my classroom and moved my students' desks to their proper places and tucked books back onto shelves. I opened the windows to let the breeze dry the mud on the carpet. Then I went out onto the landing and breathed in lungfuls of the warm air. Once I'd drunk my fill of spring, I went inside and unlocked the lab. I sketched a rough timeline of the weekend on my yellow legal pad and placed it next to the typewriter. With the timeline as my guide, I typed out every conversation I'd heard, every facial expression I'd seen, and my impressions of what I'd observed. I put the original reports into an envelope for Rick and the carbon copies in the case file folder in the filing cabinet. By then it was noon, so I fixed myself a sandwich and opened a jar of the home-canned applesauce Mom had sent home with me after Christmas vacation.

I gazed out the window while I ate. The sunshine and blue skies beyond the glass were tempting. Impossible to resist. I slipped into my jacket and was about to go outside when the image of Beanie lying in the hospital in a coma colored the prospect of a walk around town basking in spring's return. I removed my jacket, went into the lab, and shot the bolt. I took the envelope from the locked filing cabinet where it had been living since Rick dropped it off the evening before the blizzard. I drew out the thick sheaf of papers and began reading them.

My desire for sunshine and warmth faded as I read slowly, searching for threads to tease out. At the same time, my desire to find the thread that would tie Beanie's attacker into knots grew inside me. Spring would still be here once the case was solved. The same might not be true for Beanie.

Chapter 24

Rick's report about his time at the dig site after Bean-ie's attack was on the top of the pile. His account was straightforward and concise, as his always were. Because the time I was at the dig site overlapped with his, I could vouch for his accuracy too.

"Nothing new there." I set Rick's account aside and picked up a thick set of papers bound together with a bulldog clip. The heading in the top right corner of the cover sheet was detailed and professional.

Interview Transcripts: Morningside College Dig Team
Interview Site: Old Lindgren Place
Interviewer: Ricardo Columbo
Date: April 24, 1978

Though Cardo and I had rubbed shoulders during the blizzard, my opinion of him remained ambivalent. On the one hand, he had thrown himself into board and card games and helped with dishes after breakfast on the

first morning. He'd even done some shoveling now and
then. On the other hand, he'd been silent during most of
the table talk. He'd disappeared when any other household chores arose. He'd declined to play in the snow or
participate in making plaster casts. He was first in line
for every meal, dessert, and snack. Despite Rick's high
opinion of his deputy's interview skills, I expected to be
unimpressed by what I was about to read.

To the contrary, the transcripts of his interviews
drew me in. They showed that he had a knack for connecting with people and putting them at ease. First,
he used small talk to make them feel comfortable.
Once they were, he asked them to account for their
movements between two forty-five, when Beanie had
been alive and well at Kids' Camp, and three o'clock,
when I'd found her unconscious and bleeding in the
lab tent. Victor had been with me and my students.
I could vouch for him. Teresa said she'd gone to the
women's tent to change clothes and hadn't encountered Beanie during that time. Donald claimed he'd
been at the dig site and had seen Beanie enter the lab
tent. Sheila said had been in the kitchen making supper preparations with her back to the lab tent. Frank
alleged that he'd been changing into shorts in the tent
he shared with Donald. Like Teresa and Sheila, he
claimed not to have seen Beanie during the time in
question either.

After taking care of those preliminaries, Cardo asked
a series of soft ball questions and gradually shifted to
curve balls. He lobbed them skillfully. Each person forgot that silence was an option, one they would have been
wise to employ. They all let slip their version of what had

gone wrong since they'd set up camp at the old Lindgren place. Thanks to Cardo's skillful transcriptions, I could almost hear each team member talking.

Victor had been pleased with the fossil evidence the team had excavated. It convinced him that dinosaur fossil gold lay not far below the surface. He was less pleased with his students. He complained that they didn't dig carefully enough. They couldn't tell the difference between dirt and fossil remains. They were lazy. They questioned his authority and ignored his instructions.

"Except for Beanie," he qualified. "She was a natural. She had—has—the head knowledge too. She's been accepted into the master's program in geology at the University of Kansas for next year. Sheila had the same promise once, but she seems to have lost her drive. I don't know why."

Teresa respected Beanie. In fact, Beanie had been training her to be her lab tent assistant. She'd learned the artifact labeling and storage process. Beanie had been about to explain the filing system but got hurt before she could. After the accident, as Teresa consistently called it, Victor had put her in charge of the lab tent.

"He expects me to put in my regular shifts at the dig site like Beanie did," she complained. "But she wants to be a paleontologist and had the dedication to put in extra hours after supper. I'd rather play cards or sit around the fire in the evenings with the guys. And Sheila."

Sheila was more realistic about the students than Victor. She dismissed Teresa as a boy-crazy underclassman who didn't know who she was or what she wanted to be when she grew up. Donald had true potential and was wasting it by becoming a science teacher. Frank was a lightweight—not college material. Sheila said she and Beanie weren't really friends. While Sheila respected her, she was tired of hearing her talk about going to the University of Kansas graduate school. And Victor?

"He's got good instincts as a paleontologist, but he's no administrator. I didn't mind taking on those duties at first. But they don't leave time for me to hone my skills at the dig site. Without those, I won't get into a top-flight graduate program."

Frank resented Victor's refusal to sleep in the men's tent. "He says that as our professor, he deserved privacy. I say it's not fair to smash me and Donald into a tent smaller than his. But we're not as bad off as the three women. Their tent's so small, they don't have room to turn around."

The sleeping arrangements didn't faze Donald. Instead of answering Cardo's questions, he asked his own questions. How badly was Beanie hurt? Had she made it to the hospital? Had the doctors called with a report? Who would want to hurt her? When Donald ran out of questions, Cardo waited for him to speak again.

Finally he did. "Beanie ran the dig more than the prof and Sheila."

"Why was that?"

"She cared more. About the dig, not about other stuff."

"What other stuff?"

"Keeping her side of the tent clean. Food and meals. She was a terrible cook. She made breakfast once. That's all it took for Sheila to pull her off KP duty. Put her in charge of organizing the lab tent instead. I volunteered to be her assistant, but the prof said no."

Cardo's report was dense with details worthy of a second read. Before doing that, I made a chart on a new page of my legal pad. I made a column for each member of the dig team and wrote their names at the top. The first row was for their alleged whereabouts at the time of Beanie's attack. The second row would contain ideas about how to double check their statements. A third row was to record their opinions of one another, and in a final row, I would jot down my follow-up questions. I was rereading the transcripts and filling out the chart when the sound of someone rattling the doorknob broke my conversation and set my heart to pounding.

"Jane Newell, I got to talk to you."

What Velma called a talk ended up being more of a rant. She revved up while I undid the bolt and slipped out of the room. She was too consumed with anger to demand the key.

"You ain't gonna believe what it took to clean the room where the men bunked down. They didn't bother with newspaper in the entryway, so I had to mop it on my hands and knees. They flung mud ever which way. The walls, the cubbies—all covered in dry mud. I been scrubbing down ever inch of it, starting at the very top."

She put a hand in her pocket and drew out what looked like a tree branch about two inches in diameter and six inches long. "I found this pushed real far back on the top shelf. For all I know it coulda been sitting there since the school went down to two teachers instead of three. Or it coulda been left by those men. You can ask 'em about it or throw it away. I don't care. I gotta finish cleaning up after them pigs." She brandished the tree branch like a club and slapped it into my palm. Then she left, muttering and waving her arms as she went.

I turned the branch over and over again until I recognized what it was. Velma had just handed me the fossil I'd found in Renny's jacket. The one that had disappeared after I found Beanie in the lab tent. I locked the fossil in the lab and ran to the other building.

I flung open the door. Velma was perched on a stepladder with a wet rag in her hand. "Velma," I shouted, "step away from the cubbies."

She glared, sniffed in protest, and went back to scrubbing the shelf where she'd found the fossil.

Using a voice usually reserved for Tiege in his most catastrophic Tigger-like state, I said, "Drop the rag, Velma. Do it now."

Chapter 25

Velma's face was a study of disgust as she obeyed and threw the rag to the floor. She descended the step-ladder and advanced until the fire in her eyes was close enough to scorch my hair.

"You listen to me, Miss Too-Big-For-Her-Britches. I answer to Mrs. Dremstein, and she's the only one who can boss me around. You got no right to—"

I straightened in an attempt to look menacing and sound official. "I'm a member of the Tipperary County Sheriff's Department. As such, I am authorized to order citizens to cease tampering with evidence germane to an ongoing investigation. This entryway is now sealed off until it's been thoroughly searched for further evidence."

"Quit spouting poppycock. There ain't no evidence in here."

"There was, and you found it."

"Found what?"

"The branch you thought was nothing much isn't a

branch. It's a fossil from the dig site. Would you show me where it was?"

She pointed to the northeast corner of the top shelf. "Pushed as far back as it would go behind some empty paper sacks. Almost like it was hid on purpose."

"What did you do with the sacks?"

"Tossed 'em in that wastebasket with the garbage them pigs threw all over the floor. The basket can't hardly hold it all. But don't you worry. I'm gonna take it to the burn barrel and put a match to the whole business."

"You can't," I said in an effort to keep her from not just tampering with evidence, but destroying it. "Rick and I need to sort through the contents of the wastebasket and take photographs."

"Well I never!" she sputtered.

"I'll deal with the trash when I'm done processing evidence."

"And when will that be?"

"Let's see." I crossed my arms and leaned against the door. "I'll start with dusting the paper sacks, the entryway, and the door for fingerprints. After that, I'll move on to searching for clues that could lead us to the person who left the fossil on the shelf. Then there's the other stuff in the wastebasket to process. It'll probably take the rest of the day."

Velma pushed past me and opened the door. "You get right to it, Miss High and Mighty. I'm gonna vacuum the dried mud in your room and go home." She pasted on an awful imitation of a smile and shut the door in my face.

I went to Liv's room and used her phone to ring Betty. "Can you chase down the sheriff?"

"What kind of question is that? Of course I can."

"Would you tell him to come directly to the empty classroom as soon as he can? This can't wait."

"On it."

The line went dead. I ran over to my apartment and traded my blue jeans for bib overalls. I went into the lab and filled my pockets with latex gloves, evidence bags, and three rolls of film. Last of all, I slipped my camera on its strap over my neck and snapped the flash attachment into place. I returned to the other building, pulled on a pair of latex gloves, and climbed the stepladder. I began to photograph the top shelf, paying special attention to the corner where the fossil had been tucked away.

I was about to load the camera with a fresh roll of film when someone began to pound violently on the door. The roll of film flew out of my hand, and I teetered on the rung of the stepladder where I was standing. The door jerked open. A hand reached out and gripped my elbow. I gasped as strong fingers pressed into my flesh.

"Really Jane? You've been practicing your tightrope routine while you waited for me to get here?"

I slapped at Rick's hand and climbed down the ladder with as much dignity as I could muster. "Hardy har har, Sheriff." I made him wait until I located the roll of film and loaded it. "Velma found the missing fossil up there." I pointed up at the corner.

Rick's eyebrows shot up. He climbed the ladder and examined the area closely, then came back down and asked, "What do you need me to do?"

I pulled a pair of latex gloves out of my pocket. "Put these on." Once he did, I handed him several evidence bags. "Bag the paper sacks spilling out of that wastebasket first. Then spread some newspaper on the carpet and dump out the rest of the trash. Keep your eyes open for anything unusual."

While he did that, I finished photographing the entryway and searching for scraps of paper, bits of cloth, strands of hair, pencils stubs, and the like. Nothing. Next, I began dusting for prints. Once Rick was done with the trash, he took over the dusting. I moved on to photographing the fingerprints that had emerged in the entryway. He started to pack up the kit.

I stopped him. "Would you dust the paper sacks you bagged, too? I'll come behind you and photograph them."

The work went much faster with two people, and we were done before dark. We turned out the lights, and I locked the door. On the way to my apartment, I savored the warm breeze and the gurgle of running water on the playground.

Wait a minute!

"Rick, do you hear water running?"

"Yep. Probably a burst pipe."

I cocked my head. "That doesn't make sense. The sound's coming from the schoolyard and not the school."

We scanned the playground. Rick spotted the narrow channel that stretched from the pond made of snow melt to the ditch beside Main Street. Water gurgled in the channel until it dumped into the ditch.

Who had thought to drain the pond that would have tempted children to splash through it and make recess duty a muddy hell? The action had Dick Phillips' fingerprints all over it.

I had hardly thought about him since I'd found the

note to Trudy soon after Dick and I had argued. I'd left him hanging for five days, yet he'd done this anyway. With the work Rick and I had ahead of us tonight, there wasn't time to call and thank him today. But I vowed to let nothing stop me from calling tomorrow after school.

Once Rick and I were in my apartment, he called Cardo and told him to drive over from Tipperary. "Stop at The Bend and pick up supper for us on the way. We've got a lot to do."

While we waited for the deputy to arrive, Rick said he hadn't heard from Beanie's doctor. "The storm hit The Hills pretty bad. Lots of people were injured in snow-related accidents. I'll give him a call in a day or two."

He began reading my reports about the events of the past few days. I developed the negatives from the film I'd just shot. I put them in their chemical bath and unclipped the negatives of Renny's lunch bag that had been on the line since Thursday, then hung up the new negatives to dry.

Once Cardo arrived with our food, we ate and discussed the case and what our next steps should be.

I went first. "I'll make prints of the latest photographs I shot and then enlarge any with fingerprint evidence."

Cardo spoke next. "Tomorrow, I'll write my report about the weekend. Depending on what else comes up, I may have time to read the reports you both wrote. Tuesday, I plan to show up at the dig unannounced and conduct further interviews."

Rick jumped in. "I've scheduled an interview with Richard Wentworth for tomorrow. I'd like to know why he and his ranch hands didn't check up on the dig team when the storm started. On the return trip to Tipperary,

I'll look in on the dig crew to see how everyone's getting along. It'll be my good-cop visit to soften them up for Cardo the next day. I want to call Morningside College when I'm in the office on Tuesday. I'd like to learn more about the members of the dig crew, Victor and Sheila in particular."

The two men left a little before nine, after promising to call later in the week to schedule a time for us to reconvene. I returned to the darkroom and made prints from the first batch of negatives. I hung up the last of them around eleven and locked the lab. I went into my room, left my overalls in a puddle on the floor, and got ready for bed. Comforted by the absence of Velma sleeping in the living room with my butcher knife, I slept like a baby and didn't wake up until morning.

Chapter 26

Though the playground pond shrank during the night, it was the main attraction before school on Monday. Kids from both classrooms ringed its shoreline, scooting closer and closer to let the water lap at the toes of their boots. I spent a few frantic minutes spreading extra layers of newspaper in the entryway before ringing the bell. It was a good thing I did. The kids on the far side, who knew better than to splash through it, did so anyway. With enthusiasm. The children on the school side of the puddle ran to the far side and splashed on through. With equal enthusiasm. My students came inside, leaving a trail of muddy boot prints on the landing stairs and on the newspapers in the entryway. My last-minute precautions had been worth the effort. I almost wished Velma had been there to see it.

The entryway was pure mayhem as the kids shed their jackets and kicked off their overshoes. Tiege's jacket cuffs refused to release his arms. As he struggled to free them, he pulled the sleeves inside out, and somehow the body of his jacket wrapped itself around his head. I stepped into the fray and caught him before he could bowl over his classmates, holding him upright while Elva untangled the jacket.

When his head broke free, he asked, "Is it my turn for show-and-tell, Miss Newell? I got a lot to say about the blizzard."

"Tiege, you always have a lot to say," I replied.

"But not about blizzards," he protested.

His classmates elaborated their own variations on the same theme, everyone speaking at once. Even shy, quiet Beau Kelly chimed in. I chose to be unusually magnanimous and announced, "All right, everyone gets show-and-tell today."

Winter Skye's eyes widened. "On a kindergarten day?"

"On a kindergarten day," I assured her before doing a double take. "Wait a minute! Why are you here? Aren't your parents branding today?"

She waggled her index finger and spoke in a singsong voice. "You gotta wait and find out."

The children skipped to their seats and recited the pledge in full voice and at double the usual speed. Then they came up one by one for show-and-tell, employing a maximum of excitement and a minimum of brevity. When all was said and done, we knew that Winter Skye's branding had been moved to Thursday so the corral could dry out. We knew that Elva and Stig's parents had lost a couple lambs in the storm but nothing more. We also knew that Beau's grandparents had donated every package of lunch meat in the store to the dig team over the weekend, that Keeva and her horse Baby got their livestock to shelter with a little help from the rest of her family, that Renny and Grace had played board games with their parents Friday night when the bar was closed, and that Cora and Bennan's dad had taken them for a spin on a Forest Service snowmobile after the storm died down.

"My dad did too," Jeremy said during his turn, which immediately followed theirs. He ended with a mighty kapow. Whether he was going for emphasis or variety was unclear. Either way, it worked.

Tiege grew increasingly wild-eyed as classmate after classmate was called upon before him. When his turn arrived summersaulted to the front. He began by drawing a picture of the snowdrift he had used as a snowmobile ramp on the chalkboard. Then he re-enacted a series of daring jumps he'd attempted on Saturday.

"Do your parents and brother know what you were up to?" I asked.

"Please don't tell."

In the end, longest show-and-tell session in the history of the world had gobbled up half of reading time. I silently vowed to never again be magnanimous. Then I explained how the remainder of the day would go down. "If we zip through lessons and seatwork starting right now, last half hour of the day will be for making Mother's Day cards decorated with your photographs, fingerprint animals, and glitter."

Beau shouted, "Let's do it!" His response was so out of character that we all stared at him, dumbstruck.

Cora recovered first. "Get busy, you guys."

The classroom buzzed with industry until two thirty when the art and fingerprinting supplies came out. The kids bought my story about the cards with only black ink fingerprints being for me, while the cards with brightly colored tempera paint fingerprints, explosions of glitter, and their photographs were for their parents.

Only Grace voiced concern. "Don't you want pretty colors and glitter on your card?"

"That's thoughtful of you Grace, but I like black."

After art class, the children shrugged into their jackets, pulled on their boots, and splashed through what was now more puddle than pond. Their muddy footprints branched off toward where ranch parents waited in vehicles and town parents waited in their homes. I went inside and surveyed the day's damage. The entryway was littered with sodden, muddy newspapers. Glitter covered the carpet around the back counter where the students had set their cards to dry.

While Velma was still not allowed to complain about vacuuming glitter when she cleaned on Fridays after art class, this was Monday. Therefore, glitter removal was my responsibility, as was removing the dirty newspapers in the entryway. My desk was piled high with papers to be graded. But my first priority was to enlarge shots of the fingerprints found on the fossil and the entryway where it had been hidden.

I changed clothes and went into the darkroom, where I made enlargements and hung them up to dry. When the clothesline in the darkroom was full, I pulled down the black shade over the window of the lab and hung the remainder on the clothesline there. I locked the lab and glanced at my watch. Six thirty. No wonder I was hungry. I fixed a peanut butter and jelly sandwich and took it into my classroom where I would, once again, eat at my desk.

The first bite was going down easy when Velma shouted from the entryway. "I got a bone to pick with you!"

When had she come in? I turned around. Her halo of cigarette smoke lent her a devilish air.

She came closer. Slowly. Deliberately. Her words kept time with each step she took. "You. Will. Be. The. Death. Of. Me."

She might be the death of you too, Jane. Now would be a good time to pray for deliverance.

She was breathing fire when she came to a stop beside my desk. "First, you put fingerprint powder in every nook and cranny of the empty classroom. Then, you didn't bother to pick up these dirty newspapers. You let those kids use glitter on a Monday so it'll be good and ground into the carpet by Friday. To top it all off, you dropped your sandwich. It's dripping peanut butter and jelly on the floor and waiting for you to step on it."

I glanced at my hand. Empty. When had that happened?

I pushed my chair back and stood, careful to avoid the sandwich. "It's not as bad as it looks. I'm going to take care of the newspapers and the glitter after I finish grading. I must have dropped the sandwich when you came in. I'll take care of that too. As for the fingerprint dust, just keep track of how long you spend cleaning it up and submit your hours to the sheriff's office. Rick'll reimburse you."

"Oh." She looked deflated. "You go git yourself a new sandwich. I'll git rid of this one."

She was gone when I returned with another PB&J.
All that remained of Velma's presence was the lingering
odor of cigarette smoke and a damp spot on the carpet
where the sandwich had died. I settled into my chair and
worked without interruption until both my meal and the
correcting were done. After that, I vacuumed up glitter,
discarded the soiled newspapers, and lined the floor with
fresh ones. By then, I was too tired to look over tomorrow's lessons or lay seatwork on the kids' desks.

"It can wait until morning," I yawned as I turned
out lights and locked the building. I was in bed before
I thought about calling Dick. Drowsiness refused to
loosen its grip on me. "In the morning," I muttered and
fell asleep.

Chapter 27

Merle's rooster woke me from a dream in which the vindictive bird was crowing, "Caw-Dick-yoo-fool-yoo!"

I was groggy on the way to the bathroom and explained away the strange message as part of the dream I couldn't recall. I didn't give it another thought until I fixed my hair and looked in the mirror. It was the style I'd worn on my first date with Dick. I gave it as second thought while I poured Life cereal from the box I'd bought on our date. That's when I went to the phone and rang Betty.

"Could you connect me to Dick Phillips?" I asked. "Is he at Fly Ranch or at home?"

"I bewieve this is his day off. Wet's try his aunt and uncwe first. He might be at their pwace. They are the nicest peopwe."

The phone rang twice before a man's voice, deep and melodious as Tennessee Ernie Ford's, came down the line and tickled my ear.

"Henry Strider speaking." His twang, more Kansas than Tennessee, sounded similar to Uncle Tim's. I pictured Dad and my uncle shooting the breeze at our kitchen table. Tim was going on and on about his favorite country western singer . . .

"He sings old gospel songs like nobody else."

"I'll grant you that," Dad said between puffs on his pipe.

"Then why won't you listen to this?" Uncle Tim held up his well-worn album, Great Gospel Songs. I guarantee it'll move your soul and make you cry."

Dad laid his pipe in the old glass ashtray he'd bought during his and Mom's honeymoon to the Chicago stockyards. "The last time I cried over country-western music was when Hank Williams died. I don't intend to do it again." He picked up the cards Tim had dealt and exclaimed, "Woo-woo-woo-woo-woo!" . . .

"Hello? Anybody there?" The man's musical voice interrupted my reverie.

"Um . . . yes. Is Dick Phillips there?" My words were harsh and tuneless compared to his.

"He is. May I tell him who's calling?"

"Jane Newell."

"That'll stop his moping." Henry's chuckle bubbled into my ear and made its way into my heart. "Hang on while I fetch him."

The receiver clunked. After a few seconds of silence, a woman asked, "Is it for me, Henry?"

"Naw, it's for Dick. It's that new teacher in Little Missouri he can't quit talking about."

I tried to imagine Dick talking nonstop about anything and couldn't do it. Maybe he had a garrulous twin with the same name.

Stop being silly, Jane. You just found out Dick's been talking nonstop about you. Enjoy it.

A tiny bud of delight began to open inside of me. "Hello?"

Dick's one word, served up with a side of silence, almost kept the bud from flowering.

"Dick?"

"Uh-huh?"

I wanted to hang up on him and don't know why I didn't. Instead, I plunged ahead and said, "Hi. Listen, I want to apologize for not calling you sooner." I had plenty of excuses to explain my neglect. The investigation. The blizzard. My job. But Dick deserved better than a string of excuses. I took a deep breath and went on. "I had no right to come down on you like I did. I don't even know why I lost my temper."

"Because cancelling our date hurt you." His six words shone a light on what I'd hidden from myself. He *had* hurt me by cancelling our date. He went on before I could identify *why* his actions had caused so much pain. "I'd like to make that up to you once Joe . . . you know, the counselor with the broken foot—"

Um yeah, I knew. I also knew that no son of mine would ever be named Joe.

"—once his foot heals, and I don't have to cover his weekends. Unless I ruined things, and you're not interested in going out again . . ."

I put him out of his misery. "Another date sounds fun."

"Want me to call when Joe's back?"

I could hear the grin in his words. Before I could answer, the woman I'd heard in the background spoke again. "Dick, see if she can come here for supper some night this week."

"Did you hear that?" he asked.

"Uh-huh. I think any night but tonight is good."

"Tomorrow, then?"

"Yes," the woman and I said in unison.

"I'll pick you up at five." The sound of Dick's grin widened.

"It's a date."

I hoped he'd heard my goofy grin as well. It was on my face throughout the school day, even after I decided to have my students make handprint fossils for their moms for Mother's Day along with their handprint cards. Even when the logical part of my brain voiced several perfectly sane objections to the fossil idea.

Their fingerprint cards were enough. *But they can't be hung on a wall.*

Wait until tomorrow when the kindergarteners are here. *Doing it in two smaller groups will be easier.*

You haven't thought this through. *Spontaneity is a good thing.*

You hate arts and crafts. *It's time to stretch myself.*

Your last mess is fresh in Velma's memory. *She can deal with it.*

My goofy grin remained even after the kids had pressed their hands in wet plaster and chased each other around the room pretending to be zombies and depositing blobs of wet plaster on the floor in the process. Once the children left and I took in the extent of the damage seven small zombies had inflicted on Velma's precious carpet, I returned to my senses and pulled out the vacuum cleaner. It took several passes before the zombie leavings gave up the ghost. Only after the vacuum cleaner sucked up every broken chunk of dried plaster was I certain my efforts would meet Velma's high standards. I thought about emptying the vacuum bag but decided to wait until after the kindergarteners made their hand fossils tomorrow. I also came up with two potential anti-zombie measures sure to curb the spread of more plaster chunks. The first was to duct tape my students to their seats. The second was to spread newspaper over every inch of the carpet. Since I was out of duct tape, I chose the second option.

The zombie cleanup took longer than expected, so I started grading papers much later than usual. It was after six when I went into my apartment and made a peanut butter and jelly sandwich. This time I ate in the lab. Between bites, I removed photographs from the clotheslines and sorted them into two piles, one of all the photographs to be enlarged, the other of all the rest. When my sandwich was gone, I went into the darkroom and began making enlargements to analyze later. I hung them on the line to dry, locked the lab, and set my dinner plate in the sink. I'd done all the investigating I could until Cardo brought the new fingerprint cards he was collecting at the dig site.

My stomach growled. It did not appreciate the steady diet of peanut butter and jelly I'd been subjected to in the last few days. I boiled a couple eggs and chased them down with an apple.

"Hang on one more day." I patted my belly. "Hilda's

making supper tomorrow night. Fingers crossed that she's a good cook."

My stomach couldn't see the goofy grin spreading across my face as I thought about seeing Dick again. I couldn't see it either, but I could feel it. It felt like glimpsing the first daffodils each spring—hopeful and grateful and a portent of more to come.

Chapter 28

The next afternoon, Dick arrived at five o'clock on the dot. His smile, once I opened the door, led me to believe I looked more put together than I felt. Thanks to the kindergarten portion of the fossil handprint project, the past thirty minutes had been a mad dash.

My proactive zombie precautions had been mostly successful, but stray bits of plaster still found their way onto the carpet. It took less than fifteen minutes to vacuum them. That left plenty of time to avoid spilling dust and dirt on the clean floor by lugging the vacuum outside to empty its bag. However, I forgot to stand upwind of the burn barrel. When I opened the bag and began shaking the dirt and dust into the barrel, a gust blew in and plastered the contents of the bag on my face and clothes. I moved to the other side of the barrel to finish the job, but the damage to my clothing had already been done. I hauled the vacuum to the entryway and made sure the door was locked before I stripped down to my underwear. I bundled up my clothes and threw them in the washing machine before entering the bathroom and using the mirror to assess the extent of the disaster. Plaster powder and a sprinkling of South Dakota dust coated every strand of hair on my head, along with every inch of my scalp and skin.

I began my mad dash by stripping off my underthings and hitting the shower. Next was a brief stop in my bedroom to pick out clean clothes. After that was a return to the bathroom. Fixing my hair and doing my makeup took longer than I'd anticipated. Dick's pickup truck came down Main Street before I could set the vacuum cleaner to rights according to Velma's meticulous expectations. I shoved it in the janitor's closet and vowed to take care of it before school tomorrow. Dick knocked on the apartment door. I raced over to let him in.

"You look nice." Dick blushed hard. His resemblance to a tomato was striking.

A little plaster dust would tone that down nicely, I thought. Then I thanked him and said, "I could have driven out to your uncle and aunt's place and saved you the trip."

"You won't be saying that once you see how high the river on the spillway is with all the snow melt. It could sweep your little tin can right into the river."

I'd never met a spillway before and wasn't all that keen to meet one now. I did, however, want to meet Dick's uncle and aunt and see where they lived. So I let go of my indignation over the insult he'd leveled at my beloved Beetle. As for my growing apprehension about crossing the spillway, I kept a tight hold on it.

Dick got behind the wheel. I gripped the edge of my seat as though my life depended on it as he took Highway 20 east out of town. Then he turned south onto the Norwegian Cut Across.

"The ranch is south and west of Fly Ranch on the Montana side of the Little Missouri," he informed me.

I redoubled my grip and tried to sound casual when I asked, "You trust this truck to cross the spillway?"

"It got me from the ranch to your apartment. I think it'll do fine going the opposite direction."

There was no disputing that logic. My hand relaxed, and my knuckles pinked up. Still, I didn't let go completely. I wasn't a crazy woman. "How long have your aunt and uncle been on the ranch?"

He considered the question. "I don't know exactly. After they graduated from college in the 1940s."

"They didn't grow up here?"

"Nope. Kansas."

That explained his uncle's twang.

He turned west onto a rutted gravel road and grasped the wheel with both hands. The truck descended into a shallow, green river valley. Cottonwoods appeared and loomed over us. "Hang on now. One spillway coming right up!"

I white-knuckled the seat again and held my breath for good measure. When water began to splash and spray on both sides of the truck, I almost shut my eyes. Only Dick's expression of pure glee stopped me. A whimper escaped my lips, though even I could barely hear it what with all the splashing and engine noise and Dick yelling, "Isn't this a blast?"

I swallowed a second whimper and replied, "It's something all right!"

The truck soon left the spillway behind and drove out

of the river valley and up a steep incline. Dick steered onto a lane that meandered along the rise and ended in front of a neat yard and a newer split-foyer home.

The front door burst open. A man and a woman rushed out. His smile was welcoming, his frame tall and thin, his posture erect, his head bald but for a fringe of dark hair. He had dark eyes, a beaked nose, and wore a long-sleeved shirt and blue jeans. She came up to her husband's shoulder. Her eyes were dark like his. Her hair, almost black, was cut in a chin length bob with bangs. She wore an apron over a cotton housedress. She clapped her hands while we climbed out of the truck. He beckoned for us to come inside.

"They're kinda excited to finally meet you," Dick whispered during our approach, then raised his voice as we drew nearer. "Uncle Henry, Aunt Hilda, this is Jane Newell. Jane, meet Henry and Hilda Strider."

Henry shook my hand. Hilda dispensed with such formalities and drew me into a hug. A long one.

"I'm so glad you could come for supper," she said when she finally let go. "It's nothing special. Come on in."

Conversation flowed as we devoured beef and noodles, home-canned green beans, and fruit salad. Compared to the cold cereal and sandwiches I'd eaten for two days running, the meal was special indeed, and that was before Hilda brought out dessert.

"Blueberry pie!" I exclaimed.

"Not blueberry," Hilda corrected. "Juneberry."

"That's a new one on me."

Henry said the Long Pines were full of juneberries. "Dick knows where to find them. He can take you berry picking next month."

Dick stared at his plate.

Hilda served the pie and stood. "Let's take our plates into the living room so we can enjoy dessert and visit a little longer." She insisted that Dick and I sit next to each other on the couch, "so you get the best view of the river valley."

The view through the huge picture window was lovely. I couldn't stop looking at it. Their stories about coming to ranch along the Little Missouri fascinated me. I had so many questions. What brought them from Kansas to here? Why had they stayed? Had they left parents and siblings behind? Dick stood before I could ask how exactly he was related to them.

"It's ten o'clock, Jane. I better get you home," he said.

Ten o'clock? Already?

I checked my watch. Yup. Dick was right. I didn't want to leave but rose and stacked his plate on top of mine.

"I'll take care of those." Hilda took the dishes out of my hands and took them to the kitchen. Then she and Henry walked outside with us.

"Will you come again soon?" Henry asked as I climbed into Dick's truck and pulled the door shut.

I rolled down my window and said, "I'd like that," and then added, "Thanks for a wonderful evening," before rolling the window up again.

Dick reversed and turned the truck toward the road. Other than warning me to hang on as we neared the spillway, he reverted to his frustratingly silent man-of-mystery persona. I matched his silence with my own until he turned onto Highway 20 and the lights of Little Missouri twinkled ahead of us in the dark.

"You've been awfully quiet," I said. "What are you thinking about?"

"Oh—" he frowned and exhaled long and loud.

I braced for bad news.

"—I wish my uncle and aunt hadn't been so pushy."

"What are you talking about?"

"You know. Henry saying I'd take you berry picking. Hilda forcing us to sit on the couch together. Him insisting you come again soon." He drove across the bridge and into town.

"I thought they were charming. And kind. Not pushy at all." The subtext of his words hit me. "Is this your way of telling me you want to end our relationship?"

"No," he said. "Not at all. I want to see you again." He pulled in beside my Beetle and cut the ignition. "Can I walk you to the door?"

"That would be nice."

He took my hand as we walked along the sidewalk and climbed the steps to the landing. In the glow of the outside light, he kissed my cheek, then turned to leave.

"Would you wait until I'm in my apartment?"

He paused while I dug out my key and unlocked the door. Instead of going inside, I felt for the light switch and flipped the outdoor light off. I pulled his face toward mine until our lips touched, gently at first, and then more insistently.

When we came up for air, I said, "I can be kinda pushy too. You okay with that?"

He kissed me again. He didn't say a word, but his answer was an unequivocal yes.

Chapter 29

Thursday morning arrived too soon. I drank three cups of coffee before, during, and after eating my bowl of Life cereal. Even so, when I opened the door to let my students in, my eyelids still felt heavy. They bounced into the entryway with voices that seemed higher than usual, their energy level overwhelming, and their footfalls far too loud. All the signs pointed to this being a rough day. Then the caffeine kicked in and the hours whizzed by. The children paid attention during their lessons and completed their seatwork a full thirty minutes before dismissal time.

Elva was the first to notice. "What are we going to do now?"

Good question.

Cora, queen of all things sparkly and bright said, "We could spray-paint our hand fossils gold."

Tiege jumped up. "Great idea! Can we?"

The others picked up on the chorus. "Can we? Can we? Can we?"

"Sit down and give me a minute to think, please."
They sat. I stood and tapped my chin, partly for effect
and partly to decide if being magnanimous would open
another can of worms.

Tap. Tap. Tap.

"Yes, I think we can—"

Hoots, hollers, and hoorays.

"—but only if you wait quietly until your turn and
follow my instructions about how to use spray paint."

"Like this?" Renny folded his hands and sat still.

I bowed. "Well done, young man."

The others mimicked him. I complimented each child
in turn and then went to where their plaster handprints
waited on the counter beside the sink. "When I call your
name, you are to pick up your handprint and line up at
the door. Wait there until I lead you outside."

They followed the instructions to the letter. Once
outside, I arranged them so each child faced a square of
sidewalk. I spread a sheet of newspaper on each square.
They quickly placed their handprints down so they acted
as paperweights. Finally, I gave a can of spray paint to
every other child and told them to take turns shaking
the cans until their arms felt like they were going to fall
off. Once they were worn out, the spray-painting commenced. We wrapped things up a few minutes before
dismissal time. By then, their handprint fossils were a
lovely golden color, as were the toes of Beau's cowboy
boots, the tip of Stig's nose, the fingers on Bennan's right
hand, and Tiege's hair. Cora and Elva had dabbed paint
on their earlobes to fashion their versions of gold ear-
rings. The sidewalk resembled a glowing, though patchy,
yellow brick road.

We left their projects on the sidewalk to dry while the kids went inside to gather their things. After they'd been dismissed, they ran across the playground shouting, "There's nothing on the sidewalk, Mom, so don't look!"

The warm sun and soft breeze tempted me to sit on the landing stairs and watch the paint dry. Instead, I went in to correct papers, going out once in a while to see if the handprints were ready to move. When they were, I brought them in and finished my work sooner than expected. I was congratulating myself about clocking out early for a change when Velma came inside.

"Good thing you done the spray painting outside. I'da put on my ruby slippers if I'd known what you was up to." She smiled. It was the real deal. "I gotta get the vacuum from the janitor's closet."

Her joke took me by surprise, so it took a second for the implications of what she'd said to sink in. Then I raced over to the janitor's closet where she stood glaring at the vacuum cleaner, its guts spilling out, and the scattering of dust bunnies and dirt on the floor.

"Are you responsible for this?" she asked, enunciating each word with terrible precision.

"I was going to take care of it before you came to clean on Friday. But you're here. On a Thursday."

"Are you blamin' me for the mess you made?"

"Not at all. I'll take it outside and do it now." I pulled the vacuum from the closet. More dirt shook loose as I wheeled it toward the entryway.

"That's making things worse." She blocked my progress. "You spread out some newspapers, and I'll do it myself."

"Can I watch how you do it?"

"I guess." She acted pleased during her demonstration and explained how to tuck the inner bag into the outer one. "It's easier to zip the outer bag shut if you yank down on the bottom of the inside part first." She grasped the bottom but stopped mid-yank and felt around. "I think there's something in there. We gotta get it outta there so it don't blow a hole in the bag. You reach your hand inside and try to pull it out while I hang on here so it don't slide around."

I stuck my hand into the filthy inner bag. Right above the spot Velma was holding, I felt something. It was hard and thin and smooth. Maybe a dime?

"Can you can scoot your fingers down a little so I can get a better grip on it?" I asked. "Yes, just like that." I pinched the dime between my thumb and forefinger and pulled it out with a flourish to show to Velma. It wasn't a dime. It was a key.

"Wonder what it opens?" She snatched it out of my fingers, blew off the dust, and headed for my apartment. "I'm gonna try it on that dead bolt of yours."

I wasn't going to stop her. She could try all she wanted, but she wouldn't get anywhere. "Go right ahead," I shouted and rinsed the dirt off my arm at the classroom sink. Then I went to check on how she was doing.

"You can have it back. It don't fit." She slapped the key down on the kitchen table. "I'm gonna git what I come for in the janitor closet and go on home." She walked over to my classroom. I heard her roll the vacuum across the floor and then slam the outer classroom door.

I picked up the key and turned it over. It could have been stuck in the vacuum bag for a while. It could belong to anyone and open anything. But . . . we'd found it after cleaning the room where Sheila and Teresa had slept. It could be a coincidence. Or not.

I went to the window and saw Velma putting the vacuum cleaner and its carpet cleaning attachment into the trunk of her car. Once she drove away, I took the deadbolt key from its hiding place and entered the lab. I put the small key we'd just found in an evidence bag and put the bag in the file cabinet. While I was at it, I took the photo enlargements off the line and locked them in the file cabinet, too. My part in the investigation was now at a standstill because Cardo had yet to drop off the fingerprint cards. I walked to the post office to see if he or Rick had sent them. Nope. Neither man had called to set up a follow-up meeting as they'd promised either. For that matter Rick hadn't called about how Beanie was doing lately. I went home and asked Betty to ring his office.

"It's after hours," she reminded me.

"Try anyway."

She did. No one answered. She offered to call Cardo's home. No answer there either. She tried Rick's house in Tipperary. Again, no answer. She called the Sternquist ranch.

Cookie picked up. She didn't know where Rick was but promised to have him get ahold of me next time she talked to him.

I stared at the phone while I ate supper. My frustration mounted with every minute it failed to ring. Finally, I got a departmental requisition form from the lab and filled it out. I wrote "police radio" in the item column and "cost is not an issue" in the dollar amount column. I signed my name at the bottom, addressed and stamped an envelope, and tucked the form inside. Then I walked to the post office for the second time in one day and dropped it in the mailbox.

My frustration waned on way home, but the reprieve was only temporary. It would return in full force tomorrow unless Rick or Cardo got back to me. If they didn't, I would do some investigating on my own. My initiative wouldn't be to their liking. Then again, considering the dearth of initiative on their part, what else was I supposed to do?

CHAPTER 30

Friday morning, I had a difficult choice to make. Should I call the sheriff's office before school or spray-paint the kindergarteners' plaster handprints by myself? I decided spray-painting anything with four kindergarteners was to be avoided at all costs and went with the latter. If only I had known that granting eleven students access to my Scotch-tape dispenser to wrap their Mother's Day gifts later in the day would be disastrous as well.

That realization dawned about a half hour before dismissal when Stig dangled a foot-long length of tape from his finger. "I don't think this is gonna be enough, Miss Newell. Can you get me some more?"

More seemed like a bad idea, so I cut his tape into four smaller lengths and showed him how to pull the wrapping paper tight before taping it shut. He was getting the hang of it when a howl erupted on the other side of the room. I left Stig to his own devices and hurried over to where Grace was slapping at her brother's hand.

"Stop it, Renny," she begged. "That hurts."

Renny saw me and lifted his hands in the air as he stepped away from his sister. "I'm not trying to hurt her. I just want to get the tape out of her hair before Mom sees it."

While I assessed the damage, the other students ran over to take a gander. "How did it get tangled in your bangs?" I asked.

Grace blinked away tears. "I didn't know it would jump on my hair when I scratched my forehead."

Winter Skye hugged her. Elva asked if I had any peanut butter.

Peanut butter?

"School will be out soon enough," I snapped. "You can have a snack when you get home."

"Not to eat it." She sounded offended. "I remember how Mom used it to get gum out of my hair when I was little. It might work on tape, too."

Lo and behold, the peanut butter did the trick. Grace and the other children went back to wrapping their gifts. About fifteen minutes and three rolls of Scotch tape later, a lumpy package covered with more tape than paper and sporting tempera paint and glitter-encrusted homemade cards sat on each child's desk. They slid the packages into their backpacks with great care and eased their arms through the straps. They avoided bumping into one another as they lined up for dismissal and navigated the landing steps cautiously.

All was well until Tiege saw Cookie's vehicle parked beside Main Street. He threw caution to the wind and sprinted across the playground screaming, "Mom, there's a surprise for you in my backpack. You can't look until Sunday!"

His reaction set off a frenzy among his classmates. They streamed across the schoolyard, all bouncing backpacks and ear-piercing screams. From the shocked expressions on their parents' faces, I could tell they weren't nearly as glad it was Friday as I was.

I went in and called the sheriff's office. The secretary answered right away. She said Rick and Cardo had been running in circles for days. "A lot of ranchers in the eastern part of the county lost livestock during the storm. The snow melted so fast, there's dams and culverts and roads washed out all over the place. Flooding in the low spots too. A couple ranchers and their families haven't been able to get out. The road crews got their lanes shored up today so Rick and Cardo are out checking on them. Rick said he's sorry for the delay, but it couldn't be helped. He's going to interview Richard Wentworth tomorrow and Cardo will get to the dig team on Sunday."

The delay in the investigation was equal parts understandable and frustrating. To my credit, I didn't slam down the receiver until after she hung up.

My phone rang. I picked up.

"That hurt my ear," Betty said.

"Did you know Rick and Cardo were dealing with the aftermath of the storm all week?"

"Yes."

"Why didn't you tell me?"

"I didn't want to put you in a bad mood before Dick took you to meet Henry and Hiwda. Did you wike them?"

"Very much, but don't change the subject. Have you heard anything about how Beanie's doing?"

"Not a peep." Pause. "Did you put Doris's Mother's Day card in the maiw?"

Oh shoot!

"Gotta go, Betty!" I slammed down the receiver and scoured my apartment for Mom's card. I found it on top of the refrigerator, right where I'd put it for safekeeping while Dick and I brought in my groceries. Hoping to make up for the card's late arrival, I sat down and wrote Mom a long letter about the spillway adventure with Dick and meeting Henry and Hilda. I left out the part where Dick and I lingered on the landing in the dark after he brought me home. I also didn't mention his jumping off the dorm roof and why our next date was another two weeks away. Mom might believe that motherhood gave her the right to know every detail of my dating life, but I didn't. I ran to the post office and hand delivered the card to Dale Cunningham.

"Mother's Day?"

I nodded.

He sighed. "It won't arrive in time. May I suggest you mitigate the damage by calling your mother bright and early on Sunday morning?" He clicked his heels together and saluted briskly. "Bright and early."

I returned his salute. "I will."

When I got home, I wrote a reminder note to call Mom on Sunday and set it next to the phone. I couldn't tape it in place because my students had used every last sticky inch of it. Next, I went into my classroom. I mopped the floor of the janitor's closet and began peeling tape off the carpet, counters, and desks before Velma arrived to clean. I was on my knees picking at a particularly stubborn strip when Liv came in.

"Keeva used a year's supply of tape to wrap whatever she made for Mother's Day," she chuckled. "I shoulda warned you about letting the kids wrap presents by themselves."

"Too late now." The strip of tape came loose. I stood and rolled it into a sticky ball. "The precedent's been set. I wish I'd taken out stock in Scotch tape. The kids used enough today to fund my retirement."

She laughed. "Would you like to come for Sunday dinner? Keeva's worried about you being away from your mom on Mother's Day and getting homesick."

"That's really nice of her. You too. But you shouldn't have to cook on your special day."

"Rosalie's fixing the meal. Frost and Fannie are coming, too."

"What's she making for dessert?"

"Cherry pie."

"What time should I be there?"

She said one o'clock would be plenty early.

I asked if she knew where Velma was. "She's usually here by now."

"She's got company from out of town."

Well, that explained the vacuum and the carpet shampooer heist.

Liv went on. "She told me she's coming tomorrow morning at eleven to clean."

Perfect! I could sleep in and sneak away before Velma demanded a copy of my Saturday itinerary. Not that I intended to tell her or anyone else what I was up to. That would not be wise.

We talked for a few more minutes. Liv went back to her room, and I sat down to complete the tasks I usually did on Saturday morning—grading, finishing lesson plans, making seatwork packets, and organizing new centers. I was tired when I finally entered my apartment. Before calling it a night, I piled the unfamiliar socks I'd found in the clothes dryer, my camera, and my rattlesnake shovel next to the door. Then I stuffed the pockets of my overalls with extra film, a flashlight, empty evidence bags, the evidence bag containing the little key, and latex gloves.

I took the bag with the key out of my pocket and stared at it. My plan for tomorrow morning might be a wild goose chase. I could still call the whole thing off. Most likely I wouldn't find what I was looking for anyway. Then again, I asked myself while turning the bag this way and that, what if I did?

Chapter 31

When my alarm rang on Saturday morning, I jumped out of bed feeling sharp, rested, and capable. I put on a sweatshirt and jeans. In the bathroom, I stood in front of the mirror and forced my hair into a ponytail.

"You stay right there." I gave my rebellious hair the stink eye. "Don't you dare try to escape."

I opened the living room windows and invited the sunshine to join me for toast, bacon, and eggs. The day's agenda demanded a substantial breakfast. I washed the dishes and checked the time. Ten o'clock. Too early to leave. Might as well scrub down the kitchen cupboards and walls. Merle had demonstrated his ability to fling non-skid pancake batter hither and yon the previous weekend. If I ignored his handiwork much longer, the batter would fossilize.

Once the cupboards and walls were clean, it was time to load the car. I swapped out my jeans for overalls and put on socks and tennis shoes. A cool, soft breeze caressed my face when I walked outside. This harbinger of spring elevated my mood from capable to invincible. Today I was going to find the lock that matched the small key in my pocket and move this case along, sans the sheriff and his deputy. Then I packed everything into the Beetle and was on the road shortly before eleven. I drove out of town east on Highway 20, belting out my favorite Helen Reddy song, "I Am Woman, Hear Me Roar". My voice was nothing compared to hers, but her lyrics captured my sense of determination and independence.

When I reached the old Lindgren place and turned onto the lane, I stopped singing and started watching for people. If anyone was around, I would pull out the socks and say I was returning them. At the ranch house, I slowed down and shuddered. The piles of antlers and weathered animal skulls in the yard creeped me out. This wasn't unusual in Tipperary County, but the total absence of bushes, trees, and flowers was. The lack of anything green and growing made the house look dead. The lack of both lights switched on inside and vehicles parked around it gave it a deserted air. Presumably that meant the dig crew had moved into their tents again, so I would check their camp first. The Beetle crept along until I reached the dig team's parking area. The van wasn't there, a good sign that everyone had gone to town, but I wasn't taking any chances.

I cut the engine, found the socks, grasped the rattlesnake shovel, and got out. "Anybody here?" I called.

Silence.

Another good sign. I walked to the kitchen tent. "Anybody here?"

No answer.

I went to the dig site and looked around. No one. I checked the women's tent, the men's tent, Victor's tent. No one. No one. No one. I checked the outhouse. No one.

I wasn't done yet. I got into the car, returned to the ranch house, and parked. With the socks stuffed in a pocket of my overalls and the shovel in hand, I climbed the steps onto the front porch and pressed the doorbell. Piles of antlers and animal skulls ringed the porch—as dandy a place for a rattlesnake to hide as I'd ever seen. I tightened my grip on the shovel. If a ranch hand answered, I would pull out the socks and ask him to give them to Victor. I rang the bell a couple more times. Satisfied that no one was there, I got in the car and drove to the camp. I tossed the socks onto the passenger seat and then changed my mind. It's always wise to have a plausible explanation handy when snooping at a place you have no business being. It's also wise to leave no trace of having been in such places. I stuffed the socks in my pocket, wriggled my hands into a pair of latex gloves, and put my camera around my neck until I had second thoughts.

Photographs could prove you've been here, Jane.

Good point. I set the camera on the passenger seat and gave it a pat. "You wait here. I'll be back before you know it."

Thus prepared, I picked up my rattlesnake shovel and made the lab tent my first stop. The entrance was unzipped. Excellent. I wasn't breaking and entering.

Are you sure?

That was one second thought too many. I went inside

and scanned the shelves for anything with a lock—a
cash box, a portable file cabinet, a small safe, a diary
even—and came up short. My next stop was the open-air
kitchen tent, which was asking for people to enter with
no breaking required. I searched every bin and container, the refrigerator and freezer, and came up emp-
ty-handed.

To be thorough, I walked through the dig site and
searched the lean-to where tools were kept. As expected,
I found nothing in there. On the way to the tents where
everyone slept, I passed the outhouse. Its door was open,
swinging in the breeze. Searching it was tricky, what
with holding my nose and the rattlesnake shovel in one
hand and the flashlight in the other. I shined the light in
every cobwebby corner and the rafters of the tiny building. Nothing.

The zippers to the men's tent and Victor's remained
in one piece when I opened them. No breaking, just
entering. Most of Frank and Donald's clothes were scattered on the floor. I peeked under them to see if anything
was hiding beneath them and found nothing. I searched
the wooden fruit crates stacked one on top of the other
beside their cots. They held books, a few clothes, and
nothing with a lock. I looked under their cots and found
only dead bugs. The same was true for Victor's tent,
though his clothes were folded and tucked inside his
crates, along with an impressive number of books.

I moved on to the tent occupied by Sheila and Teresa.
Beanie, too, before her attack. It was unzipped, and I
entered with a clear conscience. This tent was more of
a mess than either of the men's. The floor was strewn
with clothes, and more were stuffed under their cots and

draped across their crates. I worked my way across the floor, checking under each item of clothing, without success until I came to a sweatshirt near one of the cots. The slight mound in its middle made me suspect something had been hidden beneath it. My heart began to pound with excitement. The reverberations made my ears buzz. When I lifted the edge of the shirt, the buzzing intensified.

I shrieked and let go of the shirt. I grabbed the shovel with my sweaty hands and brought it down hard on the wiggling, rattling sweatshirt. I smacked at it repeatedly.

"Take that, and that, and that!" I screamed until the sweatshirt stopped moving and the rattling ceased. Snake slime seeped out from under the ruined sweatshirt. That was reassuring, but I poked at it with the shovel a few times to be sure.

Once I was certain the rattlesnake was deader than the Wicked Witch of the West, I scooped the shirt up with the shovel. I carried it to the outhouse and dumped it down the hole. Considering the chaotic state of the tent, I didn't think Sheila or Teresa would notice it was missing. I returned to the tent, scooped up a good percentage of the snake carcass, and tossed it down the hole too. Then I got a rag and bucketful of water from the kitchen and mopped up the snake slime, gagging with every swipe. Never had I been so thankful to be wearing latex gloves. When I'd removed all the evidence, I took the water, the rag, and my latex gloves to the outhouse and deposited them in the hole.

I pulled on a new pair of gloves and returned to check the tent one last time. A ponytail holder with one end sprung free of the metal fastener that connected the two elastic ends was lying on the floor a few feet from the ex-snake's hiding place. I felt for my ponytail and discovered it had come undone. The holder must have broken while I pounded the snake into oblivion. I stuck the ruined hair tie in my pocket and checked for anything else I might have dropped. When I was sure no traces of my visit or the snake remained, I picked up my trusty shovel and ran for my car. I climbed inside and stared straight ahead, immobilized by the reality of what had just happened.

I had killed a rattlesnake.

Without warning, my stomach lurched. I pulled an evidence bag from a pocket, lifted it to my face and barfed. And barfed. And barfed some more. Once my substantial breakfast was in the bag, I sealed it shut and carefully placed it on the passenger seat. I started the car and drove home, my hands shaking, my mouth sour tasting, my mission an abject failure. Even so, I felt more invincible than I had this morning because I was a woman who had killed a rattlesnake.

See me roar!

Chapter 32

As it turns out, killing rattlesnakes has unexpected consequences. For one thing, it takes a while for a person to realize the excitement made her forget to look for a lock box or diary in the women's tent. Second, using yout kitchen sink to wash reptile slime off of a spade kills the appetite. Last but not least, once the adrenaline rush dissipates, all a person wants to do is sleep. Which is why I skipped lunch, took a nap, and slept the afternoon away.

When I woke, my grumbling stomach announced it was suppertime. I had no desire to cook. Eating anything at my kitchen table was out of the question until I had the energy to disinfect the sink where microscopic bits of rattlesnake slime still lurked. I grabbed my purse and walked to The Bend.

The weather was perfect. The sun lingered to the west in a cloudless sky. The breeze kissed my cheek. I reveled in the loveliness of spring and the aroma of cut grass. Someone had attached new nets to the basketball hoops on both ends of the cement slab and mowed the area outside the fence. When I entered the café, I went to the cash register and asked Trudy to bag my meal so I could eat outside on the bench near the slab.

"Jane!" Victor's voice boomed from the bar side of The Bend. "Want to eat with us?"

Yes, I did!

"Cancel the paper bag, Trudy." I gestured toward Victor and the students. "I've changed my mind."

I went into the bar and joined the dig crew. They scooted closer together to make room for me. Donald hopped up and asked Frost and Fannie McDonald if he could borrow the empty chair at their table. He dragged it over and slid it into the open space between his chair and Sheila.

"Long time no see." He motioned for me to sit down. "What have you been up to since we cleared out last Sunday?"

Regaling them with stories about my students making fossil handprints as Mother's Day gifts was a much better idea than saying I'd spent the morning snooping at their camp. My description of our plaster of Paris and Scotch tape adventures made them laugh out loud.

Teresa chuckled. "Hand fossils. I'll have to remember that."

I shrugged. "With kids, it's all about how you sell it. What's new at the dig site?"

Before anyone could answer, Trudy approached our table, her order pad and pencil at the ready. "What can I get started for you all?" she asked pleasantly. When Victor requested separate checks for everyone, the pleasantness vanished.

Her good mood returned when she asked me, "You want what you ordered a minute ago?"

"Yes."

"Put her meal on my tab," Victor said.

"There's no need for that," I protested.

"Compared to you putting us up last weekend, it's nothing."

I couldn't argue with the truth.

"Do what he said, Trudy." After she stuffed the order pad in her apron pocket and left, I gestured for everyone at the table to come in close. "Big tips are the rule tonight. It's how we can thank Trudy and Glen for delivering supper every night during the storm. Are you in?"

"In," they said in unison, but with varying levels of enthusiasm.

"Good," I said. "Did the storm do much damage at the dig site?"

Sheila ran through the details like a research assistant in charge of a dig should. "The lab and the kitchen were fine, but the tents where we sleep were soaked. And the trenches in the dig site were full of water."

"Were any new fossils exposed?"

She shook her head. "We were hoping nature might give us a leg up, but no."

"So," I said as though I didn't know the answer, "are you still staying in the house?"

"If only," Teresa sighed. "Victor made us say goodbye to soft beds and running water as soon as the ground and our tents dried out. We've been back in them and using the outhouse since Tuesday. We got into the trenches again the day after that."

"How'd you drain the water?"

Sheila answered. "Mr. Wentworth let us borrow a pump to bail out the trenches."

We stopped talking when Trudy brought our food. After that, our conversation was limited to "Please pass the ketchup" and "Where's the salt?" as we plowed through our meals.

Frank paused before biting into his second cheeseburger. "You oughta come to the dig site and see for yourself. It's like the blizzard never happened." He stuffed half of the burger into his mouth.

"I just might take you up on that. There's a teachers' meeting in Tipperary this Tuesday after school. Would it be okay if I stop by afterwards on my way home?"

Teresa's eyes sparkled. "Maybe you could stay for supper."

"Who's cooking?"

"I am," she said.

"Is she a good cook?" I asked the entire group.

"Almost as good as Sheila," Don said. "Way better than Beanie."

Beanie. The mention of her name popped the bubble of good humor that had enveloped our conversation until now.

The fry I'd just dipped in ketchup didn't look appetizing anymore. I set it down. "Have you heard anything? How is she doing?"

"We visited her this morning." Victor drew in a deep breath. "She looks like she's sleeping."

Tears welled in Sheila's eyes. "More like dead."

"Stop being so melodramatic," Victor told her. "She's in a coma, not dead. And Beanie's mom says more is happening below the surface than we can see. The doctor keeps telling her that all signs point to a full recovery."

That sounded like Mrs. Lavender. "How is she doing?"

Victor spoke again. "She told me that she and her husband don't hold me responsible for what happened."

That also sounded like the Lavenders.

Victor frowned. "She's more forgiving than I would be in her shoes. More than I'll be if what happened to her daughter was due to a deliberate act and not acciden-tal. I swear to God that if that turns out to be the case, and the sheriff finds the person who hurt her, I will show no mercy."

That person was sitting at the table. I was sure of it. Victor's expression said he was, too. For a long, silent minute, I studied each member of the team in turn. Don met my gaze without blinking, Teresa reddened and broke away. Frank looked ready to burst into tears. Sheila shifted in her seat to rub Victor's back. Without acknowledging her touch, he buried his face in his trem-bling hands.

No one was in the mood for more casual conversa-tion. I went to the register and asked Trudy for a doggie bag and returned to the table to pack up the rest of my food. I picked up the bag and my can of Diet Coke and said, "See you Tuesday afternoon. Enjoy the rest of your meal." Which I didn't think they would, but one could always hope.

The pall that had descended when I brought up Beanie had not affected the weather. Outside, the sun still hung in the western sky, though it had moved further west. The breeze remained soft and sweet, the sky cloudless. The lovely evening begged me to sit down and keep it company. Its charms made me an easy touch. I crossed the street and sat on the bench next to the cement slab. The fresh air revived my appetite. I opened the doggie bag and ate the rest of my meal while replaying our conversation in the bar.

Victor suspected Beanie had been attacked by a member of his crew. I had no idea who that was, and I believed Victor didn't either. Still, my gut told there had been something said, something implied—a facial expression, a tone of voice, or body language—that contained a sliver of truth.

Watch your back, Jane. When Beanie's attacker realizes the slip up, there's going to be trouble.

I wadded the doggie bag into a ball and drained the last of my Diet Coke. I got up and glanced over my left shoulder and then my right. The sun was sinking. Soon it would be dark. Time to go home.

CHAPTER 33

On the short walk home, I thought about calling the sheriff to suggest a few extra avenues to pursue during his interview with Richard the First tomorrow.

After you lock your apartment up tight, Jane.

I argued with myself about the idea while checking every window and door in the building. Finally I decided against it. I didn't want to advertise Rick's plans to whoever might be listening on the party line. Besides, he would be at church in the morning and we could talk then. Come to think of it, I could write my report about supper with the dig crew right now and give it to him in the morning. Maybe the act of putting it on paper would reveal the sliver of truth that had so far eluded me.

The sliver hadn't become any clearer by the time I took the completed report from the typewriter, folded the original, put it in an envelope, and stuck it in my purse. Still, it was a good job to have done.

On my way to the bathroom, the scrap of paper next to the phone jogged my memory. I took it into my bedroom and set my alarm for an hour earlier than normal. Then I set the note next to the clock so I would see it first thing when I woke up. I should call Mom before she and Dad left for the early service at church.

The plan proved to be fail-safe. Sunday morning at six o'clock on the dot, I rang Betty and asked her to put me through to Mom.

"That'ww be seven o'cwock for her. Doesn't she sweep wate on Mother's Day?" Betty asked.

"She doesn't sleep late," I said. "Not ever."

As if to prove my point, Mom picked up at the first ring. "What's wrong?"

"Nothing," I assured her.

"Then why are you calling this early?"

"To wish you a happy Mother's Day."

"You forgot to get me a card, didn't you?"

"I did not forget. In fact, I bought your card over a week ago. I just didn't send it on time. Dale Cunningham said it'll arrive in a day or two."

Or three. At least by the end of the week.

"Are you doing anything special today?" I asked.

"Your father is treating me to a dinner at Archie's Waeside in Le Mars. Your brother Jeff is driving."

Archie's was the most famous steakhouse in northwest Iowa and Dad's favorite restaurant. His instincts, and Jeff's as well, were impeccable, though their motives were suspect.

The thought of not being home to celebrate with Mom made me weepy. I brushed away my tears and said, "Yum!"

"Are you coming down with something, Jane? You sound a little stuffy."

"Hay fever, most likely. People have been mowing their lawns lately. It's quite a change from shoveling snow last weekend."

"What do you expect? People don't live in the godforsaken wilderness because the weather's good."

And she's off.

Except she wasn't. Her next words took the conversation into unexpected territory. "Did you put the kibosh on Velma and Betty talking to me about your social life? They won't say a word about whether or not you ever made up with Dick Phillips, just that he's a very nice young man."

Way to go, Betty and Velma!

"We made up. He even took me to his aunt and uncle's for supper on Wednesday."

"Oh?" She held onto the "oh," raising its pitch higher by the second until it reached dog whistle territory. It might have gone higher had I not taken pity on her and described my date in detail. Mom hung on every word and asked a thousand questions. Her final one—"Do you think your father and I will get to meet him?"—made my eyes water again.

"I'd like that, Mom. He's really nice."

"I can hear that in your voice, Jane."

"Have a good Mother's Day."

"I already am. Bye now."

After we hung up, I went outside and sat on the landing steps. I soaked in the sight of the sun climbing in the east. Then I went inside and ate breakfast. More than an hour remained until church, so I made an Early Bird Coffee Cake to take to the McDonald place as a thank you to Liv. Dinner with her family would ease the

sting out of being away from mine on this beautiful day.
Between good weather and good friends, this country
didn't feel the least bit godforsaken.

I got ready for church while the coffee cake baked.
It came out of the oven in plenty of time for me to walk
to church. The place was packed, though neither Dick
Phillips nor the Sternquists, Rick included, were there.
Dick, I knew, was working Joe's shift again. Pam Barkley
said the Sternquists were spending the day with Bud's
mother, who was in a nursing home in Belle Fourche.

I said all the right things about the importance of
spending time with loved ones while they were here.
Inside, however, my frustration was rising again. Mrs.
Lavender's Mother's Day was a living hell of sitting with
her daughter who was in a coma. Weren't the Lavenders
equally worthy of our attention and time? Shouldn't
Rick be here reporting on his interview with Richard the
First and reading my latest report? When would our case
become his top priority?

Such thoughts made following Pastor Petersen's sermon difficult. It was a mix of an homage to the presence
of mothers and the Holy Spirit in our lives. I couldn't
connect the two until he said Pentecost Sunday was
two weeks away. His sermon convinced me of a couple
things. First was the undeniable power and influence
of my mother's constant presence as I grew up. Second
was my pitiful inability to recognize the presence of the
Holy Spirit. When the pastor began his closing prayer, I
whispered my own.

"Father, Jesus, Holy Spirit. I don't know which one
of you is in charge of this kind of thing. Whoever it is,
would please you take the lead on this one? I don't have

much practice in this area, so bang me on top of my head to get my attention if you have to. Thanks." I opened my eyes and immediately regretted the "bang me on top of my head" bit, but what was I to do? The prayer had been prayed.

I didn't want to make the McDonalds wait for me to get there for dinner, so I hustled out of church. What if, I wondered on the walk home, my gut instincts fell into the realm of the Holy Spirit? What if He was keeping the sliver of truth out of reach and would reveal it in his right time? I chewed that over for the rest of the walk, while I changed clothes, and during the drive to the McDonald ranch.

Keeva was waiting outside as I pulled up in front of their house. She grabbed my hand when I got out. "We been on a trail ride with Mommy this morning. She says that's her favoritist thing. On the way back, Daddy showed us where there's dinosaur bones. They're in the pasture in back of the barn. I thought they was just cow bones like at Elva and Stig's ranch. Daddy said I could show you and then we gotta go in."

Her stream of chatter continued as we passed the barn and crossed the back end of the pasture. Then she stopped talking and walking and pointed the toe of her boot at the protrusion in front of us. "Daddy says that's the biggest one."

The fossil and the landscape around it were similar in appearance to what the Gibsons had taken me to see. I had questions when we went into the house, but I waited until after Rosalie's delicious meal to ask Liv's husband, Axel, and his father, Frost, how long they'd known the bones were there.

"Since my dad bought this place when I was a kid," Frost said. "He didn't think it was anything to write home about. Once he passed in 1957 and the place came to me, I contacted the School of Mines. They been sending professors real regular since Axel took over running the ranch."

"Their head geologist called me a year or two ago," Axel said. "He said a college in Iowa was looking for a dig site, and he mentioned our place."

"Did anyone from the college come out?"

"Uh-huh. A young gal showed up last summer. She got real excited when me and Dad showed what we got. Kinda went into a tizzy when I told her the team could stay in the old bunkhouse. When she heard it has electricity and indoor plumbing, she was ninety-nine percent sure her professor would take us up on the offer."

"And after that?"

Father and son exchanged a glance, and Axel said, "I never heard from her again."

"Me neither," said Frost. "But I seen her."

"Where?" I asked.

"At The Bend."

"When?"

"Last night. She was sitting right next to you."

CHAPTER 34

I drove home buzzed by what Axel and Frost had said and shown me. They had taken me on a complete tour of the bunkhouse and the fossil area behind the barn. It was far superior to the site at the old Lindgren place. I couldn't imagine why this one hadn't been chosen. Unless Frost had mistaken Sheila for the woman who'd done the scouting. I peppered him with questions, but he remained certain that Sheila and the woman who'd visited the McDonalds' were one and the same.

I examined the situation from a different angle. I could understand why the Gibsons' site had been ruled out. It lacked both running water and a level area for setting up camp. But no matter how I looked at it, choosing the old Lindgren place over the McDonalds' made no sense at all. Sure, it had a decent area for camping, but tents and an outhouse didn't hold a candle to a bunkhouse with indoor plumbing and electricity. And would a research assistant be given the authority to nix one site in favor of another? Wasn't that the prerogative of Victor as supervising professor?

Deep in thought, I buzzed past the school and missed my turn. After doing a U-turn on Main Street and heading back to my apartment, I saw a pickup truck in my parking spot. The truck was unfamiliar. The indolent posture of the man leaning against it was not. He wore a wrinkled linen duster reminiscent of the rumpled trench coat Peter Falk wore as Columbo. Deputy Cardo was back in town.

I pulled in next to him. Only when my Beetle nearly ran over his toes—served him right for taking my spot— did he stand tall.

I got out and walked over to him. "Long time no see, Cardo. Are you here to drop off fingerprint cards?"

"Indeed I am." He put a hand in the front pocket of his duster and produced a thick, nine by six manila envelope. He presented it to me with a little flourish.

I plucked it from his hand before it could disappear. "Thank you very much." I began hurrying away, eager to get to work in the lab. Then I remembered my manners and returned to where he still lounged against his truck. "Did your interviews produce anything of interest?"

"I believe rubbing elbows with the dig team last weekend gave them a false sense of security concerning my role in their lives. They treated me more like a friend than a deputy. Don invited me to eat with them this evening. I had to say no, as I'm expected to arrive home and grill venison steaks for Mother's Day within the hour." He held up an index finger and grinned. "I did not tell them of my intentions to swing by your apartment with their fingerprint cards. Perhaps that explains why they let a few things slip during the interviews. Give me twenty-four hours to transcribe my recordings, and you can see for yourself."

"Sounds promising." I motioned toward the cab of his truck. "You should get on your way. Your wife and kids must be getting hungry."

I raced to the lab without waving goodbye and shook the fingerprint cards onto the table. Analyzing fingerprints is slow, tedious work for a team with top-notch equipment. For one person with only a magnifying glass, it can take days or weeks. We didn't have that long.

I got to work and lost track of time as I matched fingerprints lifted from where the men had slept last weekend to those on the cards. My eyelids began to droop long before I was close to done.

Keep at it, Jane. It's too early to turn in for the night.

I slid another photograph under the magnifying glass. My eyes refused to focus. I checked my watch. How could it be midnight already? I set down the magnifying glass, locked the lab, and went to bed.

When my eleven students bounced in the next morning, they were jazzed by their parents' enthusiastic reactions to the handprint fossils. Bottling their enthusiasm required every ounce of my energy. At the end of the day, I was trashed. I felt like I'd borrowed energy from tomorrow at an exorbitant rate of interest, and it was bleeding me dry. I slogged through my after-school work and went to the crime lab, where I spent an hour accomplishing very little.

Try eating something, Jane.

I went to the kitchen and made a PB&J sandwich. Then it was back to the crime lab, where I discovered that everything I'd done before fixing the sandwich had been done wrong. In other words, the very little I thought I'd accomplished was, in reality, nothing whatsoever.

I gave up and shoved the photographs and fingerprint cards into a folder. Then I stuck it in the filing cabinet and locked it. After that, I locked the lab up tight and went to my bedroom. Everything related to the case was safely tucked away until I could work on it again.

My bed beckoned me to rest for a minute or two before brushing my teeth and changing into pajamas. The next thing I knew, Merle's rooster was interrupting a dream that left a pleasant aftertaste but was short on delicious details. My bladder was screaming, I was wearing yesterday's clothes, and my teeth felt fuzzy. According to my clock, I'd slept for twelve hours straight. I ran for the bathroom and landed on the porcelain throne without a second to spare.

Before school, I went to Liv's room and told her I'd been invited to the dig site for supper this evening and would drive to Tipperary on my own.

"Doin' a little investigating, are you?" She grinned. "Axel said you interrogated him and Frost pretty good on Sunday."

"Once a snoop, always a snoop," I laughed before going to my room and ringing the bell. The day passed quickly and left me with energy after the kids went home. I enjoyed the scenery on the drive to Tipperary and listened carefully while Mrs. Dremstein explained how to fill out final report cards and went through the end-of-year check-out forms. The meeting ran late, but since only seven school days remained for the year, no one seemed to mind. After the meeting, there wasn't time to stop at the SuperValu for cones and ice cream and still make it to the dig site by five. I stopped anyway, knowing my contribution to the evening meal would be like ambrosia to college kids who'd worked all day in the sun.

When I handed the goods to Teresa, she said we should eat dessert first. "There's no room for it in the freezer, and it would be a shame to have it melt."

"But Don's not here yet," Sheila objected. "We should probably wait for him."

Frank opened the box of cones. "He said he not to wait for him since he didn't know how long he'd be in town."

"I guess that means we're going wait on him like one pig waits on another." Sheila got a large spoon and opened the square of ice cream. "Everybody line up."

Victor elbowed his way to the front. The way she filled his cone was slapdash at best. She was more careful with the others. When Don arrived, she was spooning ice cream into her own cone.

"Did I miss supper?" he asked.

"Just dessert," Teresa said as she carried a large casserole pan to the picnic table. "Better get yours quick before it melts away."

Sheila handed hers to him. "Take this one. I'll make myself another one."

"Nah," he said, "you don't have to do that. I can get my own."

"I insist. It's my job to make everyone happy." Her gaze was directed not at Don, but at Victor as she spoke. "Even when they're in the wrong."

Don accepted the cone, looking like he'd been caught in the crossfire of someone else's battle and wanted to escape. Victor looked like he understood the subtext of Sheila's comment but wasn't about to admit it. Sheila looked like she wanted to grind her ice cream and cone into Victor's face. The others looked like they wanted to be anywhere but at the supper table with Victor and Sheila.

I sat down at the picnic table, dished some of Teresa's casserole onto my plate, and started to eat. I planned to stick around and figure out exactly what had made the ice cream hit the fan.

CHAPTER 35

Teresa and Don began tossing a Frisbee after supper. I picked up a kitchen towel and chatted with Sheila and Frank while they did dishes. They didn't chat back, so I tried my hand with Teresa and Don. Before I could get them talking, the breeze lifted the Frisbee Don had thrown my way, and it smacked me between the eyes.

"Ouch!" I yelped, more from surprise than pain. Don and Teresa came running and insisted on having me sit down at a picnic table. Teresa insisted on bringing ice. I insisted that was unnecessary. Don insisted it had been an accident and apologized profusely. Sheila brought the first aid kit and insisted on taking a look. She offered to drive me home. I refused but promised to ice my eye on the drive to Little Missouri.

When I got home, I dumped the melted ice in the sink and went to my classroom. Because of the teachers' meeting, there hadn't been time to prepare after school. By the time I finished, I was tired and in no shape to analyze fingerprints.

My eye ached a little, so I took a Tylenol before bed and dreamed vividly. The members of the dig team challenged Rick and Cardo and me to a game of softball. The bases and home plate were made of deer antlers and positioned on the dig area marked by the twine and tent peg grid. The pitcher's mound sat at the center of the grid and consisted of the sun-bleached skull of a longhorn.

Our team was outnumbered. I struck out whenever I was up to bat. If it hadn't been for the sheriff and his deputy, we wouldn't have gotten past the first inning. They hit a series of home runs that sent the other team's outfield hunting for the ball and returning with it, breathless. When they were up to bat, Rick struck out their batters in short order, and it was our turn again. That set the pattern for each inning until Victor ordered Sheila to replace Don at the pitcher's mound. I went up to home plate and cinched the bat, at which point the ball morphed into an ice cream cone.

"Whatever," I muttered with a swing and a miss.

"Chocolate," said the catcher. "Yum!"

I turned and saw Don licking the ice cream dripping from his mask. Sheila lobbed her next pitch before I was in position. A cold, pink blob hit my left shoulder and splattered onto my chin. I licked it.

"Mmm," I said. "Strawberry."

With that, the outfielders released a torrent of ice-cream balls. Rick, Cardo, and I were soon covered with sticky, melting, delicious goo.

"Guys, use the cones to catch them!" I yelled to Rick and Cardo.

My alarm rang, and I woke up craving ice cream. I checked the freezer. No ice cream there, but I took the lab key out from under the ice cube tray. Then I made do with oatmeal with brown sugar and dollops of Snippy cream for breakfast. Delicious.

My hunger satisfied, I went into the lab. My class-room was in order, so I had a free half hour before school for reviewing the fingerprint cards and photographs. A shiver of excitement ran through me as I anticipated the uninterrupted hours I would have to devote to analysis after work. This could be the day when I narrowed our small pool of suspects down to one. A breeze touched my cheeks, and the scent of fresh air and damp earth reached my nostrils as I entered the lab.

That was weird. I rarely opened the window when I was in this room and always made sure it was shut before I left. I looked up. The small window was more than open. It was destroyed. The screen and glass had been wrenched free. They lay on the carpet at my feet. The filing cabinet was in bad shape too. The lock was broken. The drawers had been pried open. My carefully organized files and evidence bags had been removed and strewn all over the floor. My heart sank through the trailer floor and into the crawl space below. Sorting through everything to determine what, if anything, was missing would take hours. I had thirty minutes before my students arrived.

I went to the phone and asked Betty to connect me to Rick.

"That couwd take a whiwe," she said. "He could be any number of pwaces this earwy in the day."

"This is urgent, Betty. Start calling around. When you locate him, tell him to call me immediately. Even if school's underway. I have to talk to him."

I replaced the receiver and entered the lab to check the contents of the closet and the darkroom. Both appeared undisturbed. It was a small consolation, but better than nothing.

The phone rang, and I ran to answer.

"Jane, what's going on?" Rick asked.

"Someone broke into the lab."

"Are you okay?" he and Betty asked in unison.

"Not a word to anyone, Betty," Rick barked.

"You know I can keep a secret," Betty said. "Miss Neweww, are you reawwy okay?"

"Not a word of this to my mother, Betty. And I'm fine."

"Rewieved to hear it."

When she got off the line, Rick asked, "Any idea when the break-in occurred?"

"The room was intact yesterday morning before school, and I didn't hear anything out of the ordinary while the kids were here. So it must have happened when I was at the teachers' meeting in Tipperary in the afternoon."

"Cardo and I will be there soon."

"I'll lock the lab and put the key in the top drawer of my desk. Sneak into my classroom and get it once you're here. Liv has morning recess duty, so I'll check in with you then."

A bloodcurdling wail rose outside. Oh, for crying out loud. The last thing I needed now was playground drama. "Gotta go. Bye."

I rushed outside. Winter Skye was escorting Grace up the steps. Blood dripped from the little girl's elbow onto the cement. Drops spotted the gravel behind her too.

"You aren't gonna need surgery." Winter Skye patted her friend's shoulder. "But you might need stitches."

Grace howled. I took her into the classroom and settled her on a chair beside the sink. I handed Winter Skye a bucket and instructed her to fill it with water and sluice the blood off the steps. While she did that, I tended to Grace's elbow. Winter Skye's assessment had been spot on. Her friend might need stitches.

I gave her a gauze pad. "Hold it right here while I call your mom."

Trudy came immediately and took her daughter home. Liv rang the bell, and I collected my students. Winter Skye and her bucket of water had nearly erased the trail of blood. All that remained were pale pink traces on the gravel. The children came inside, and the school drama faded away.

The crime lab drama, on the other hand, gained steam as the day progressed. Rick and Cardo were photographing the lab and dusting for prints when I stopped by at recess. "Have you been around back yet?" I asked.

"I put up crime scene tape and will process that area once we're done in here." Cardo said.

Rick frowned. "That'll be pretty quick. Our intruder wiped down every surface he touched. Probably wore gloves too. We haven't found a single fingerprint. Not so much as a partial. It'll be the same outside, I wager."

Cardo eyed the hole where the window had been. "Once we finish our work here, I'll go to Tipperary and talk to Mrs. Dremstein about how she wants to handle the damage to school property. We must have someone come out here to patch the hole before nightfall."

Rick said, "While you do that, I'll stay here and sort through files to determine what's missing."

What I wanted to say was, "Leave them alone. They're my files. I can figure out what's missing faster than you." What I actually said was, "This is my last break until after work. I'll be in then."

The minute the last student left the schoolyard, I hustled to the crime lab. The file folders and papers that had been on the floor were in neat rows on the tables. Rick sat with the case file open in front of him.

"You've been busy," I said. "Do you know if anything is missing?"

He massaged his forehead. "I can't find the fingerprint cards."

My heart skipped a beat. "The enlargements of the prints from the other building were with the fingerprint cards. Are they gone too?"

"Yes."

"Can you think why anyone other than a member of the dig team would break in and take them?

Rick shook his head.

"Are the case file reports still here?"

He pointed to a stack of papers on the table. "They appear to be intact. You can check for yourself a little later. For now, I want you to come out back."

We went outside and circled the building. Merle's scrawny rooster was perched on the high fence between his garden and school property. The rooster squawked in agitation while I examined the area. From the indentations in the gravel and marks on the siding under the window, it appeared our culprit had climbed a ladder to reach the window. Marks on the siding indicated the use of a crowbar to remove the screen and window frame.

"Whoever broke in had to be small enough to get through the window," I said. "The opening is too small for either Frank or Victor. Which leaves Dan."

"Or Sheila. Or Teresa." Rick added.

"Do you think they have the upper-body strength to remove the window and haul themselves inside?"

"Probably not." He crouched next to the patch of gravel where the ladder indentations were. "What do you think of this?"

I knelt beside him. Other than where the ladder had been, it looked normal to me. I said as much.

"Look at the dirt between the rocks, not at them," he said.

The rooster clucked. I could almost feel him breathing down my neck. I studied the area for a few seconds and noticed pale pink patches around the gravel. They were similar to the place around front where Winter Skye had washed away the evidence of Grace's injury.

I rose. "He drew his own blood during the break-in and tried to wash it away."

Rick straightened. "All we have to do is find the person on the dig team with a deep scratch or a puncture wound and we've got our man." He grinned and raised an arm. "High five?"

Our palms met with a resounding slap. The rooster lost his balance and tumbled backwards. He disappeared behind the fence with another squawk. Served the old bird right.

CHAPTER 36

I knelt down again. "It doesn't look like Cardo bagged a dirt sample."

"He wanted you to take a look before disturbing it." Rick pulled a bag and latex gloves from his pocket. "You want to do the honors or should I?"

I gloved up and used a piece of gravel to scrape a sample of pinkish dirt and nudge the rocks surrounding it into the bag. After sealing it shut, I asked Rick, "Do you have a Sharpie on you?"

He patted his pockets. "Don't think so."

"No big deal. There are plenty in the lab. I'm done out here. Are you?"

"For now anyway."

On the way inside, I asked Rick if his interview with Richard Wentworth had turned up anything.

"Nothing that makes our investigation easier. He said now that he's semi-retired, his business manager made the arrangements with the college. I asked for the business manager's name and contact information, which he provided willingly enough. He walked me to my truck, friendly as could be. After I got in, he mentioned that the business manager had gone on vacation and would be out of the country until mid-July. He regretted the delay but promised the manager would contact me when he returned." Rick scratched his head. "I gotta say his expression was more sly fox than regretful."

"Like normal, then."

"Uh-huh."

Once we were in the lab, I labeled the bag and looked around. "Where did you put the other evidence bags?"

"They're in here." He dragged a small cardboard box out from under the table. "They haven't been sorted or cross-checked with the case file yet."

There was nowhere to set the box. Folders covered every inch of the worktables. I suggested we take them to the kitchen so we could spread out the bags and make sure they were all there.

He carried the box. I picked up the case file and joined him in the kitchen. He had already laid the evidence bags on the counter beside the sink. One held the dirt I'd just collected. Another contained what must be wood splinters from the destroyed window and frame. After that were bags with the paintbrush from the lab tent, the paper sacks Rick had salvaged from the wastebasket in the empty classroom, loose trash from the same wastebasket, and the key Velma and I had found in the vacuum cleaner bag.

I stiffened. "Where's the bag with the fossil? Tell me it's still in the box."

He tipped the top of the carton toward me so I could see it was empty. "I wish I could."

I slammed a fist on the counter. "Damn!" The bag of dirt bounced and skittered onto the floor.

Rick retrieved it and set it gently on the counter. "It's frustrating, but its disappearance isn't all bad. The theft proves our hunch. The break-in is definitely related to the dig team."

His calm tone set my teeth on edge. "At least in *our* minds it does," I snapped. "But we can't make an arrest on a hunch. We need tangible evidence to back us up."

"We've got these." He gestured toward the bags on the counter. His voice was as irritatingly calm as ever. "We can collect their fingerprints again. And you can make new photographs from the negatives. That's tangi—"

The negatives!

I ran into the darkroom, got on my hands and knees, and peered into its dimmest corner. I stuck my head under the workbench and felt around for the bin where my negatives were filed. I pulled it out and opened the lid. The negatives in their envelopes were like rows of tiny soldiers, their backs straight and in perfect order. Not one had broken rank. I took out one of the packets in question and ran into the kitchen. "They're all here!"

"Good. We've lost a little time. That's unfortunate, but we now know that Beanie's attacker is getting nervous. And careless."

A knock sounded from the landing. Cardo shouted, "Anybody in there who can hold the door open? There's a special delivery for Miss Newell!"

"I'll go," Rick said. "You put the negatives where they'll be safe."

I went to the darkroom and tucked the bin into the corner where it lived. The packet I'd pulled out went into my pocket. Until the investigation was over, it would be on my person during the day and sleeping with me at night. I came out of the darkroom and saw Cardo wheeling a dolly with a file cabinet strapped onto it through the lab door. He and Rick slid it off the dolly and were easing the ruined cabinet onto it when a stranger stuck his head through the opening where the window used to be.

His hair and once-white T-shirt were gray. His teeth were sparse, his smile broad. "I'm Darryl, one of the school janitors from over in Tipperary. Nice to meet you, Miss Newell."

"Likewise," I replied, standing on tiptoe to check the fence behind him for Merle's rooster. No sign of him.

The man spoke again. "Miss Dremstein said we gotta get this fixed up soon as we can. She don't want none of her teachers in harm's way is what she said. That and it's s'posed to rain on Friday, and she don't want water damage. Me and Larry here—say hello to Miss Newell, Larry—"

A cheery, disembodied hello interrupted Darryl's soliloquy.

Darryl wobbled from side to side. "Garsh darn it, Larry. Can't you hold a ladder and talk at the same time?"

"Sorry."

The wobble subsided. Darryl continued. "We gotta measure for a new window first. Then we got to seal the hole with plastic inside and out before we board it up. We'll get outta your hair quick as we can. You just pretend we isn't here."

Rick, Cardo, and I followed his advice as best we

could while scooting the new cabinet against the interior wall. We deposited files into its drawers and locked it shut. Ignoring the men became impossible when Larry and Darryl came into the lab bearing plastic sheeting, duct tape, and a stepladder. The room wasn't big enough for five, so the sheriff, deputy, and I retired to the kitchen.

"Want some coffee?" I asked.

They nodded, and I started filling the carafe with water. "I get it that the person who broke in wanted to wash away the blood. But why not brush away the indentations in the gravel and the scuff marks on the siding while he was at it?"

"My supposition is that he was running out of time," Cardo said. "He wanted to be at the dig site when you got there."

"Don Gaddy!" The carafe slid from my fingers and into the sink. Water splashed up and hit me full in the face. I gasped and used a dishtowel to dry off. "He didn't get there before me. He was late!"

Cardo whistled. "You want me to take his fingerprints again tomorrow? Interview him about where he was?"

Rick thought before answering. "Let's not draw attention to him until we're ready. Take everyone's fingerprints. Then pull them aside one by one. Ask where they were between three and five on Tuesday. Maybe that'll could flush out whoever might be holding something back about Don."

A loud squawk came from the lab. Its door flew open. Darryl tromped out with Merle's rooster under his arm. He thrust it at Cardo. "Take it wherever it come from." After handing off the rooster, Darryl patted my shoulder. "Don't you worry about nothin', Miss Newell."

The chicken poop dotting his shirt and the rooster feathers in his hair didn't inspire confidence. I picked at a hangnail while we waited for Cardo to get back. I was on hangnail number three when he returned and went straight to the sink to wash his hands.

"Now, where were we?" he asked.

Rick took charge. "Jane, you take the evidence bags and files into your classroom while Cardo gets us food from The Bend." He turned to his deputy. "Get something for Larry and Darryl too. While you do that, I'll help board the window before Merle's rooster dive bombs and bumps one of 'em off the ladder."

An hour later, every stomach was full. The window was rehung and rooster-proof. Larry and Darryl bid us goodbye. I was not sad to see them go

Cardo said, "Sheriff, how do you want us to proceed?"

"You go to the dig site tomorrow like we discussed. I'll man the office in Tipperary and write an incident report about the break-in. Jane, you write up your trip to the dig site yesterday and then start on the photos. Let's meet here again tomorrow around four to go over everything. I have a feeling things are going to move fast from here on out."

He rose and motioned for Cardo to do the same. They left. I went into the lab to get my typewriter. I plucked rooster feathers from between the keys and added them to those scattered on the floor. From the smell of things, Merle's rooster had left behind more than feathers.

The phone rang as I carried the typewriter to the

kitchen table. I set it down and hurried to answer. The caller spoke before I did.

"You okay?"

"I'm fine, Dick."

"Betty said the school janitors got the window boarded up."

"They did."

"Would you feel safer if I camped behind the building tonight? I get off work soon."

This guy's a keeper, Jane.

"That's thoughtful, but there's no need. Larry and Darryl used so many nails when they boarded the opening, it would take a crew to pry it off."

"You sure?"

"Yes. With the extra shifts you're covering for Joe, you need to sleep in your own bed. Not on the ground."

"He's back on the schedule again starting the weekend after next. I gotta work with him that Saturday to be sure he's up to it, but I have Friday off. Do you want to go out?"

"Are you kidding? Friday morning I have to drive to Tipperary to check out for the year. That makes's Friday afternoon the start of summer vacation. Of course I want to go out." I felt the return of my goofy grin.

"Me too," he said before hanging up.

I could still hear breathing on the line. "Those of you listening in better not breathe a word about my upcoming date or the break-in to my parents. Is that clear?"

"Absowutewy." Betty quickly disconnected.

I hung up and returned to the job at hand. Despite the disgusting task ahead of me, my grin stayed firmly in place. I filled a bucket with hot water, found a rag, and went into the lab. After putting on latex gloves, I got on my hands and knees and began scrubbing the carpet.

"Chicken poop," I groused. "Oh God, please don't let it be the new glitter."

Chapter 37

I worked in the darkroom until the wee hours of night locating the negatives of fingerprints lifted from the fossilized bone, the cubby shelf where it had been sitting, and the paper bags it had been hidden behind. After finding them, I made eight by tens and hung them up to dry. We needed them ready to be analyzed when Cardo brought the new sets of fingerprints tomorrow. Now that Don was our chief suspect, the business of comparing his prints against those on the fossil wouldn't take long. I agreed with Rick. Things were about to move quickly.

What didn't move quickly was school on Thursday. I dozed during show-and-tell. A comment Renny made during his dramatic retelling of Grace's trip to the clinic in Tipperary roused me.

"The PA said it was a good thing Mom brought Grace in. She got three stitches, and I heard her screaming bloody murder—"

I came wide awake and rooted around on my desk for my memo book. *Call the clinic to see if anyone from the dig team went in for a tetanus shot Wednesday or later,* I wrote.

I watched the clock, eager to follow up on this new lead and phoned the clinic when morning recess rolled around. The receptionist said that only the PA could release information about patients, and that he was a real stickler about it. The sheriff would have to call and request it himself. The bell rang before I reached Rick. I was on duty for both lunch and afternoon recess. The matter would have to wait until he and Cardo got here after school. Between me nodding off and Tiege waking me with his frequent announcements about the end-of-the-year school picnic being six days away, dismissal time couldn't come soon enough. When it finally arrived, the children tore through the door. Tiege led the charge yelling, "Four more days of school and I'm free!"

My thoughts exactly.

Unless I took drastic measures, I would be snoring at my desk when Rick and Cardo showed up. I went into the kitchen, made a pot of stiff coffee, and poured myself a cup. Next, I mixed up an Early Bird Coffee Cake and put it in the oven. I chugged down my coffee and poured another cup, which I took into my classroom. As a result, my desk was in order, I was awake and highly caffeinated, and the coffee cake was cooling on my kitchen counter when the sheriff and deputy walked into my classroom.

Cardo inhaled and beamed at me. "It smells like heaven in here!"

I stood and closed my grade book and went to the kitchen. I dished up generous squares of coffee cake

while Rick poured coffee. Cardo laid the new set of fingerprint cards next to my plate.

The cards could wait a little longer. I wanted to know
about the dig site. "How did your interviews go?"

Cardo sighed. "Victor vehemently objected to my
presence. He claims my constant interruptions are
keeping them from their work. Everyone acted surprised
when I told them about the break-in and the theft of
the fingerprint cards. It was hard to tell whose reactions
were genuine and whose were feigned. They all rattled
off alibis like they'd prepared them ahead of time. One
of them surely had."

"Did you ask about injuries?"

Cardo downed several bites of his coffee cake and
washed it down before answering. "Don had a recent
wound big enough to have bled profusely. So did Frank.
And Sheila had a nasty scratch on one arm. It seems
paleontology is a dangerous profession."

Rats! I'd hoped for just one wound to confirm just
one suspect. Still, the field was down from five to three.
That was progress. "What about Don? Was he nervous?
Evasive?"

"Nervous, yes. Evasive, no. He said he was at the
clinic in Tipperary Tuesday afternoon. Claimed he'd
tripped on a rake laying in some tall grass and cut his lip
and arm. Both bled pretty badly, and Teresa insisted he
get them looked at."

"Did her story match his?"

Cardo nodded. "It did, but she appeared very nervous. When I asked the others, they didn't mention that
Don had been injured. They thought Sheila said they

were low on plaster of Paris and sent him to the hardware store for more."

Rick broke in. "Do you think we have enough evidence to get a warrant to search the dig site for the fossil?
I'd like to do it Saturday. Every day means another
chance for the culprit to remove the fossil from the
property."

Cardo considered the question. "We might. Do we
have anything else to back up our suspicions other
than the break-in? Fingerprint evidence? Confirma-
tion from the clinic about Don's whereabouts Tuesday
afternoon? The record of someone from the dig site
receiving a tetanus shot this week?"

Rick sighed. "The PA's out of state for a family emergency. I can't contact him in time."

"Then let's start looking for a fingerprint match." I
stood. "Bring the food and the cards into the lab. I'll lay
out the photographs."

We got to work and soon found Don's partial print
on the fossil and several complete ones he'd left on the
cubby shelf, though they weren't close to where the fossil
had been. The problem was that the other prints on the
fossil matched those of every other member of the dig
team, plus a few prints we couldn't identify. Probably
Beanie's. Victor and Frank's prints were also on the
shelf. Sheila and Teresa's were not. There were unidenti-
fied prints on the shelf too.

"They could be Velma's," Rick said. "Which one of
you wants to take her prints?"

Silence.

Finally Cardo cleared his throat. "Perhaps we now

have enough to get the search warrant. No need to bother her."

Rick rose. "This is what we've got. Let's hope it's enough to convince the judge tomorrow. Jane, can you write up the analysis tonight? I'll pick it up by six tomorrow."

"It'll be waiting for you."

Cardo cleared his throat. "Might you have time to copy out the coffee cake recipe too?"

"Consider it done."

The analysis and the recipe were on the table when Rick arrived the next morning "Cardo and I will be here after school to discuss the search."

"In that case, leave the recipe. I'll give it to Cardo then. Tell him I'm making more coffee cake for tonight."

It rained all day. Grace showed off her stitches during indoor recess. Tiege was so impressed he forgot about his countdown to the end of the school year. I stared out the window at the rain and imagined how uncomfortable the dig team must be. I hoped their misery made them turn on one another and out Beanie's attacker.

A girl can dream.

Rick and Cardo parked along Main Street when school dismissed. They splashed across the playground, dodging children and puddles along the way. Velma was on their heels. Once inside, the men removed their galoshes and set them on the newspaper under her watchful eye. She complimented them effusively. Knowing a good thing when he saw it, Cardo invited her to join us for coffee cake in the kitchen as soon as he took her fingerprints. She agreed without complaint and didn't wait for the ink to dry before she heaped three pieces on her plate.

"Jane even wrote out the recipe for you." Cardo handed her the card meant for him. She thanked him, not me, before going into my classroom to clean.

I didn't trust her to not eavesdrop on our conversation and suggested we discuss tomorrow's search in the lab. Once we were in our cone of silence, Cardo said Victor mentioned the entire dig team was going to the Swensens' branding on Saturday morning.

I was surprised. "Winter Skye said they rescheduled their branding for last week."

Rick drained his coffee cup. "They had to reschedule again after they found a whole section of their fence got tore up by a snowplow after the blizzard. A bunch of their cattle got out. They've been finding them all over the place and fixing fence since then. Garth said they're branding tomorrow come hell or high water."

"Do you want me to go out there and keep tabs on them?" Cardo asked.

Rick considered the offer. "Best not. I need you in Tipperary to keep tabs on the crew operating the one-lane traffic on Highway 85. That second string of theirs gets pretty lax on the weekends. You better get out there every hour or so to keep them on their toes. I'll stop at the Swensens' in the morning and make sure the dig crew's there. Jane, you stay here until I pick you up. Then we'll go out together and conduct the search."

We got up. I opened the door. Velma fell into my arms.

She regained her balance and took the recipe card

from her pocket. "Do you use white or brown sugar when you make it?"

"Brown." I pointed at the ingredient list. "Just like it says right here."

She rubbed her eyes and blinked. "Guess I better get an appointment with the eye doctor."

"Get your hearing checked too," I suggested. "So you know whether leaning against the door is absolutely necessary when you eavesdrop or if you can hear just as well while standing up straight."

The malevolent glint in Velma's eye rivaled that of Snow White's stepmother. When I didn't blanch, she did an about face and marched away. One thing was for certain, I thought while watching her retreating back. If she left an apple on my desk when she finished cleaning the school, I wasn't going to eat it.

CHAPTER 38

Sunshine streamed into the living room on Saturday morning. The sky was a cloudless blue, of a color Crayola had yet to capture. Yellow and pink tulips waved merrily in front of the house across the street. Muddy puddles and bright green grass were the only remnants of yesterday's rain. I opened the windows to let the outside air blow in, as clear and cool as a mountain stream. The beauty of the day caught in my throat and stirred a mysterious longing inside me, as new as morning and as ancient as time.

I put on an old T-shirt under my sweatshirt before climbing into my overalls. After breakfast, I set my rattlesnake shovel, a thermos of water, and my camera beside the door. Then I went into my classroom to wait for Rick's call. He hadn't said when he would pick me up. I doubted he would arrive before nine, perhaps not until ten. I distracted myself by averaging my students' final-quarter grades. Whatever work they did in class from Monday until the school picnic wasn't going to change their averages, so why not get started on them? I calculated their reading, phonics, and spelling grades before my brain went into math overload. It was time to take a break.

Rick still hadn't phoned from the Swensen ranch, so I threw a load of laundry in the washer and cleaned my bathroom. I was about to attack the kitchen when he finally got ahold of me around nine.

"I've gotta keep an eye on things here a little longer." He was breathing hard. "How do you feel about driving out to the site by yourself?"

"Fine. After all—" I caught myself before blurting out that I'd been there alone the previous Saturday. My fingers trembled. I squeezed the phone receiver to make the shaking stop.

"After all what?" Rick asked.

"Um . . . After all, I'll have my rattlesnake shovel for company."

"Good. Everyone from the dig team's here. Victor says the ranch hands who live in the house are in the Hills for the weekend. Still, this is no time to get careless and give yourself away. Drive around to the back of the house and park as close to it as you can. You can snoop while you wait for me, but don't touch anything until I'm there. I wouldn't be surprised if the fossil's been hidden in plain sight. Maybe among the others in the lab tent. Try starting there. I won't be more than a half hour behind—"

An excited shout came down the phone line. A door banged shut. A burst of excited chatter crescendoed. "Just a second." He mumbled something and then spoke to me again. "I gotta go." The call ended.

I made a quick trip to the bathroom—no way was I using the outhouse at the dig site. Next, I filled my overall pockets with evidence bags, Sharpie markers, latex gloves, and film. I put the camera around my neck and grabbed the shovel. Finally, I closed the windows and locked the apartment. The scent of lilacs tickled my nose on the walk to my car. I hunted for its source and found it. The big bush next to Merle's mudroom door was in full bloom. Maybe he would let me cut a bouquet later this afternoon. The thought made me smile.

The countryside was a green delight on the way to the dig site. The windbreak of lilacs at the Wentworth place was forming buds, a week or more behind Merle's. Clusters of tulips lined their lane. Corinne's doing, no doubt. I couldn't imagine Richard the First or Junior lending her a hand. A few miles later, I made the turn onto the old Lindgren place and bumped down the gravel path. The grass in the ditches had grown at least six inches since Tuesday.

By contrast, the area around the ranch house was ugly as sin, a mix of piles of antlers and animal skulls, plain dirt, mud puddles, and tire tracks. At least the Beetle's wouldn't stand out, I thought, while driving to the back of the house. The landscaping here on the south side was no better than out front. The lack of shade had bleached the antlers and bones a ghastly white.

The creepiness factor made me shudder. I opened the door cautiously and scanned the ground for snakes. I didn't get out until I had a firm grip on the shovel. I leaned out and banged it on the ground several times and counted to ten. When nothing slithered into sight, I got out. The scent of mud, dirt, and septic gas danced on the breeze. What had possessed Victor to choose this location over the McDonald ranch? It didn't hold a candle to what that place had to offer.

I hurried on foot to the dig site. *Better Homes & Gardens* wasn't going to use it for a feature article in the near future, but it was paradise compared to where I'd just been. There was more grass here than mud and dirt. Blocks of shade cast by the tents offered relief from the warming sun.

Following Rick's suggestion, I entered the lab first to see if the stolen fossil was hiding among the clutter on the tables. They were covered with fossils. Some were recognizable as bones. Others were fragments that looked like the alligator skin, carapace shells, petrified wood, and reeds the dig team had shown us during our field trip. Many specimens had been added since that trip. A few of the bone fossils were as big as or bigger than the one that had been stolen, but the stolen one wasn't there. We were going to have to search harder once Rick arrived.

I checked my watch. Nine twenty. He should be here soon. I was getting thirsty and decided to get my thermos from my car. I hadn't expected the sun to warm things up this early or I would have brought it with me. After I got to the car and quenched my thirst, I checked the time again. Nine twenty-five. Rick would be here any minute. I might as well hang out here until then. Not here on the sunny side of the house though. I circled the building and found plenty of shade on the west and north sides. That was a bummer because those sides were visible to anyone coming down the lane. But I would hear a vehicle long before the driver saw me. There would be plenty of time to hide.

I went around to the front and sat on the porch stairs with the rattlesnake shovel at my side. I got bored and checked my watch. Nine forty. What was keeping Rick? I removed my camera's lens cap and took pictures to pass the time. The antlers and the animal skulls were fascinating—in an Addams Family kind of way. I circled the house, leaning my shovel against the side of the house and taking photos as I went. The antler pile next to the back door was the most visually pleasing with the direct sunlight casting a mass of curving light and shadow. I studied it, searching for the perfect angle before snapping a shot. I moved closer and snapped again, then straightened. Something about the shot disturbed me. What was it? I let the camera dangle around my neck and bent for a closer look.

There it was. A straight line among the curves. I picked up the shovel, stepped back, pounded it on the ground several times, and counted to ten. No movement. Good. I leaned the shovel against the house. Then I reached into the pile of antlers, grasped what had caught my eye, and lifted out the fossilized bone.

"Well hello there! You weren't quite in plain sight, but darn close." I smiled and stood up straight.

A hand clamped over my mouth. The barrel of a gun pressed between my shoulder blades. "Drop it," a raspy voice hissed, "and put your hands on your head."

CHAPTER 39

I obeyed without hesitation. The gun pressed harder on my back as its owner moved the hand covering my mouth to my wrist and yanked my arm into a hammerlock. I was pushed toward the back door of the house. "We're going inside."

Again, I obeyed and stumbled forward as I tried to identify the voice. Despite its raspiness, I was sure it belonged to a member of the dig crew. It was too high to be Don. Or Victor. Or Frank. That left only Teresa or Sheila. Teresa wasn't tall enough to hold my arm as high as the person behind me was doing.

"Sheila, the sheriff will be here any minute," I warned.

"Don't count on it." She shoved me through the door and into a straight-backed kitchen chair. She pointed the gun at me while rummaging through cupboards and drawers. "Last I saw him, he and a bunch of bulls were in a staring contest on the road. The bulls weren't giving him any leeway, but I cut a fence and chased a herd of sheep onto the road just to tie him up in knots. The sheep were milling around stupid as could be when I took off."

"How'd you get here with the road blocked?"

"I'd helped myself to Victor's van earlier and parked a good distance east of where I intended to release the animals."

"Why did you attack Beanie?"

"Aha!" Sheila held up a roll of duct tape. "Mike said he left this in the kitchen." She tore off a length with her teeth and bound my hands behind the back of the chair.

She had the power to limit my movement, but not my curiosity. "Why did you attack Beanie?" I repeated.

"An accident." She knelt in front of me and taped my legs to the chair's front legs. She stood and dragged another chair in front of me, then sat and began to talk. "Really, it was Beanie's fault for being so anal about her recordkeeping. The minute we brought our finds to the lab tent, she was documenting and organizing them. She hovered in and around the tent all day long. I had to wait until late at night to go in and claim the fossils that were rightfully mine. About a week before the field trip, she was in there at night, taking the logbook from where Vic demanded it be kept. After she left, I went in to see what she was up to. She'd been cross-checking the items in the logbook with the artifacts in the tent. She'd stuck a list of what was missing in the front of the book. All of them were ones I'd brought in. Unless I returned them, she would make the connection and go to Victor with what she knew. I'd hidden my finds in different places around the camp until I could arrange for my contact person to collect them. I had to put them back, at least until I could put someone less organized in charge of the lab tent so I could reclaim them.

"I hid my best find in the rafters of the outhouse and returned the others. On the day of the field trip, I put that one into Renny's lunch bag with a note for Trudy and stuffed it in his jacket pocket. My contact person and I had done a few test runs using her as a go-between. I'd led her to believe the two of us were an item and needed to keep our relationship on the down-low. In a way, that was true, just not in the way she was thinking. Vic was doing his final dog-and-pony show for you and the kids when I went into the tent. Beanie was in there again. She said several artifacts that she thought had been missing had shown up again. She wondered if I could help her determine what had happened. I said sure. She climbed up on the collapsible step stool to get the logbook, leaned too far, and lost her balance. She fell and smacked her temple on the side of a table. When she hit the floor, I panicked, put the step stool where it belonged, and left."

I believed what she said, but not what had been left unsaid. "Why didn't you go for help?"

"I already told you. I panicked."

"But why? Were you afraid to draw attention to yourself and risk having your thefts discovered?"

"Enough!" She jumped up, tore off a length of duct tape, and slapped it over my mouth. "I have to get a few things from my tent before I get rid of you."

That didn't sound promising. I had no illusions about her intentions. She wouldn't have spilled her story if she thought I'd live to pass it on. She would be back for me soon. I wanted to die with a clear conscience. I prepared to meet my Maker by begging him to forgive my many daydreams about duct taping Tiege to his chair. I was searching my soul for other sins—and was appalled by how many surfaced—when a light rapping sounded on the door.

"Miss Newell, are you in there?" the visitor whispered.

I breathed in through my nose until my lungs were bursting. Then I screamed as loud as my duct taped mouth could. It sounded pretty puny to me, but a ray of light appeared and the door swung open.

"Oh my gosh, Miss Newell, are you all right?" Trudy Berthold ran inside with Renny at her heels.

"Mmm, mmm, mmm," was the best I could manage.

Trudy ripped away the duct tape. The pain made me gasp. I vowed to never again tell a student that tearing off a Band-Aid didn't hurt.

"I'm fine. But we don't have much time. Sheila will be here soon. She's got a gun."

Renny's eyes widened and his face blanched.

Trudy pressed her car keys into his hand. "Listen, Renny. You got to go to where we left the car. Don't let nobody see you. Walk in the ditch, not on the lane. Drive home fast as you can. Flag down the sheriff if you can. Otherwise find your dad and tell him to get out here."

He left without a word. Trudy started opening drawers. "Soon as I find a knife, I'll cut you free."

"I have another idea. My rattlesnake shovel—"

"Your what?"

"I'll explain later. Just go outside and get the shovel. It's leaning against the wall."

While she fetched it, I fleshed out my plan. When

she came in, I explained it to her. She did as I suggested without hesitation. We were ready with seconds to spare when Sheila returned.

She pointed the gun at me and pulled a pair of scissors from her pocket. "After I free your legs, stand up. Try to get away and you're dead. Got it?"

I nodded and squeaked, "Mmm, mmm," through the duct tape Trudy had reapplied to my mouth. When Sheila bent over me, Trudy came from around the corner into the hallway. She brought the shovel down on Sheila's head. At the same time, I kneed Sheila in the chin. She dropped the gun. It spun across the linoleum, hit the wall, and stopped next to the back door. Sheila lay unmoving at my feet. Blood trickled from her mouth.

Trudy sliced through the duct tape on my legs and wrists. I jumped up and tore off the tape. Ouch! I sprinted to the phone and rang Betty. "We need an ambulance at the ranch house on the old Lindgren place."

"Miss Neweww?"

"No time, Betty. Just do it." I hung up.

Trudy leaned the shovel against the wall and knelt beside Sheila. Her mouth flopped open. "I think she bit her tongue," Trudy said. "I'll see if there's a first-aid kit in the bathroom."

"Bring a towel to soak up the blood, too." I took Sheila's pulse. It was strong and slow. I felt along her skull where Trudy had beaned her on the head. She had quite a goose egg! I got ice from the freezer and dumped it in a plastic bag I found in a kitchen drawer. I was holding the ice to Sheila's head when the door opened. A man entered. He was one of the ranch hands Junior Wentworth had sent to round up the bulls on the playground last fall. The man's name escaped me, if I'd ever known it, so I couldn't greet him by name when he picked up Sheila's gun and aimed at me.

"Stand up and put your hands on your head," he ordered.

I obeyed. Funny how staring down the barrel of a gun opens the mind and jogs the memory. "Fancy meeting you here, Mike Hansen," I said, as loud as I dared without sounding suspicious. I've always pictured you packing a rifle rather than a pistol. If I promise not to move, will you point that thing at the floor instead of at me?"

CHAPTER 40

"Junior told me you don't know when to shut up. I thought he was just bad-mouthing you for getting him sent to prison. I was wrong."

Mike's little speech sparked a host of questions. How often did he talk to Junior? Did he call him? Write letters? Visit him at the prison? Bring him cakes with files baked inside? Mike didn't give me an opportunity to ask even one.

"She dead?" He gestured to Sheila.

"Unconscious. The EMTs are on their way. They should be here any minute."

"We'll be outta here before they make it. Put your hands behind your back."

Once again, I obeyed.

He bound my wrists with duct tape, took me outside, and forced me into the back seat of his truck's club cab. "You sit tight. I'll be back with Sheila." He fastened my seatbelt and locked me in. As he walked away, he stuffed the pistol into his waistband. He went into the house a few feet. I saw Trudy step from behind the door and whack him on the head with my spade. He went down like a rag doll. She taped his wrists together and then his legs before dragging him further into the kitchen. Then she ran toward the truck.

"I'm locked in," I shouted through the window glass. "Get his keys. And the pistol while you're at it. It's in his waistband."

Before long, we were in the kitchen. Trudy and I propped Mike up against a leg of the kitchen table. It was a huge piece of furniture, heavy as a Sherman tank, and we taped him to it. We hadn't expected to use an entire jumbo roll of duct tape doing it, but we did. My students were rubbing off on me.

Mike regained consciousness and alternately hurled invectives and complained of a raging headache. Trudy took his colorful language in stride. I assumed that was a perk of waitressing at Round the Bend. My vocabulary expanded with every sentence he uttered. Sheila still lay on the floor but began to moan and stir. I got a pillow from a bedroom and slid it under her head. While I was at it, I repositioned her ice pack.

Trudy and I sat at the table, as far from Mike as we could, and kept an eye on him and Sheila while we waited for the ambulance. Trudy found a full pitcher of iced tea in the refrigerator and poured us each a glass.

When Mike paused his railing to draw breath, I asked Trudy, "What possessed you and Renny to come out here?"

"Rick called from the Swensens' and said the road to Little Missouri was blocked." She shouted to be heard above Mike. "He asked me to come out and tell you to be on the lookout for Sheila. He knew she'd left the brand-ing, but not when."

"Why didn't Betty raise a posse?"

"She was organizing a crew to clear the road between the Swensens' and town so Rick could get through."

"But why did you bring Renny?"

"He brought himself. He popped up from the back seat while I was parking along the lane. Said he was gonna come with me. You was his teacher, he said, and he was gonna help you."

My heart melted and seeped through my eyes. I took a tissue from the box on the counter and blew my nose.

Trudy went on. "He swore he wouldn't be any trouble, that he'd do anything you or I told him to do. And he did." She chewed her lip. "I sure hope he made it to town okay."

The ambulance siren sounded in the distance. As it grew louder, I ran out to the front door and pointed to where they should park. Dick jumped out from the driver's side—wasn't he on duty at Fly Ranch?—Mary Borgeson from the other.

"We've got two people with blows to the head. One male, conscious and fighting mad. One female, starting to stir," I said as they grabbed their equipment and ran inside. I was about to follow when the wail of another siren reached my ears. A cloud of dust rolled down the lane, slowed as it neared the house, and parked several yards behind the ambulance.

Rick got out. "Have you seen Sheila?"

"She's inside. Along with Trudy, Dick, Mary, and Mike."

"Mike who?"

"Hansen. He works for Junior."

"What's he doing here?"

"Giving me a vocabulary lesson for one thing."

He raised an eyebrow.

"I think he and Sheila are part of a fossil smuggling ring. She's out cold, and he hasn't been forthcoming about the details. Maybe that will change once his headache subsides and he's no longer duct taped to a Sherman tank."

Rick raised the other eyebrow. "I can't wait to hear the whole story."

"Now's not the time. Dick and Mary need direction about where to take patients who not only held me at gunpoint, but bound and gagged me—"

Rick started to speak.

I raised my index finger and continued "—until they could, as they put it, 'get rid of me.' Also, Trudy is dying to know if Renny made it to town okay." I lowered my hand. "Now what were you about to say?"

"Never mind." He closed his eyes and massaged his temples like he had a headache. They were going around this morning.

We went into the house. Trudy flew over to Rick. "Is Renny okay?"

He put a hand on her shoulder. "He's better than okay. He's a hero. You oughta be proud of your boy."

She burst into tears. I brought her the tissue box and rubbed her back. While she regained control, Rick restrained Mike so Dick could assess his injuries. Mike demanded to be released and refused medical treatment.

"If that's the way you want to do it, that's fine." Rick cuffed Mike's hands behind his back. Then the sheriff cut away the duct tape, arrested him, and read him his rights. Together, Rick and Dick led Mike to the sheriff's vehicle. Mike fought and kicked the whole way but gave up after Rick shoved him in the back seat, cuffed his ankles, and locked him inside.

Dick went into the house. Trudy came out and waited with Rick and me. Dick and Mary wheeled Sheila out on a stretcher and loaded her into the ambulance. Rick said an officer from the Sturgis police force would meet them at the emergency room to guard Sheila. I was to ride with Rick to the Sturgis jail where Mike would be booked. Once he was behind bars, the sheriff and I would go to the hospital to see how Sheila was doing. While we did all that, Trudy would drive my Beetle to the school, then go home and heap accolades on Renny's head.

Everyone got into their respective vehicles. I went inside, retrieved my shovel, and then got into the sheriff's vehicle. The ambulance left in a blaze of flashing lights. Rick waved for Trudy to go next. We brought up the rear. When we passed the dig team van in the ditch, I asked, "Does the search warrant include official vehicles at the site?"

He smiled and parked. "It does."

We got out and told Mike to stay where he was while we made our way down into the ditch. Rick charged ahead. I minced along, watching for snakes in the greening grass. We peeked through the passenger-side window. What we saw inside made us grin from ear to ear.

"You do the honors." Rick opened the door and stepped back. "You've earned it."

I gloved up and took an evidence bag from my overall

pocket. With my thumb and forefinger, I picked up the fossilized bone lying on the passenger seat and dropped it into the evidence bag. I was sealing it shut when we heard banging from the direction of Rick's truck. We scrambled up the side of the ditch and saw Mike hitting his head on the side window. He began hurling curses as we ran to the vehicle and jumped into the cab.

"Hang on!" Rick started the engine and flipped on the sirens. Gravel flew in every direction as he accelerated and turned onto the highway. Centrifugal force slammed me against the door. "No matter how fast I drive, it's gonna be a long trip with all the caterwauling in the back seat." He pressed down on the gas until we were flying down the road.

"Slow down!" Mike screamed.

"Shut up," Rick ordered.

Neither one gave an inch.

Rick's right, I thought as I tightened my seatbelt and tried to ignore the constant cursing from the back seat, *it's going to be a very long trip.*

Chapter 41

My vocabulary had expanded exponentially by the time we got to Sturgis around noon. Mike's voice grew hoarse from all his shouting but remained as offensive as ever. He accused Rick and me of all manner of wrongdoing. Though he'd brought up Junior Wentworth immediately after finding me in the ranch house, he hadn't mentioned him once since Rick had entered the scene. Very interesting.

Rick had radioed the Meade County Jail in Sturgis, and two deputies were waiting when we pulled in. They helped him escort the prisoner into the building.

"Jane, call the hospital and ask if the ambulance has arrived," Rick shouted as the door opened and the jail swallowed them whole.

I waited to see if it was going to keep Mike or vomit him out whole. When I was certain he was headed toward the bowels of the building where he belonged, I went inside. I found the hospital's number in the directory beside the pay phone in the lobby. I searched my pockets for a dime and came up empty. I went to the desk where an officer was taking his afternoon nap.

I coughed and pretended not to notice him startle awake.

"How far is it to the hospital?" I asked.

He yawned. "A couple blocks."

"Could you tell me how to get there?"

"I'll make you a map." While he drew, I took a Sharpie from my overalls and wrote a note telling Rick I was walking to the hospital. The officer gave me the map. I gave him my note and asked him to deliver it to the Tipperary County Sheriff. While capping the Sharpie I realized that the evidence bag containing the fossil still needed to be labeled. I went to the sheriff's truck and took the evidence bag from the glove box where I'd tucked it for safekeeping during the drive. I labeled and dated the bag but felt uneasy about leaving it in his unlocked vehicle. I decided to take it with me. I emptied the contents of the biggest pocket of my overalls into the glove box. Then I pushed the evidence bag deep into the pocket and snapped it shut. After that, I picked up the map and followed it to the hospital.

Spring was a couple weeks ahead of Little Missouri here. The lawns were a lush green. Backyard vegetable gardens had been plowed and planted. Rhubarb poked through the ground, just like at my parents' house. I imagined Mom setting out the tomato plants she'd grown from seed while Dad sat on the patio giving her advice about how far apart to place them. Not that she needed advice. She was master of her garden and grew copious amounts of produce every year.

When I arrived at the hospital, the Tipperary County

Ambulance was parked near the Emergency Room, but there was no sign of Mary or Dick. I went inside and found them sitting in the waiting area. She was completing paperwork. He was staring at the floor.

I went and sat next to him. "How is Sheila?"

The question startled him. He looked up, and when he saw me, his whole face lit up. Mine did too.

"She's stable. Vital signs are good, but she's still unconscious. Doc thinks she's in a coma. You must have whacked her good with your shovel."

"No," I corrected. "Trudy whacked her on the head. I just kneed her in the chin."

"How did we miss that detail?" Mary asked. "I better tell the ER doctor to add that to her chart before we take her to Rapid." She jogged off and went through a set of double doors.

"When do you leave?" I asked Dick.

"Soon as the ER doc gives us his report and the X-rays he took."

Mary burst through the double doors. She had a large manila envelope in her hands, a large Meade County deputy at her side, and two large orderlies pushing Sheila's gurney at her heels. Dick rose and swung into step behind the gurney. They loaded Sheila into the ambulance. Mary and the officer climbed in next to the gurney. Once they were settled, the orderlies shut the doors. Dick got into the driver's seat, and off they went.

Rick had missed everything. I'd better go to the jail and fill him in. On the return trip, I wondered if Sheila and Beanie would be on the coma floor together. Did hospitals have coma floors? The police officer who was guarding Sheila would need to find out where Beanie's room was. Mrs. Lavender wouldn't want Sheila moving in next door to her daughter. Rick wouldn't either.

Rick was in the jail's lobby signing documents when I got there. Committing crimes and apprehending bad guys—or in Sheila's case, bad gals—cut a wide swath. For one thing, the paperwork involved killed a lot of trees. Didn't the criminals think about the trees?

Rick looked up and saw me. "Give me a minute." He reviewed the documents and passed them to the officer behind the desk. He handed me a manila envelope. "Those are Hansen's fingerprints to keep on file in our lab."

I unsnapped the pocket with the evidence bag, added the envelope, and snapped the pocket shut again. "Where to next?"

"The hospital."

"Too late," I said on the way outside. "She's been transferred to Rapid City."

The trip was barely long enough to tell him why Sheila was being moved and relay the broad strokes of what had happened at the ranch house before he got there.

"You've set a new record," he said while turning into the hospital parking lot.

"What do you mean?"

"You apprehended two suspects without being injured." He nosed into a parking space and cut the engine.

"Maybe not injured. But being gagged and bound with duct tape is no picnic," I said as we hoofed it to the emergency room. "My wrists and cheeks are sticky with residue."

He held the door open. My stomach rumbled. Rick's growled in reply, reminding us that we had skipped lunch. I checked my watch. Two o'clock.

Dick was sitting in the lobby staring at the floor. Again. Mary was sitting next to him doing paperwork. Again. Crime sure didn't pay if you were a tree.

Rick pointed to the row of vending machines along the wall. "I'll get snacks to tide us over for now. You get a status report from Dick and Mary."

I walked over to Dick and tapped him on the shoulder. He looked up and said that Sheila had regained consciousness. A specialist had examined her and ordered more tests. She'd been moved to Room 305.

Rick brought chips and candy bars for us. After I told him where Sheila was, we got on the elevator and tore into the food. When we reached the third floor, we got lost once and asked directions to Sheila's room three times before we finally found it and went inside.

She was in the bed closest to the door. A curtain blocked the bed on the far side of the room. Rick asked me to stay with her while he and the deputy from Sturgis went into the hall to discuss the procedure for scheduling round-the-clock guards outside the room.

I went to the side of Sheila's bed. An ice pack sat on her head at a rakish angle. Her eyelids were puffy, and the skin around her eyes was turning purplish black. Her chin was bruised, and her swollen, bloody tongue protruded from between her lips. Knowing that she was in no state to hurt me or Beanie or anyone else was a relief, but I took no pleasure in her condition.

I put a hand on her shoulder. "Sheila," I whispered. No response.

I bent closer. "Can you hear me, Sheila?" Then a little louder. "Sheila?"

Her eyelids opened a fraction of an inch. When she saw it was me, her eyes widened. She winced.

"Ay," she mumbled and winced again. "Ay."

"Are you trying to say my name?" I asked. "Are you saying Jane?"

Sheila nodded.

"Can I get you something?"

Before Sheila could answer, the person in the bed behind the curtain said, "Jane? As in Jane Newell?"

Sheila and I exchanged puzzled glances.

"Yes." I tugged at the curtain until the patient in the other bed came into view. "Beanie?"

Beanie's gaze went from me to her new roommate. "Sheila?"

Sheila turned away and began to sob.

CHAPTER 42

"Beanie?" I went over to her and squeezed her hand. "You're awake . . . what . . . when . . ."

"I think . . ." Her eyebrows furrowed. ". . . yesterday morning? My brain's still fuzzy. I keep forgetting things. Mom'll be here soon. You can ask her. How did Sheila get hurt?"

I held up my index finger. "Will you excuse me for a moment?"

I pulled the curtain between the two women and went into the hall, where I interrupted Rick and the deputy. "Beanie's awake."

"Who told you that?" Rick asked.

"She did."

He looked skeptical. "When did you see her?"

"Come with me." I took him by the elbow and escorted him through the door and over to Beanie's side of the room.

"Would you tell this guy who you are?" I pointed at Rick.

"My full name is Colleen Lavender, but my friends call me Beanie." She extended her right hand toward him. "Have we met before?"

"We have not." He went to her bedside and took her hand in both of his. "I'm Rick Sternquist, Tipperary County Sheriff. It's wonderful to finally talk to you. I'm leading the investigation into the accident that put you in the hospital. I'll visit with you more later. Right now, I need to confer with my team." He released her hand and turned to me. "Jane, would you come with me?"

We joined the deputy in the hall. Rick introduced me to Deputy Minor as Tipperary County's forensic expert.

"Cole Minor," the Rapid City deputy said after we shook hands. "My parents thought it was funny."

Rick explained the situation to him. "These women need to be in different rooms. I'm going to order the floor nurse to move one of them. Until then, Deputy Minor, I want you to pull the curtain all the way around Beanie's bed so she and her parents don't have to see Sheila. You are to sit between their beds on Sheila's side of the curtain. Jane, you are to keep Beanie company. Don't tell her anything about Sheila or the investigation yet."

"Can I tell Beanie's parents?" I asked.

"Yes, as long as they know not to tell their daughter until we give the go ahead."

Rick walked toward the nurses' station. The deputy and I returned to the room. He did as Rick had ordered. I sat beside Beanie. A nurse came in to check her vitals, which gave me a few minutes to choose a topic of conversation that wouldn't stray into Sheila, the dig crew, or dinosaur territory. I settled on reminiscing about high school. We were giggling about riding the school bus to speech contests when we heard a knock and looked up.

"Why if it isn't Jane Newell!" Mrs. Lavender exclaimed when she pushed aside the curtain and stood next to the bed. "Beanie said she'd seen you at the dig site, but I didn't know you had come to visit. How thoughtful of you!"

In order to follow Rick's directive, I said nothing about being part of the investigation and let her misguided opinion of me stand.

Mrs. Lavender went to her daughter's side and kissed her cheek. "You've got more company, Beanie. Do you want them to come in in?"

"Sure, Mom."

"Surprise!" Teresa entered and stood at the foot of Beanie's bed. "Your mom called the switchboard operator in Little Missouri and said to tell us you were awake. We came as soon as we got word."

The other members of the team clustered around Beanie's bed. Victor brought up the rear. "The gang's all here," he said. "With the exception of Sheila. We're not sure where she is."

Beanie gestured toward the curtain. "She's—"

"Shhh." I took her hand and squeezed it.

Beanie hesitated and squeezed in return.

Her friends crowded closer. I led Mrs. Lavender into the hall and told her about the room mix-up. "The sheriff is trying to get Sheila moved."

"Oh that poor girl. I'll sit with her and the deputy until Beanie's company leaves."

My gut said I should object but she disappeared behind Sheila's curtain. Rick returned before I could go after her. An orderly with a gurney was right behind him. They went into the room, where the orderly announced he was taking Sheila to radiology for some tests. Soon, he, Sheila, and the deputy were on their way. I introduced Rick to Mrs. Lavender. Then he crashed the dig team party by informing them that due to new evidence in the case, Sheila was a suspect. He also told them that she had been injured earlier in the day and was now hospitalized.

"When you're done here, Jane and I will accompany all of you to the Meade County sheriff's office in Sturgis to answer questions that have arisen in light of these new developments."

"But," Victor protested, "we have errands—"

Rick cut him off. "They can wait. Also, I've ordered pizza. It'll be waiting for you when get there."

That silenced him.

Mrs. Lavender kept a close eye on her daughter during the visit. When Beanie began to tire, her mother thanked the dig team for coming and whisked them into the hall. About an hour later, they were sitting in a conference room eating pizza under the supervision of another Meade County sheriff's deputy.

Rick took Victor to the interview room first. The professor returned silent and visibly shaken. Rick then asked Don to go with him. A few minutes later Mr. Gunderson, the county attorney, whom I'd met back in February during a previous case, came into the conference room. When he asked me to go with him, I reluctantly set down my second piece of pizza and followed him. We went into a small room with one grimy window. The walls were a depressing gray, as were the small table and chairs around it. A woman wearing a bright red pantsuit sat at the table. I knew her too. She was Mrs. Knight, the court reporter who had come with the attorney to Little Missouri in February. He motioned for me to sit in the empty chair across from her, then went around the table and sat beside her. She gave me a businesslike nod as her hands hovered above her stenograph.

"Miss Newell," Mr. Gunderson said, his sad smile as much in evidence as it had been when I'd last seen him. "Since you are present in our fair county, I would like to take advantage of that fact and have you recount the events of what you experienced today at the dig site."

"Is this my deposition?"

"Precisely."

I launched into my account. He stopped me occasionally to ask for clarification. When we finished, I was tired and hungry again. I stood, eager to return to my half-eaten, cold pizza.

Mr. Gunderson dismissed Mrs. Knight and asked me to take my seat again. He shut the door and said, "There's been a peculiar development that pertains to you. It involves the Mr. Hansen whom you mentioned in your deposition. On the advice of his lawyer—"

How had Hansen secured a lawyer on a Saturday afternoon?

"—he is not answering our questions. However, he has repeatedly requested to meet with you. I said I would relay the request, which I am doing now. I advise you to decline it."

Hansen had spent hours yelling at me and Rick earlier in the day. What more could he have to say? My curiosity was piqued. "If I say yes," I asked the attorney, "will you stay with me?"

"I can, but he made clear his desire to speak to you in private. I believe my presence would turn the meeting into an exercise in futility." He paused. "However, he can be seated with his back to the door so I can watch through its window unbeknownst to him. I can then extricate you from the conversation immediately if you so indicate."

"Will he be handcuffed?"

"Yes."

"Bring him in."

A few minutes later, Hansen was sitting across from me at the table. He looked pleased with himself and leaned back, tipping his chair onto its back legs. "I got a message for you from a friend of mine."

"I'm impressed. You've only been here a few hours and have already made a new friend."

"Not a *new* friend. More like a *mutual* one. And not since I been here. I saw him a few weeks ago." He paused and leaned toward me. "At the prison."

My body tensed.

He smirked. "You know who I'm talking about, don't you?"

I refused to nod.

"He wanted me to tell you what a good boy he's been in prison. So good the parole board is gonna release him early." He grinned. "You want to know the real good part?"

Again, I refused to nod.

"Soon as he's out, he's gonna make you wish you'd

never come to Little Missouri. He's gonna run you outta town."

Junior's threat was an empty one. Arvid Drent, an old bachelor rancher I'd met when I came to Little Missouri, had put measures in place to keep me safe from Wentworth. Arvid no longer lived in Tipperary County, but his best friend Merle did. He knew to contact Arvid's lawyer and start proceedings against Junior should he try to harm me.

I stood. "Can you get a message to our mutual friend while you're in jail?"

"Me and my friend have our ways," he boasted.

I bet you do.

"Tell him his scare tactics won't work on me. Not with Merle and Arvid on my side."

Mike smirked. "He said that when you mentioned them, I was to tell you he's got a real good lawyer. He's prepared to take his chances."

I stood and walked to the door. Mr. Gunderson opened it. I went into the hallway."

"You weren't with him for long," the attorney said.

I shrugged. "He didn't have anything worthwhile to say. Where's the nearest restroom?"

"Right this way." He walked me down the hall and asked me to join him and Sheriff Sternquist back in the conference room when I was done. "He and I have much to discuss until you return. Take your time."

I went into the small bathroom, stood in front of the mirror, and braced my arms against the sink. My body began to tremble. The sink shook so hard I feared it might detach from the wall.

Somehow, neither the sink nor I fell to the floor.

CHAPTER 43

"I was ready to send out a search party," Rick said when I entered the crowded conference room. He sat next to Mr. Gunderson, who handed him a document to read. Victor and his students sat at the far end of the table finishing the pizza. My hands began to shake again. I balled them into fists and put them behind my back.

Rick frowned. "You okay?"

"I'm fine."

I pretended to look fine and went to the other end of the table to get my half-finished slice of pizza. It was gone, so I began stacking the pizza boxes and sneaked a glance at Rick. He didn't look like he was buying my act.

Teresa began to gather dirty napkins and toss them in the trash. "The sheriff said he's going to be here a while longer, but that we can go back to camp. Do you want to hitch a ride home?"

And not have to pretend I was fine in Rick's vehicle all the way to Little Missouri? "Yes, please!"

Teresa dropped her voice to a whisper. "Just let me sit next to Don. Okay?"

"You've got yourself a deal."

We were a subdued bunch in the van on the way home. I couldn't tell if the others were still digesting the news about Sheila, or if they were keeping their mouths shut because they were co-conspirators and didn't want to incriminate themselves.

I balled my sweatshirt into a pillow and wedged it between my head and the window. I tried to sleep, but my brain refused to switch off. Junior's message was on constant replay, interrupted only when a litany of my own questions rose to the surface.

Did I need to tell Rick and Cardo about Junior's threat? *Yes.*

Immediately? *No.*

Why not? *They might kick me off the team and close down the forensic lab.*

Then when? *Before Junior is released.*

Should I tell Dick? *Not until we know each other better.*

Was I being wise? *God, will you tell me if my decision is wise?*

Silence.

My internal hamster wheel of anxiety and the unending kaleidoscope of the day's events eventually wore me down. Teresa nudged me awake and said we were crossing the bridge into Little Missouri.

She passed me a couple tissues. "You might want to wipe up your drool. I've got more if you need them."

Ew!

Victor pulled the van into the schoolyard to drop me

off and was gone before I reached the landing stairs. My stomach growled as I unlocked the apartment. That half slice of pizza hadn't come close to satisfying my hunger. I was too ravenous for sleep and too tired to cook. A delectable aroma lured me into the kitchen where I saw a note on the counter. My name was written at the top in Dick's scrawl. I picked it up and began to read.

> *Jane,*
>
> *Aunt Hilda said you'd be hungry when you got here. There's ham and scalloped potatoes in the oven and salad in your refrigerator. She said to tell you that Velma let me in so you wouldn't worry. See you at church.*
>
> *Dick*

I devoured the food and went to bed. Had it not been for Merle's rooster, I would have slept through church. Instead, I woke after a sleep too short to make me feel rested and worried about falling asleep during Pastor Petersen's sermon.

I went into the kitchen, started the oven, and took butter from the fridge. I set it on a plate and put the plate on the warmest section of the stovetop right above the pilot light. It might be soft enough for me to make a coffee cake before church. Not for my breakfast, but for Dick to take to Hilda as a thank you for last night's supper.

The timing did indeed work out. I left the coffee cake cooling on the kitchen counter and drove to church. The mingled scents of cinnamon and nutmeg clung to my clothes as I walked into the foyer. I'd selected my outfit with great care and redone my hair several times. Dick and the sheriff were talking in the foyer when I walked in. From the way Dick looked at me when I came in, I knew my effort had been worth it. He grinned. Rick yawned.

"How long did you stay in Sturgis?" I asked him.

"Too long. Don't call this afternoon. I'll be taking a nap." He yawned again. "Gunderson is driving up tomorrow afternoon to depose Trudy and Renny. He'll do her first and him after school."

"Where at?"

"The Forest Service. Same as our last case. Would you mind bringing Renny after school and then sticking around to confer with me and Gunderson afterward?"

"I can do that."

Tiege bounded over and elbowed Rick in the ribs.

He yelped. "What'd you do that for?"

"Mom said I should practice for keeping you awake during the service." Tiege took aim again.

Rick caught his brother's arm. "Save it for the sermon, buddy. See you tomorrow, Jane. Good to talk to you, Dick." He led Tiege into the sanctuary and plunked him onto a pew.

I took Dick's hand. "Can you stop by my apartment after church? I have a gift for your aunt. To thank her for supper."

"What about me?" he teased. "I delivered it."

"Maybe she'll share it if you say please." I paused. "Hey, weren't you supposed to work for Joe at Fly Ranch yesterday and today?"

"Uh-huh. But when the ambulance call came in, one of the counselors who lives in the staff house volunteered to cover for me. When I got to the ranch this morning, he said he'd take my shift today too."

"Sounds like a nice guy."

"He is."

Pastor Petersen burst into the foyer and hurried into the sanctuary. We followed him down the aisle as Cookie began playing the introduction to the first hymn. Throughout the service I listened attentively, waiting for God to answer my plea for wisdom in light of Junior's threat. God remained frustratingly silent. Furthermore, he made not a peep when Dick stopped by to pick up Hilda's coffee cake. He didn't so much as chuckle when Velma barged in on us kissing in the kitchen.

"You talked to Corinne Wentworth lately?" she asked after Dick left, blushing a brilliant red I found quite attractive.

"No."

"I was out at her place yesterday dropping off a quilt for her to repair. She asked how you been doing." Velma dug a sealed envelope from her pocket. "She said to give you this soon as I could. I come right over when I seen you get here after church."

I took the envelope. "Thanks."

She crossed her arms and waited. "You gonna read it?"

"As soon as I'm alone."

Her eyes narrowed. "I could tell your mother what you and Dick was doing when I come in."

"Go ahead. She'll be thrilled."

"Hmph." She slammed the door on her way out.

I tore open the note.

Jane,

I thought you should know that Junior's first parole hearing is this fall. Perhaps as early as September. He and his lawyer are confident he has a good chance of being released. I advise you to share this turn of events with Rick Sternquist very soon. I will keep you informed of changes as I become aware of them.
Your friend,
Corinne

God had postponed his answer until I was by myself and he had my full attention. I had to admire how he'd used Corinne Wentworth as his still, small voice. He knew I respected her and would listen to what she had to say. Why he'd used Velma as his hands and feet to deliver the note was a mystery I had no desire to solve. If he decided to share his reasons, he knew where to find me.

Chapter 44

I had to tell Rick and Cardo about Junior's threat soon. With Junior's release still months away, soon was a relative term.

Could you clarify that, God? How soon is soon?

Silence.

Oh well. No harm in asking.

I took Corinne's note into the lab and locked it in the file cabinet for safekeeping. I'd wait to put it in an official folder until God provided an unambiguous timeline in the form of a second note or a lightning bolt, the note being my first preference. Though if the member of the Trinity in charge of special effects went with the lightning bolt, I hoped he would make Velma the delivery person again. I'd never heard of anyone who had wrestled lightning into submission, but I had no doubt our school janitor could.

At that point, I ran out of gas. The events from the day before caught up with me. Standing became a test of endurance, coherent thought a pipe dream. My body clamored for food and sleep. I spent the afternoon snacking and napping. And reading when I could keep my eyes open. I went to bed early and woke up ready for the last week of school. First up on the day's agenda was show-and-tell, starring Renny Berthold. Had roses been in bloom, I would have strewn his path with them as he strode to the front like a conquering hero.

"You know that house we saw right before the dinosaur dig?" he asked his classmates.

Their heads bobbed up and down.

"Me and my mom was inside there on Saturday. We found Miss Newell taped to a chair!"

The children swiveled their heads in my direction and waited for me to contradict him.

"He's telling the truth," I assured them.

"Want me to bring duct tape tomorrow so I can show what the bad guys done to her?" Renny asked.

"Yes," they said.

"No," I said.

They protested.

I held firm. "Renny," I said, "tell them how you drove your mom's car to town."

He jumped at the chance, and I let him go on longer than usual. The kid deserved every iota of glory and attention he received. When he wound down several minutes later, I said show-and-tell was over. His classmates didn't object, though he was the only student who'd had a turn.

The children waited until calendar time to go bonkers. I pointed out that this was not only Monday, but also the final Monday of the school year, and tomorrow was the final Tuesday.

"We only got today and tomorrow and then the pic-nic before school's done?" Cora marveled.

Jeremy kapowed. Renny sang backup on the second kapow. After that, the other boys added to the beat.

A wail rose above the din.

I glanced over at the kindergarteners. They were fine.

"I don't want school to end. Miss Newell won't be me and Renny's teacher anymore," normally self-possessed Elva sobbed.

Renny quit kapowing and buried his head in his arms. I reminded the two third graders that I would still be their music teacher, that they would see me on recess duty, and that they could stop by after school anytime they wanted. My reassurances sounded like cold comfort to my ears, but satisfied Renny and Elva for the moment. Both of them hugged me before and after every recess for the rest of the day. Elva broke down again at dismissal time and couldn't stop crying. I took her hand and walked with her to her mother's vehicle to explain why Elva was sad. Mary and I tried to comfort her but failed.

"You broke my heart, Miss Newell, and it can't be fixed"—she sobbed and blew her nose—"unless you say you'll be my fourth-grade teacher."

My heart broke knowing I couldn't give her what she wanted most. I returned to the school, fighting to maintain my own control and not break down in front of Renny. He was waiting for me on the landing, looking none too eager to talk to Mr. Gunderson. Wide-eyed and silent, he took my hand.

I gave it a squeeze and bent down. "You worried?"

His face crumpled. "I'm scared." He wrapped his arms around my neck and began to sob.

I rubbed his back and said, "You know how you told your story during show-and-tell this morning?"

I felt his nod against my neck.

"Was that scary?"

"No."

"Then pretend it's show-and-tell time again."

"Will you stay with me?" Each word was a puff of warm air on my skin.

"Yes. Your mom will be there too." I fished a tissue from my pocket and handed it to him. "Now blow."

He held my hand on the walk to the Forest Service office, where he sailed through the deposition. When he finished, Mr. Gunderson asked a few questions and said that was it. They were done.

Renny gave me a look that said, "You were right. Just like show-and-tell."

As he and his mom prepared to leave, she said, "You all come to The Bend when you finish up here. Your meals are on the house."

Mr. Gunderson stood and gave her a courtly bow. "How very generous. We will be there shortly." His next bow was for Renny. "Rarely have I met a young man as brave as you. I think you will grow up to do great things." After they left, he sat down and asked if I had any questions for him.

"Have you learned anything more from Mike Hansen?"

"No." He smiled sadly. "His lawyer is keeping him on a very short leash."

"What about Beanie and Sheila? Have you talked to them yet?"

"Their doctors advised we wait to question them until

Thursday to give them more time to recover. We will meet with each woman in her respective hospital room late that afternoon. The delay will also allow Miss Hundley to obtain and confer with counsel beforehand. You and the sheriff should be present. Will that be a problem for you, Miss Newell?"

"Not at all, though I do need to know which room Sheila is in now."

"Room 307 if memory serves. Right next to Bea—I mean Miss Lavender. Very convenient for her mother, I might add."

"Sheila's mother is there? That's good."

"No, no. Pardon the confusion. I was referring to Miss Lavender's mother. From what I understand, she visits Miss Hundley on a regular basis." He stood. "Shall we go to supper now? I would like to get to a hard-surfaced road before darkness falls. Driving on gravel is not my forte."

The café was almost empty when we got there. Even so, we restricted our conversation to harmless topics suitable to be overheard. Trudy hovered around our table throughout the meal. When she wasn't thanking us for being kind to Renny, she was refilling our water glasses and asking if our meals were to our liking. Had Mr. Gunderson not taken his leave, as he put it, on the early side, the customers who did trickle in would have felt neglected.

Rick and I left soon after. He offered me a ride home, but the evening was too lovely to waste. Blue sky, calm winds, cool air, and an orange sun sliding toward the western horizon accompanied me on the way home. The afternoon begged me to stay outside. I gave in and sat on the landing steps, reveling in the sounds of spring. A meadowlark singing in the vacant lot across Main Street. Someone starting a lawn mower. A dog barking in the distance.

Sheila had stolen more than fossils from a dig site, I thought as I lifted my face to the breeze. She had stolen springtime from Beanie. I hated her for it. I vowed to do everything I could to strengthen the case against her. I wanted to rob Sheila of every spring the law allowed.

My phone rang. I hurried inside and picked up the receiver. "Hello, this is Jane Newell."

"And this is Mrs. Dremstein. Do you have a minute?"

I had oodles of them, in fact, what with summer vacation just a few days away. What she had to say took thirty minutes once Betty cleared the party line and left the call.

"The first thing is that the janitors will be there later this week to install new windows in the forensic lab and your bedroom."

"Why the bedroom window? It wasn't damaged."

"True, but it would be as easy to remove as the other one. The safety of my teachers is of the utmost importance, which is why both windows are being replaced.

"The other thing you should be aware of is that the school board will be approving some staffing changes at tonight's meeting." She proceeded to delineate them and then said, "I can come over tomorrow at the end of the day to tell your students and their parents. Unless you would rather do it yourself."

"I can handle it."

"You sound quite confident."

"I am." With good reason, I said to myself after the

call ended. God was on a roll. He had spoken clearly for the second time in two days. This time, he had used my boss and a little girl whose broken heart had broken mine to show me what to do. By this time tomorrow, Elva's heart would be whole again. Mine would be too.

Chapter 45

Darryl, Larry, and the two windows arrived while I was drinking the last of the milk in the bottom of my cereal and about to pour my second cup of coffee. Boy, was I glad to have dressed before breakfast instead of leaving it until after.

I set down the bowl and held up the pot. "Want some?"

"That'd be real nice, Miss Newell." Darryl said.

"Got any more of that coffee cake from when we was here before?" Larry asked.

"It's long gone. If I'd had more warning that you were coming today, I'd have made a fresh one." I took out two mugs and set them beside the coffee maker. "Help yourselves."

I went to the bathroom and brushed my teeth. I had a sneaking suspicion that the janitors would hit me up for cereal and toast if I returned to the kitchen, so I snuck through the hallway that went past the girls' and boys' bathrooms to get to my classroom.

The day was less about teaching school and more about supervising my students as I set them to work cleaning our classroom. The noise level rose as the children cleared away the year's worth of papers and broken crayons that had gathered in their desks, as they argued with one another about whose turn it was to use the spray bottle, as they turned in their textbooks and packed them in cardboard boxes. The volume of their chatter and industry masked the sounds of hammering in my apartment as well as Darryl and Larry's bouts of swearing.

The janitors packed up and left as Liv McDonald led her students over. Mrs. Dremstein had called her after she'd spoken to me. Liv had called me after that. We decided to invite the parents to hear the announcement we would make at the end of the day. My students pushed their desks against the walls, and we arranged the students in a circle on the floor. As the parents began trickling in, some sat on the floor behind their kids. Others stood.

Mary Borgeson was the last to arrive. "Flat tire," she whispered, and then, "I better sit behind Elva instead of Stig. She's still bent out of shape about having a different teacher next fall."

Once Mary was situated, Liv announced that she and I would hand report cards to the parents before they left. Then she said, "Now, Miss Newell has news for you all."

"The school board made some staffing decisions at last night's meeting," I began.

"You're not leaving, are you?" Trudy asked.

I turned to her. "Whatever gave you that idea?"

"It's happened before," Liv said. "We kind of expect

first year teachers who weren't raised West River to get out soon as they can."

"I'm not leaving."

Cookie Sternquist clapped her hands together. "That's good." Several other parents began applauding.

I went on before the flattery could give me a big head. "You probably already know that next year's crop of five-year-olds is a big one. And that Mrs. McDonald's only losing one eighth grader. Because of that, the school board recommended hiring a part-time kindergarten teacher for next year. In the fall, Mrs. McDonald will be teaching fifth through eighth grade, and I'll teach first through fourth. Kindergarten will start in January as usual and will be held in the empty classroom. In other words, other than the eighth grader who's graduating, Liv and I will be teaching the same kids we have now."

Elva crossed the room and wrapped her arms around my waist before Mary could stop her. "I been wishing for this all year. I want you to be my teacher forever."

Her words made my heart swell until it threatened to pop out of my chest with a cartoonish boing.

My happy mood lasted until after Liv's class, my students, and their parents left the building. I went into my apartment to see the new windows. They passed muster, but the state of my bedroom and the forensic lab did not. I had hoped to finish the fingerprint analysis related to the investigation and run it to the post office before school in the morning. Rick and the county attorney would need them for Sheila Hundley and Mike Hansen's bail hearings before the week was out.

Instead, my afternoon and evening were spent picking bent nails and wood scraps out of the carpets, vacuuming up sawdust, washing and drying my bedding, putting the furniture Larry and Darryl had moved out of place back where it belonged, and dusting. In the process, I made good use of many of the vocabulary words the janitors and Mike Hansen had taught me lately. I hadn't exhausted them when I crawled between the covers and fell asleep.

I woke early the next morning and mixed batter for the two coffee cakes that would be my contribution to the school picnic. While they baked, I dressed and ate breakfast. Once they were cooling on the counter, I worked on the fingerprint analysis. The report came together quickly and contained what I hoped would convince the judge to set bail high enough to keep Mike Hansen behind bars and Sheila in police custody for the time being. On the way to the picnic, I stopped at the post office and mailed the reports.

"They'll be on the sheriff's desk this afternoon, or I'll resign my post." Dale Cunningham clicked his heels and gave me a snappy salute. "Glad to hear you'll be teaching our kids for another year, Miss Newell."

I wanted to say, "Me too," but my heart was swelling again, and the words couldn't squeeze through.

The weather was perfect for a picnic. When I pulled into the parking area at the Wickham Gulch, my students ran to greet me. They bickered about who got to carry my bag. To prevent a riot, I asked Elva to carry one coffee cake and Cora the other. I pulled a serving spatula out of my bag for Jeremy to carry, sunglasses for Winter Skye, and so on until only Tiege, Beau, and Renny remained. With great ceremony I gave the rattlesnake shovel to Renny and positioned him in front of me.

Renny held it like a royal scepter. Then, I took the other two boys' hands in mine. We walked behind Renny in solemn silence, undergirded by occasional giggles as our procession made its way to the picnic area.

It teemed with parents, grandparents, school kids, preschoolers, and babes in arms. Dick Phillips stood beside the ambulance, purely as a precautionary measure, he and Mary Borgeson assured me. Merle and Velma were supervising the parents who were cranking four old-fashioned ice cream freezers situated at the edge of the picnic grounds.

"You kids start whining," Velma announced as my students passed by, "and I'll snatch you over here to crank for a while."

I licked my lips. "Snippy cream?"

"Stupid question," Velma grumbled.

"And my eggs," Merle said.

Before lunch, there were three-legged races, egg and spoon relays, and water balloon fights organized by Pam Barkley, Linda Gibson, and Galva Swensen. Next up was a hike led by all the dads. After that, Cookie and Bud Sternquist, along with the Kellys and the Bertholds, uncovered the food.

"Time to eat," Cookie shouted. No one heard her. She was about to try again when a shrill whistle stilled the crowd. All eyes turned to its source.

Dick Phillips removed his fingers from his mouth. "I'll say grace," he said.

"Thank you, Dick," Bud said when the prayer ended. "Before we eat, I want to say a few words to Miss Newell and Mrs. McDonald. You both been through the wringer this past year. More outta school than in. We parents want you to know we admire how you kept showing up for our kids. We got you each a little something to show our appreciation."

Iva Kelly and Trudy Berthold came forward and gave Liv and me each a large box. I was speechless. Liv didn't say anything, so I think she was in the same boat.

Tiege careened toward me. "I can open it for you, Teacher!"

Bud picked him up by the shirt collar and dangled him in the air. "Let her be, Son."

Liv and I tore off the paper and opened our boxes. Hers contained a cowboy hat. I don't know much about them, but from the expression on her face and the reaction of the crowd, it had to be a stunner. My box contained a pair of pink cowboy boots. I hoped my expression didn't telegraph the vow I'd made last fall to never, ever own a pair of the ubiquitous West River foot-wear. I hoped my face didn't reveal the question that was spinning the hamster wheel in my brain. If it had only taken nine months for the residents of Little Missouri to make me break my cowboy-boot vow, how long until the other promise I'd made went out the window, the one to never, ever ride a horse?

Chapter 46

The boots fit perfectly, but I wore tennis shoes to Tipperary the next morning. Liv had warned me that checking out at the end of the school year was akin to moving out of a college dorm in the spring. She advised wearing old clothes and comfortable shoes.

"Bring your purse, too. Us country schoolteachers always go out for a late breakfast after we sign out," she said.

"Count me in," I said. "I'm driving to Rapid City in the afternoon, so I'll take my own car."

I appreciated my tennies as we lugged audiovisual equipment—film and filmstrip projectors, record players, overhead projectors, screens, stands and also wall maps—into the high school gymnasium.

My upper arm muscles were burning when I plopped the last box of textbooks on a table in the library. "I get bringing audiovisual equipment here for cleaning and maintenance, but why the textbooks?" I asked Liv.

"So we can haul them out again next fall, I guess."

We were dusty and sweaty when we walked down the hall to the school office where we were to turn in our grade books and file copies of the students' report cards in their permanent folders. Once those tasks were finished, we joined the line of teachers waiting to meet individually with Mrs. Dremstein so she could sign our check-out sheets.

"You gotta get her signature, or the business manager won't send your paychecks this summer," Liv explained.

When my turn came to meet with Mrs. Dremstein, she wanted to know how the Little Missouri parents and kids had reacted to the staffing changes.

"Very well," I assured her.

"What are your summer plans?" she asked as she gave my check-out sheet a cursory glance and signed it.

"I have some loose ends to tie up regarding the current investigation. Then I'll be with my parents in Sioux City for a few weeks. After that, I have no idea what the summer will bring. Rest and relaxation, I hope."

"I'm glad you signed your contract again, Jane. You're a strong addition to the Tipperary County Schools staff. I hope you'll be with us for many years to come." She stood and shook my hand. "Enjoy your summer."

"Same to you."

Full of warm fuzzies, stomach rumbles, and school's-out-for-the-summer vibes, I drove to the Nine Pins to celebrate. After feasting on hash browns, eggs, and bacon, I squeezed my too full stomach behind the Beetle's steering wheel and drove south on Highway 85. When I reached Rapid, I rolled down my window to enjoy the fine weather. This was the latest in the string of beautiful spring days Beanie had been deprived of because of Sheila.

What that woman had done to Beanie was unforgivable, I thought as I parked and walked toward the hospital. No matter what transpired today, I would show her no mercy. I was an hour early and considered passing the time with a snack from the vending machine. But my stomach was still full, and none of the junk food looked appealing. I settled on coffee and took it to the third-floor waiting area adjacent to Sheila's room. I sipped at my drink—it tasted terrible—and paged through a *Family Circle* magazine from December 1975. It was hopelessly out of date, but I was a sucker for Christmas issues. I was writing a sugar cookie recipe on the back of a check deposit slip when a series of noises next door, a heavy object dropping to the floor followed by something banging against the wall and a muffled shout, brought me to my feet.

With my purse in one hand and my ballpoint pen in the other, I burst through the door of Sheila's room. Her bed was elevated, and a man wearing a deputy sheriff's uniform was bending over her. He blocked my view of her from the waist up, but I could see her legs thrashing and kicking. Something about the officer's uniform felt off, but it took a few seconds to pinpoint what it was. The fabric the shirt was made of was too thin. The patches on the sleeves were carelessly sown into place. The hem of the trousers touched the floor. His appearance was not that of a professional officer of the law. It was that of an imposter.

I rummaged inside my purse until my fingers closed around my keys. Using them as makeshift brass knuckles and my pen as a miniature dagger, I tiptoed up behind the man and stabbed my weapons into either side of his fleshy neck. He bellowed and twirled around to face me. His elbow made direct contact with my left eye. It began to throb. I could feel it start to swell. My pen fell to the floor, and I closed my fingers around my purse strap. I wound the strap around his neck. He shook me off like Merle's rooster shedding feathers. Then he wrapped his large hands around my neck and began to squeeze. I clawed at them, then reached up and raked my finger-nails down his cheeks. He squeezed harder. The light around me faded. I gasped for air. I waited for my life to flash before my eyes. Instead, there was a clang above my head. The hands around my neck loosened, and my attacker slid to the floor. I bent double and sucked air into my thirsty lungs until my vision cleared.

Sheila stood and patted my back. "Do you need a nurse, Jane?"

"No." I sucked in more air and glanced at her. She wore a pretty, pink bathrobe over her hospital gown. The pink complimented the band of purple raccoon bruises around her eyes, but I was more interested in the white enameled bedpan in her hand. It looked heavy enough to crack open a skull. Which, if the pool of blood under the deputy's head was any indication, it had.

When he began to stir sooner than a person with a cracked skull should, I revised my assessment. Sheila had split open his skin but nothing more. I wanted to borrow the bedpan and thump his head in the worst way but thought the better of it. Instead, I asked Sheila to push the call button. I rummaged through the metal stand by her bed until I found several rolls of gauze bandages and one of white tape. She was swaying on her feet when I handed the tape to her.

"Get in bed," I ordered, "and tear off several lengths of gauze."

I used the gauze bandage to bind the deputy's wrists together and secure them with tape. His ankles required twice as much gauze and the remaining tape to bind and attach them to the foot of the bed. As I worked, I saw that the patches on his uniform shirt were generic, he was wearing black tuxedo trousers, and his shoes were scuffed. He was now fully conscious, watching my every move.

"You're not a sheriff's deputy, are you?"

He turned away and pressed his lips together.

A nurse breezed through the door. "What do you need, honey?" she asked Sheila. When she saw me kneeling beside the trussed-up guard, her white, rubber-soled shoes squeaked to a stop. She puffed up and pointed at the blood on the floor. "What did you do to him?"

"Has the sheriff arrived?" I asked.

She nodded.

"Go get him."

She held her ground. "You need to leave."

"Rick," I yelled. "Room 307. Get in here!"

Footsteps pounded along the hallway and into the room. They came to a halt near the foot of the bed. "What did you do to the sheriff's deputy?" Rick asked.

I didn't take my eyes off the man. "Ask me again after you take a closer look."

He knelt down. He scanned the miscreant from the crown of his poorly cut hair to the tips of his worn shoes.

"Who are you?" Rick asked. "And where's the deputy assigned to guard the patient in this room?"

The man narrowed his eyes and spit, first in the sheriff's face and then in mine.

Rick took out his handkerchief and handed it to me. "Wipe your face."

Our eyes met. His jaw dropped. He got to his feet and gently helped me up. His solicitousness was frightening.

"What's wrong?" I asked.

"You see those?" He pointed to Sheila's technicolored eyes. "You two are a matched set."

Chapter 47

The assault on Sheila convinced me that it was time to tell Rick about Junior Wentworth's threat. However, I was escorted to the nurses' station to ice my eye while he transferred the fake deputy to police custody and searched for Deputy Cole Minor. After a member of the housekeeping staff found him gagged and trussed up in a supply closet, Rick told me to inform Beanie and Mrs. Lavender that there'd been an unforeseen delay. He and the county attorney would arrive to interview her as soon as they could.

When I found Beanie in her room, she was wearing her own pajamas and a robe rather than a hospital gown. She sat in a chair rather than her bed. Victor, Don, Frank, and Teresa were with her, and all of them were chowing down on Big Macs and fries.

"Wow!" I paused in the doorway, still holding an ice pack to my face. "Beanie, you look great!"

"What did you do to your eye?" she asked.

I didn't want to go into details in front of the dig

team and made a vague reply about my clumsiness. Then I delivered Rick's message and steered the conversation back to her. "Any word on when you'll be dismissed?"

"The doctors say Mom can take me home on Saturday."

"All the way to Sioux City?" I asked.

"Yup. Dad flew there a few days ago to coordinate the therapy appointments I'll need once I go home. He says they're ready for me."

"That's wonderful! How about the rest of you?" I asked her visitors.

Victor spoke for the lot of them. "We can't shut down the dig site and leave until the sheriff gives the okay. Who knows when that'll be."

"The investigation has been clipping along lately. He may have more information later this afternoon." I gave Beanie a few seconds to mention her upcoming interview if she wanted. She didn't.

"I'll leave you to your meal." I went into the hall and saw Mrs. Lavender come out of Sheila's room. I walked over to her. "Do you visit Sheila often?"

"When I can." Beanie's mom shook her head. "Can you believe that no one from Sheila's family has come to see her?"

I believed it completely. I didn't want to see Sheila even though she had saved my life not two hours ago. What she'd done to Beanie stuck in my craw. I asked Mrs. Lavender how she could stomach being in the same room with the woman who had hurt her daughter.

Mrs. Lavender sighed. "I don't know if I can put it into words, but I'll try. For one thing, she's young and needs a mother. For another, she's repeatedly said how bad she feels about what she did to Beanie. I was very angry after Beanie's accident. I wanted to hate the person who'd hurt her. My bitterness grew with each day she was in a coma. Nursing my grudge was exhausting. I had nothing left for Beanie. I came to a crossroads after meeting Sheila. I could either hang onto my hatred and bitterness, or I could forgive her and trust God to do justice."

I didn't know what to say. My anger toward Sheila was a great comfort to me. I liked having it close at hand, though I knew better than to admit it. Mrs. Lavender met my gaze. It felt as though she was looking into the dark corner of my soul where my anger lay swaddled in a blanket of lies. My discomfort grew under Mrs. Lavender's gaze.

Rick and Mr. Gunderson came down the hall. I greeted them with a fervor I usually reserved for Cookie Sternquist's cinnamon rolls or the end of the school day.

Rick introduced Beanie's mom to the county attorney and then asked, "Is she up to an interview?"

"More than up to it. Just wait a few minutes for her company to wrap up their visit."

A few minutes turned into fifteen and then twenty. I went to the nurses' station for more ice and then to the restroom to look at my shiner in the mirror. Rick hadn't exaggerated the extent of the damage. Before leaving town, I needed to stop at a drug store for more concealer and foundation. I didn't want Dick to think he was taking a raccoon to dinner and a movie tomorrow.

Eventually Mrs. Lavender and the dig team cleared out, and we assembled in Beanie's room. Mr. Gunderson handed out coffee in paper cups. Rick spread an assortment of candy bars on Beanie's tray table. While Gunderson tested the tape recorder, we sipped, nibbled, and engaged in small talk.

"I believe all systems are now go," he declared. "Sheriff Sternquist, you may commence."

Rick led Beanie through the initial stage of the interview, asking for her name, her age, and so on. Once those details were on record, he asked, "Can you describe what happened the afternoon of Monday, April 24?"

"I'll do the best I can," she said. "My short term memory is still playing tricks on me. I do remember staying in the kids' camp area after the children left to put away the tools we'd used. It was too early for supper when I finished, so I went to the lab tent to enter the kids' finds in the logbook. Since Victor had assigned me to run the tent, I'd lost several artifacts. I felt terrible about it. To prevent it from happening again, I'd decided not to go to bed until each day's finds were recorded and stored where they belonged. What I couldn't finish before supper, I did after. When I got to the tent, a particularly rare fossil I'd misplaced a while ago was sitting on the table. At least I think so.

"See, this is where things got weird. Since the accident, my memory has been mixing up when stuff happened. Some things I remember as happening the day of my accident may have actually occurred two weeks earlier. I'm pretty sure that some lost artifacts had shown up before the day I got hurt, but I can't be sure. I do remember Sheila coming into the tent that afternoon and me telling her about misplacing the artifacts. She suggested I get down the logbook so we could cross-check them together. She got the step stool. I climbed up, reached for the logbook, and lost my balance."

She stopped to sip her coffee. "That's the last thing I remember until I woke up."

Rick asked questions to clarify a few details and to see if her story would change. As I expected, it did not. What she said tallied with the story Sheila had told me in the ranch house—with one striking difference. Beanie said she'd blamed herself for losing the artifacts. Sheila had assumed Beanie was about to accuse her. Would Sheila mention that when Rick interviewed her?

One thing was certain. Beanie had climbed the step stool at Sheila's urging and had suffered a near-fatal injury because of it. Had she lost her balance? Or had Sheila jiggled the step stool and made her fall? We might never know. Either way, Beanie had spent a month in a coma because of Sheila, and Sheila deserved to pay for what she'd done.

Forgiveness be damned.

CHAPTER 48

A nurse bustled in, took Beanie's pulse, and studied her tired, pale face. "I think you need a rest if you want to be in good shape for the drive home on Saturday. Let's get you into bed."

Rick, Mr. Gunderson, and I filed out of the room and went to the waiting area where Beanie's mom was sitting.

"Is the interview over?" she asked.

"It is for now," Rick said. "The nurse says she's tuckered out and needs to rest. Mr. Gunderson or I can stop by tomorrow if there's a need. Or we can call once you get her home."

The county attorney checked his watch. "It's past time to interview Sheila. I wonder if her lawyer has arrived."

"She's in with her now," Mrs. Lavender said.

"In that case, you must excuse us." Gunderson bowed and went toward Sheila's room. Rick and I said hasty goodbyes and fell into line behind him.

Deputy Minor was standing outside the door. He appeared no worse for the wear after his stint in the supply closet. He knew who we were but checked our drivers' licenses anyway. Sheila was sitting up in bed, still wearing the pretty pink bathrobe over her hospital gown. A woman in a conservative blue jacket and skirt, nylon stockings, and sensible blue pumps occupied the chair beside the bed. Her short, gray hair lent her a motherly air, though her eagle eyes warned us not to mess with her. She rose and said she was Sheila's lawyer. She must have said her name, but her next words pushed it right out of my head.

"Against the advice of counsel," the lawyer stated, her expression sour and her words clipped, "my client wants to make a full confession."

Sheila proceeded to do just that. She started by disclosing the sexual affair she had initiated with Victor when she was a junior in college. She stated that her sole purpose was to become his research assistant after graduation in order to advance her long-term career goal to become a paleontologist. She was awarded a twelve-month assistantship that began in the spring of 1977. Among her many duties was researching and recommending a location for a month-long dig in the spring of 1978. She scouted locations at the Swensen, McDonald, and old Lindgren ranches during the summer after her assistantship began. She recommended the inferior Lindgren site because an employee representing the ranch's new owner made her a very attractive offer. He would arrange to collect the occasional artifact from her, and she would receive cash payments based on what they might fetch from interested buyers.

Mr. Gunderson stopped her. "Who was this employee?"

"Michael Hansen."

"Did he say what he did with the fossils?"

"Just that he delivered them to the person above him in the pecking order."

"Are you certain Hansen was employed by the Wentworths?"

"Yes. He lived in the ranch house near the dig."

"Was the same true of the person who took the artifacts from Hansen?"

"I guess I assumed he did." Sheila paused. "But I don't really know."

"How did you transfer the artifacts?"

Sheila licked her lips before continuing. "When I used the outhouse at night, I would hide them in the antler pile beside the back door of the ranch house."

"How did Hansen know they were there?"

"He had me arrange sticks next to it in a certain pattern. When he picked up the fossils, he stacked the sticks behind the pile. When he was out of town for more than a day or two, I put them in packages with love letters and stupid mementos and gave them to Trudy at The Bend. He would go to the bar when he got back and get them from Trudy. I asked her to keep things on the down-low so Victor wouldn't find out Mike and I were having a fling. The system was fail-safe until the rest of the team threatened to mutiny unless Victor did something about Beanie's terrible cooking. His solution was to switch her to the lab tent and me to the kitchen. That's when the system began to break down."

She then repeated what she'd told me at the ranch house and also explained why she had taken the fossilized bone to the school during the blizzard.

"By then, I'd found it, hidden it, and nearly lost it enough times to make me paranoid. I wanted it within reach. The cupboard in Jane's classroom seemed like the perfect solution. Then that grump of a janitor came in and started searching your desk and cupboards. She kept muttering about a key. I snuck the fossil over to the other building when Teresa was asleep and the men were waiting in your apartment for the shower. The day we left, the guys from the Forest Service made us pack up and leave so fast, I couldn't get to it."

She also admitted to breaking into the forensic lab to retrieve the fossil and steal the fingerprint cards and photographs. The color drained from her face, the purple bruises around her eyes accentuating her paleness. "I put the fossilized bone in the van. Did you find it?"

"We did." Rick said.

"Thank goodness. I'm ninety-nine percent sure it's from a T-Rex. Very rare. Very valuable. Please don't let it fall into the wrong hands."

Besides your own? I wanted to ask. But the tape recorder was running, and I thought the better of it.

"Where are the fingerprint cards and the photographs?" Rick asked.

"I burned them."

Mr. Gunderson and Rick had several more questions. Sheila answered them without hesitation. When they were done, Rick turned to me. "Is there anything you want to ask?"

I looked Sheila straight in the eyes. "Why did you do it?"

She met my gaze. "I have wanted to be a paleontologist since I was a kid. My parents couldn't have cared less. I needed a way to finance graduate school while building my resume. When Hansen's offer landed in my lap, I snapped it up." She stared at her hands. "That was wrong."

"You misunderstood my question," I said. "I want to know why you decided to confess."

She lifted her chin and smiled for the first time since we'd entered the room. "Beanie's mom."

Gunderson's head snapped up. "Are you saying she coerced your confession?"

"No. Not at all. She never asked me to do anything. I tried to tell her what I'd done, and she said it didn't matter."

"In that case," the attorney said, "I would be interested to know what Mrs. Lavender did that led to your confession."

"She asked when my mother was coming. When I said my parents had written me off years ago, she volunteered to be both my mother and Beanie's while we were here. She visited every day. She sat beside me and held my hand. She said that no matter what I'd done or why, she forgave me. I asked her how she could possibly say that. She said she'd been forgiven and wanted me to experience it too." Sheila began to cry. "I'm the reason her daughter got hurt. The least I can do is to tell you and her the truth."

Mr. Gunderson turned off the tape recorder. "Thank you, Sheila." He nodded to the other lawyer. "In light of her confession, your client will be arrested. If she continues to cooperate, I'm sure we can arrange for an option other than jail upon her release from the hospital."

Rick stood and cleared his throat. "Sheila Hundley, you are—"

"Not yet!" I jumped up and went to the door. "I'll be right back. Hang on a second."

I went to Beanie's room. She was asleep. Her mother sat beside her bed, reading. I cleared my throat, and she looked up. "Can I borrow you for a minute?"

She closed her book and stood. "Of course."

We went into the hall, where I explained what was about to happen to Sheila. Together we entered her room. Mrs. Lavender went to stand beside the bed. She took Sheila's hand and didn't let go until long after the arrest was made. Until long after my tears dried. Until Rick was able to speak again. Until Mr. Gunderson bowed and smiled his sad, hopeful smile. Until Sheila's lawyer snapped her briefcase shut and stood. Until all of us, save Sheila and Mrs. Lavender, left the room quiet and awestruck by the holiness we had witnessed in an ordinary hospital room.

Chapter 49

Rick, Gunderson, and I watched Sheila's lawyer and her sensible pumps clip down the hallway. When she was out of earshot, I said, "There's something I need to tell you."

The two men looked at me expectantly.

"Can we go in there?" I motioned toward the chairs in the empty lounge area. I needed to sit down for this. Once we were all situated, I took a deep breath and made my own confession.

After hearing about the message from Junior that Mike Hansen had relayed to me, Rick came as close to unglued as I'd ever seen him. "You should have told us this immediately Why on earth did you think withholding information pertinent to our investigation was acceptable?"

"I sort of assumed Wentworth's message was about a past case and specific to me rather than pertaining to this one. Sheila's assault is making me reevaluate."

Gunderson remained silent while Rick and I discussed how to proceed. Make that *he* told *me* how it would proceed. Being the one at fault, I had no choice but to go along with him.

Rick was convinced that whoever had dispatched Sheila's attacker might send someone after me next. When we left the hospital, he bumper-hugged my Beetle on the trip to the Sturgis jail. Then he and Mr. Gunderson stayed by my side while I filed assault and battery charges against Mike Hansen and Sheila. In light of Mrs. Lavender's kindness toward Sheila, I was no longer keen on pressing charges against her until Rick spelled it out for me.

"No judge will take your charges against Hansen seriously unless you charge her too."

Mr. Gunderson cleared his throat and said, "Because she confessed, I will negotiate a plea deal with her attorney. It is my hope that our efforts will result in a lighter sentence for her. "

"I'm counting on you," I told him. He bowed and gave me a woeful smile.

Rick walked with me to where the Beetle was parked. "You might be interested to know that Sheila is pressing charges against the man who assaulted her in the hospital. She says she assumed he was a friend of Mike Hansen's, the way he went in and out of the house next to the dig site on a regular basis."

"When did she tell you that?"

"She didn't. She told Mrs. Lavender, and Mrs. Lavender called the jail here and left a message."

"Did he work for the Wentworths?"

"Don't know yet. You can bet Rapid City and Meade County law enforcement will find out. They show no mercy to culprits who attack one of their own. If a link between the Wentworths and Sheila's attacker is found, they'll show up at Junior's parole hearing en masse to testify against him."

Those words were music to my ears.

Rick stuck close to my car during the entire hundred-mile trip from Sturgis to Little Missouri. As I parked, he pulled up beside me. Darkness had fallen, and he walked me to my apartment. He had me wait in the entryway while he checked my apartment and classroom for, as he put it, "undesirable elements."

When he sounded the all clear, I went into the living room. A sleeping bag had been unrolled on the couch, and an overnight bag sat on the end table. I went closer and sniffed. The faint odor of cigarette smoke rose from both of them.

I narrowed my eyes. "Tell me you didn't."

Rick started to speak, but was interrupted by a pounding at the door. He went into the entryway and escorted Velma to the living room.

Clearly, our paradigms of what constituted desirable and undesirable elements were diametrically opposed. He considered a woman whose evil eye sent grown men and women packing to be a desirable element. I, on the other hand, considered a woman who would wait until I fell asleep to turn my home upside down in search of the key to the forensics lab to be undesirable.

She grabbed me by the elbow, steered me to the kitchen table, and plunked me into a chair like I was a five-year-old.

"You sit here and think about how stupid you've been while I make hot cocoa and heat up the cinnamon rolls

I brung. I got enough for you too, Sheriff, so sit yourself down."

Okay, so maybe she did have a few desirable elements.

She bustled around the kitchen until the food was ready. Then she sat down and spoke to Rick. "Here's what me and Betty and Merle come up with after you talked to us."

When had Rick done that?

"I'm gonna stay with Jane for two nights. Merle's gonna sleep in his truck in the schoolyard with his gun handy until she leaves on Saturday."

"I'm not going anywhere on Saturday," I protested.

"You are now," Rick snapped.

"Me and Merle was in favor of you leaving tomorrow until Betty said you had a date with Dick Phillips."

What had possessed Betty to break her promise to keep our date to herself?

Rick conceded that the extra day was for the best. "It'll give you time to pack for your trip and make sure the case file and evidence are ready to turn over when you leave."

"It works out real good, don't it? You and Dick can drop it off at the sheriff's office on your way to supper in Belle Fourche." Velma smiled her real smile, not the imitation one. Her pleasure with how she and Rick were orchestrating my life was unmistakable.

"Have you given Dick your restaurant recommendation?" I asked.

The sarcasm went over her head. "That's a real good idea. I'll call him in a bit. I ain't seen the movie they got showing at the theater. You can tell me about it tomorrow night when you get here. I'll wait up."

Leaving town on Saturday felt more attractive by the second. "Where am I going?"

"To Sioux City see your parents."

"My parents?"

Velma stared at me like I was the one who'd lost my mind. "You was already planning to visit them. Betty already let 'em know you're coming a little sooner than expected and staying longer. Doris said that's real good and don't call tomorrow when the rates are high. Just give her a ring before you take off Saturday so she knows when to expect you."

I inhaled and was working myself up to telling Velma and Merle and Betty and anyone else Rick had roped into his scheme to mind their own business. I was a grown woman, perfectly capable of managing case files, my dating life, and travel plans. Furthermore, if they so much as dared to suggest what I should wear on my date with Dick, I would—

Rick held up a warning hand. "It's a lot to ask of you Jane. I know that. But I need to find out whether or not the fossil smuggling and the attack on Sheila in the hospital are linked to the Wentworths. To do that, Cardo and I have to interview Junior in prison, locate the Wentworths' business manager, and lodge a complaint with the parole board to prevent or at least delay Junior's early release. Even with Cardo, Gunderson, Rapid City, and Meade County law enforcement assisting me, it's going to take us a good while to do that. We just don't have additional manpower to provide you with the protection needed ensure your safety here in Little Missouri. A visit to your parents in Sioux City will give us breathing room."

I had to give Rick credit. He had laid out a darn good rationale for me getting out of town. "How long do you need?"

"Two weeks. Maybe three."

"And you or Cardo will call when there are new developments, right?"

"Yes."

I hated to give in, but it had to be done. I looked at him and then at Velma. "It's a deal."

Merle pulled up in his truck about then. Velma put a plate of cinnamon rolls in Rick's hands and told him to deliver them to Merle. She immediately called dibs on the bathroom and disappeared. While she sang in the shower, I removed the key to the lab from the freezer and carried it into my bedroom along with a roll of duct tape. I changed into pajamas, crawled under the covers, and taped the key to my belly button.

Go ahead and turn my apartment upside down, Velma. I'll be sleeping like a baby while you do.

Yawning, I rolled onto my stomach and fell asleep.

Chapter 50

Neither Velma nor Merle was awake when I got up in the morning. I took pity on them after their night in makeshift beds and made Early Bird Coffee Cake for breakfast. Once it was baking and the coffee was brewing, I went into my bedroom and changed into an old T-shirt and blue jeans. The duct tape and key would remain in place until later. Then I returned to the kitchen to check the cake.

"That better not be what you're wearing on your date with Dick."

I yelped at the sound of Velma's voice and turned to look at her. All I could see were two beady eyes peering from a slit in her sleeping bag.

"Your love life ain't worth two nights with me sleeping on this sofa if you ain't gonna cooperate." She poked her head out of the sleeping bag. "Now quit standing there with your lips flopped open like a wide-mouthed bass and get me a cup a coffee, why don't you?"

I brought her coffee but didn't respond to her comment about my clothes. I had a nice outfit picked out for my date but liked the idea of letting her stew in her own juices for a while. Both my bodyguards were pulled up to the table when the coffee cake came out of the oven. When they pushed away, the coffee pot was empty and the cake pan held only crumbs.

"We-ull," Merle said after he'd scraped the crumbs from the pan and downed them. "Snippy's waiting to be milked. I suppose you ain't got time to copy out the *receipt* for what you made us with what you got goin' today, do you, Teacher?"

"I don't, but Velma will be happy to write it out after Dick picks me up this afternoon. While she's at it, she can tell you what kind of sugar to use. In case you find the ingredient list to be as unclear as she did."

She glared like the rattlesnake I'd killed. I decided it would be wise to lay off teasing her for the rest of the day. It wasn't easy, what with her dogging my footsteps while I did laundry, cleaned out my refrigerator, and packed. She removed clothes and shoes from my suitcase and replaced them with what she thought was necessary. She complained when I removed her substitutions and repacked the clothes I'd chosen in the first place. When her interference became intolerable, I went to the bathroom and ripped the duct tape—it hurt like the dickens—from my belly button. Then I locked myself in the lab and organized the case file and gathered evidence bags for Rick. Velma shouted dire warnings from the living room, which I tuned out by praying for her to lose her voice.

I came out of the lab at around one and locked it again. Velma made lunch and called Merle when it was ready. She was in a foul mood, so he shoveled down his food and limped off faster than a centipede with a peg leg. I grabbed the roll of duct tape and the clothes for my date and fled to the bathroom. Velma hollered at me through the bathroom door. To drown out her voice, I stayed in the shower until the water ran cold. I dressed carefully and taped the key inside my cowboy boots. Velma didn't stop talking while I did my hair and make-up. I stayed in the bathroom until shortly before Dick was to arrive.

When I came out of the bathroom wearing a sundress the same shade of pink as my boots, I stopped in front of Velma and pointed my finger at her. "Don't you start."

She did not.

Dick arrived a few minutes later and picked me up, along with a bunch of other stuff. First, he loaded my large suitcases into the Beetle. While he went back for the next load, I locked and guarded the car to prevent Velma from repacking the contents of the suitcases when no one was looking. Dick returned with the banker box containing the case files and evidence. He put it in his truck bed so we could hand it over to the sheriff in Tipperary. Finally, he opened the passenger door to the truck. I climbed in.

"Nice boots," he said, chuckling.

"Not you, too!" I arranged the skirt of my sundress and crossed my ankles.

A half an hour later, Rick held open the door as Dick carried the box into the sheriff's office.

"Nice boots," Rick said.

"Don't you start." I untaped the lab key, gave it to him

for safekeeping, and held Dick's hand on the way to his truck.

Our date was more comfortable than my boots. While we ate, he asked me what it was like growing up with a dad in a wheelchair. I asked him what it was like growing up in Alaska. His story was as foreign to me as my story was to him. I said I'd like to meet his parents and see where he'd been raised. He said he'd like to meet my parents and the Moys––Uncle Tim, Aunt Wanda, as well as their four kids. But not quite yet, we both agreed.

The movie *Saturday Night Fever* starring John Travolta was disappointing. We made the most of the evening by stealing kisses in the back row of the theater. Between Velma waiting up in my apartment and me leaving for Iowa tomorrow, what else were we to do?

She was waiting at the door when Dick brought me home and was not pleased with my report of the evening's activities.

"You left out all the good stuff," she grumbled.

Indeed, I had.

Her grumbling resumed when I declined her offer of breakfast the next morning.

"I want to get on the road. I'll gas up in Belle Fourche and grab food there." Before she could argue, I rang Betty and asked her to call my parents.

"Hi Mom. I'm leaving now."

"We are so excited to see you," she trilled. "You're a good daughter to visit your parents so soon after your school year ends."

If she only knew.

Merle drove ahead of me to Rick's house in Tipperary. Rick drove behind me from there to Belle Fourche.

He stood guard while I filled my tank and bought break-fast. Once he felt sure we hadn't been followed, we said our goodbyes.

I got in the car and turned the key. "Will you call and issue an all clear the minute you know its safe to come home?"

"Missing Dick already, are you?"

"A little," I admitted. "Mostly I don't want Junior and his crew to think they can scare me off."

"There's not a person in Tipperary County, including Junior, who thinks you frighten easy, Jane. He's the one who's worried about what you're gonna dig up against him." He gave the hood of my car two quick pats. "Get on your way now. You got good people in Iowa waitin' to see you."

I waved, rolled up the window, and settled in for the long drive. It was long and blissfully uneventful until I walked into my parents' home.

"Surprise," they yelled.

"Surprise!" yelled Uncle Tim and Aunt Wanda, Danielle, Gabrielle, Juliette, and their youngest, five-year-old Donatello.

"Surprise!" yelled Mr. Lavender, Mrs. Lavender, and Beanie.

"Did we surprise you?" Mom asked.

"Completely."

"Supper's ready." Mom announced. "Are you hungry?"

"In a minute. I need to let Betty know I'm here."

Uncle Tim stopped me. "Before you do that, we've got one more surprise. Donatello, would you like to do the honors?"

Donatello waited until we were all looking at him. "Me and Mom and Dad and my sisters and Uncle Harold and Aunt Doris are gonna come to Little Misery this summer. We're gonna be there two whole weeks!"

Once I recovered from this second surprise, I went to the phone, rang Betty, and asked her to connect me to Rick Sternquist, wherever he might be.

"Jane," he said, "what's wrong?"

"You sound like my mom." In a few short sentences I acquainted him with my family's vacation plans. "Before they come, I need to know they will be safe."

"They'll be safe."

"How do you know?"

"Because Little Missouri's citizens take care of their people. And their people's people, too."

I hung up, called Betty, and asked her to ring the Striders. Hilda answered, and I asked if Dick was there.

"Give me a minute," she replied.

"Did your parents puww off the surprise party?" Betty whispered while we waited for Dick to come to the phone. "Wouwd you wike me to hang up?"

"Totally surprised. Would you hang up once Dick's on the phone?"

His voice came on the line. "Hi, Jane."

"I'm at my parents'."

"I miss you already."

I missed him too and said so. "One more thing," I added.

He waited.

"My parents and the Moys are coming to Little Missouri for two weeks this summer. At my apartment."

Silence.

"It's a total surprise, way sooner than either of us expected. I won't be offended if you make yourself scarce while they're here."

More silence.

"Please say something, Dick. Tell me what you're thinking."

"Oh!" He sounded like he'd assumed I could read his mind. "I'm thinking I should start building your dad's ramp."

We said our goodbyes, and I sat down to eat with my family. We bowed our heads, and Dad prayed. He was thanking God for the meal set before us and the hands that had prepared it and was well into further thanks for the previous night's bountiful precipitation in the form of three-quarters of an inch of gentle rain when my own still, small voice spoke up.

Dick's a keeper, Jane. You know that, right?

Did I ever.

Early Bird Coffee Cake

- 2 1/2 cups flour
- 2/3 cup softened shortening
- 2 cups brown sugar
- 1 cup buttermilk
- 1/2 teaspoon salt
- 2 eggs
- 1/2 teaspoon soda
- 1/2 teaspoon nutmeg
- 1/2 teaspoon cinnamon
- 2 teaspoons baking powder

1. Heat oven to 350 degrees.
2. Mix all dry ingredients thoroughly in a large bowl.
3. Cut in shortening.
4. Remove one cup of the mixture and reserve for topping.
5. Add eggs and buttermilk, stirring by hand until batter is still slightly lumpy.
6. Pour into greased 9 x 13 pan.
7. Sprinkle dry mixture on top.
8. Bake for 35 to 40 minutes. Do not over-bake!

Author's Note

The northwest corner of South Dakota is home to numerous dinosaur finds. It, along with southeastern Montana and southwestern North Dakota, are part of the Hell Creek Formation. Geologists and paleontologists have been digging up fossils there for over one hundred years. South Dakota Stan, one of the most complete T-Rex skeletons found to date, was discovered by Stan and Steve Sacrison in 1987. They were residents of Harding County, South Dakota, which is known as the T-Rex capital of the world due to the large number of fossils discovered there. The Sacrisons were assisted by Pete Larson of the Black Hills Institute of Geological Research. In 2020, Stan was sold through Christie's Auction House for a record $31.8 million dollars to the future Natural History Museum Abu Dhabi. Stan will be the museum's centerpiece when it opens in 2025.

My husband, 3-year-old son, and I moved from Harding County to Iowa in 1985. For years afterward, I followed the dinosaur discoveries through articles in the county newspaper, *Nation's Center News* (NCN). My thought after reading each article was always the same: My students would have loved a field trip to a dinosaur dig! As time went on, NCN reported more dinosaur discoveries. The national news reported on the astronomical prices fossils from the area had garnered.

The idea for *See Jane Dig!* came after reading about smuggled dinosaur bones being sold on the black market to private collectors. My story is a total fabrication. Creating an authentic setting required research to stay true to how dinosaur digs were conducted in the late 1970s and 1980s. John R. Horner's book, *Digging Dinosaurs*, provided many details about dig camps in southeastern Montana during that time period.

I'd also like to thank John Carter, Harding County's local paleontologist, for sharing his experiences in our long and fascinating phone interview. Many thanks to Wally and Linda Stephens, the long-time owners and editors of NCN, for their faithful reporting on dinosaur discoveries in the area, and to Nancy Sainsbury Johnson, who stepped into the Stephens' shoes when they retired. Many thanks also to Darrah Steffen, geologist and paleontology curator at the Pioneer Trails Regional Museum in Bowman, North Dakota. Hiram and I still talk about the day we spent with you on a paleontology site tour followed by an afternoon in the museum's fossil lab. It was an informative, eye-opening, and magical day. I am grateful for how you translated your expertise and knowledge in ways we could understand.

If you're ever in the area and have a chance to go on one of the museum's paleo tours, it's well worth your time and money. Hiram and I advise taking plenty of water and snacks. Jane advises taking a rattlesnake shovel. You probably won't need it, but what if you do?

About the Author

Jolene Philo discovered Laura Ingalls Wilder and Encyclopedia Brown in elementary school and has been fascinated by the prairie and mysteries ever since. She's a voracious reader of fiction, biography, and creative non-fiction. Imagine her surprise when she became the author of several non-fiction books for the special needs and disability community. The *West River Mystery Series* combines her love of mysteries and northwest South Dakota's short grass prairie, where she and her husband Hiram lived for seven years when they were first married. Jolene and Hiram live in central Iowa with their daughter, son-in-law, and their two children. Jolene instills book love into her grandchildren by reading to them as often as she can. You can keep up with her reading and writing adventures at her website, www.jolenephilo.com.

PLEASE WRITE A REVIEW

Dear Reader,

At Midwestern Books we have worked hard to make this excellent book available for you. We truly hope you have enjoyed it. It is our mission to tell stories from a Midwestern perspective that honors its culture. Thank you for including us in your reading selections.

Please, would you consider going to the Amazon website and write a review for this book. Reviews are crucial for helping others to know about this book and encouraging Amazon to promote it. We very much need help from readers like you to get the word out about our books and the enjoyable stories they share. Thank you for helping us.

Midwestern Books

OTHER TITLES FROM MIDWESTERN BOOKS

See Jane Run! Book 1 of the West River Mysteries. Amidst the scenic wonder of a quirky corner of western South Dakota, Jane Newell starts her career in a country school. She soon discovers that someone close to her is a killer, and she is determined to find out who it is.

See Jane Sing! Book 2 of the West River Mysteries. Just back from Thanksgiving break, Jane Newell stumbles over the body of a teenage boy while hunting for a Christmas tree. Jane ignores Sheriff Sternquist's warning not to investigate when she discovers a tangle of clues.

See Jane Dance! Book 3 of the West River Mysteries. What do Kindergartners and square dance lessons have to do with murder? Jane Newell is at it again, braving snowstorms and town gossip as she and the sheriff zero

in on a killer dancing too close for comfort in the newest
West River Mystery.

Stay Out of that Room! Two sheltered teen aged girls
spend a summer on lake Minnetonka with their wacka-
doodle great aunt when a secret room lures them to
break her rules, while hunky neighbor boys heighten the
stakes.

Cosmic Background Radiation. Grieving his brother,
Josh confronts rural life to save his family. Strange
dreams take him back 2,700 years to a parallel life with
his brother alive and a girl he just met as part of the
household.

Your Alaskan Daughter 3rd Edition. Three months
pregnant with her first child, Harriet Walker traveled to
Alaska in 1953 to establish a homestead with her husband, Harold. She tells the story through the letters
she sent to her family and friends, from the hair-raising
trip over the Alcan to the exciting events surrounding
the birth of Tommy, their first child. While camped in
a small summer cottage, the intrepid couple finds a new
home in tiny Hope, Alaska, where they brave the pinch
of an Alaskan winter.

www.ingramcontent.com/pod-product-compliance
Lightning Source LLC
Chambersburg PA
CBHW030140310726
48970CB00005B/1515